"I'm not here because

Allison took a deep breath before clarifying. "About the money or the contract."

Red smiled. "What contract?"

She couldn't help smiling back, but she gave it a wry twist, so that he would know she was onto slick guys like him. He'd promised he wouldn't talk about the contract, and he wouldn't—at least until he thought he had her softened up. He wasn't a fool. But neither was she.

"But the truth is...I got the impression that you really cared about Victor, that the two of you were close. And that you might be sincerely concerned about the welfare of his family."

He nodded. His expression was guarded, now, less slick but no less handsome. That great bone structure and that dramatic Black Irish coloring weren't dependent on a twinkle or a grin. As she poured the thick cream into her cup of coffee she found herself wondering whether he was married, or engaged.

Then she told herself to stop wondering things like that.

Dear Reader,

One of my favorite quotes says, "If you don't make mistakes, you don't make anything." I heard it long ago, at a time when I really needed it. I'm not much of a risk-taker, and that quote opened my eyes to a new way of looking at my life.

Even though taking risks is daunting, always playing it safe can be scary, too. Isn't every important move forward a risk? Wouldn't it be safer never to fall in love, have children, start a business, travel the world or even write a book? And yet...how boring utter safety would be! Think how much we'd miss!

Allison York has just made one of the biggest mistakes of her life, and she wants only to hunker down and protect her infant son—and her heart. No more risks. No more blunders.

But then sexy, charismatic Redmond Malone enters her world—the one man who poses a threat to everything she holds dear. Letting him in might well be the ultimate mistake...but does she have the strength to send him away?

I hope you enjoy their story. And I hope that, as you go through life, all the mistakes you make turn out to be blessings in disguise!

Warmest wishes,

Kathleen O'Brien

P.S.—I love to hear from readers! Visit me at KOBrienonline.com, on Facebook or Twitter, or email me at KOBrien@aol.com.

The Cost of Silence
Kathleen O'Brien

TORONTO NEW YORK LONDON
AMSTERDAM PARIS SYDNEY HAMBURG
STOCKHOLM ATHENS TOKYO MILAN MADRID
PRAGUE WARSAW BUDAPEST AUCKLAND

Recycling programs
for this product may
not exist in your area.

ISBN-13: 978-0-373-71746-0

THE COST OF SILENCE

www.Harlequin.com

Printed in U.S.A.

ABOUT THE AUTHOR

Kathleen O'Brien was a feature writer and TV critic before marrying a fellow journalist. Motherhood, which followed soon after, was so marvelous she turned to writing novels, which could be done at home. A born sentimentalist, she believes a person can never have too many old friends, sad movies, spoiled pets or corny songs. She's never met a book about a baby that she didn't love.

Books by Kathleen O'Brien

HARLEQUIN SUPERROMANCE

1015—WINTER BABY*
1047—BABES IN ARMS*
1086—THE REDEMPTION OF MATTHEW QUINN*
1146—THE ONE SAFE PLACE*
1176—THE HOMECOMING BABY
1231—THE SAINT†
1249—THE SINNER†
1266—THE STRANGER†
1382—CHRISTMAS IN HAWTHORN BAY
1411—EVERYTHING BUT THE BABY
1441—TEXAS BABY
1572—TEXAS WEDDING
1590—FOR THE LOVE OF FAMILY
1632—TEXAS TROUBLE
1668—THAT CHRISTMAS FEELING
    "We Need a Little Christmas"
1737—FOR THEIR BABY

*Four Seasons in Firefly Glen
†The Heroes of Heyday

HARLEQUIN SINGLE TITLE

MYSTERIES OF LOST ANGEL INN
        "The Edge of Memory"

Other titles by this author available in ebook

To Ann Evans.
Your friendship, your generosity and your talent
have made all the difference.

CHAPTER ONE

REDMOND MALONE HAD BEEN PARKED in front of the Windsor Beach Peacock Café for a full five minutes. He kept going back and forth, one minute gazing at the ocean—which glittered invitingly between the buildings—and the next minute glaring at the restaurant, with the blue-and-green-striped awnings and kitschy matching outdoor umbrellas.

So what was it going to be? Hit the gas, find a beach shop that sold surfboards and trunks, and wash his cares away in the Pacific? Or open that shadowy café door and scope out the mysterious, adulterous Allison York?

Yeah, right. As if he had any choice.

With a heartfelt, under-the-breath curse, he met his own eyes in the rearview mirror. *Note for next time: don't make deathbed promises. First, obviously everyone's too emotional to think straight when a good friend is dying. And second, promises like that are set in stone. Impossible to renegotiate them when you wake up and realize you've stepped in a big pile of—*

The thought broke off as, without warning, his parked car lurched forward sharply. Simultaneously, he heard a grating, metallic sound. Harsh, piercing, up close and personal…

Aw, hell. He swiveled to look out the back window.

Some jackass in a fat black Rolls Royce just rear-ended him.

God, could this damned errand get any worse? He yanked the keys from the ignition, shoved open the door and climbed out. Luckily for the blind fool in the Rolls, Red wasn't the yelling, punching kind, or the "ouch, my neck" kind. But the fool had better have insurance.

The other driver was slower to emerge, so Red was almost at the door of the Rolls when it opened. Great. The guy must have been eighty, easy. Suit, tie, pocket kerchief…definitely overdressed for early-morning pancakes, so maybe he hadn't been headed to the Peacock Café. Maybe the bank down the street.

"You all right, son?" The man's long, seamed face looked worried. He reminded Red of a wood carving of an ancient Chinese philosopher.

"I'm fine. How about you?"

"Nothing broken." The old guy slowly eased out his legs, as if he balanced raw eggs on his knees. Where his hand gripped the door, his fingers trembled on the shiny black paint like long, pale flower petals.

He tilted his chin to see over the huge hood of his own car, all the way down to Red's low-slung Mercedes.

"Oh, dear. That is a shame. I am sorry, young man. I didn't see your little automobile until it was far, far too late."

On a normal day, Red might have been amused by the old-world style. Unfortunately, he, too, had gotten a good look at the rear panel of his SLK 300, which he'd bought only three months ago and still liked better than any woman he'd ever dated. So, yeah. Not amused.

The old man tottered over to the sidewalk and gingerly mounted the curb, balancing himself on the parking meter. Apparently drawn by the sound of the collision, people had started to gather in front of the café. A couple of men grimaced when they saw Red's car, but most of the onlookers clustered around the old guy, clucking sympathetically, as if he were the victim.

"Are you okay, Bill? Did you hit your head? Does anything hurt?"

Red might as well have been invisible. Which suited him fine. He dialed the operator on his cell phone. "Windsor Beach Police Department," he said, propping his phone between his shoulder and his ear so that he could search for his insurance card and registration. "Nonemergency."

"No, wait!" A female voice raised itself above the general hubbub of curious gawkers. "Wait. Don't call the police."

He glanced up from his wallet. A young woman had emerged from the crowd and was heading toward him. She wore a blue-and-green-striped uniform, so he assumed she worked at the café. She waved her hand vigorously, as if to demonstrate that he absolutely must hang up.

Yeah? He didn't think so.

When he didn't lower the phone, she frowned and moved faster. She reached him two seconds later, while the unanswered call was still ringing against his ear. And ringing. And ringing. For the Windsor Beach police, apparently *nonemergency* meant *no response*.

"Please," she said, slightly breathless. She was cute. Mid-twenties, with a chin-length brown bob, freckles and an imploring smile. "Please, hang up. There's no need to involve the police, really." She glanced back toward the sidewalk. "The man who hit you…that's Bill Longmire."

"Okay." Red smiled, too. He nodded toward his car. "And that's an eight-thousand-dollar repair."

She gave the Mercedes a cursory look, but Red could tell she didn't think his car was the important point here. Maybe it wasn't, to her. Maybe the old guy was her grandfather, or the grand pooh-bah of Windsor Beach. Red didn't care. The man shouldn't be behind a wheel.

He glanced at her name tag.

Without really thinking, he lowered the phone from his ear. *Oh, great.*

He'd been so riled by the accident he'd almost lost track of why he was here in the first place. He'd almost forgotten he was on a ridiculous spy mission, trying to find out everything he could about a waitress named Allison York.

Well, James Bond. Meet Allison York.

In his defense, he'd been expecting a home-wrecking sexpot. He had only a few facts about her. She was twenty-seven. She was divorced. And last year she'd given birth to his best friend's baby.

His *married* best friend.

The one who had died of cancer two months ago. The one who had, even on his deathbed, been terrified that his big mistake—that would be Allison York— would somehow find a way to destroy the loved ones he was leaving behind.

This woman was pretty, but no sexpot. She looked more like the one who would get cast as the sexpot's worried best friend. Skinny, with no-fuss, healthy hair.

A little pale for a California gal. The kind of long neck he always associated with ballet lessons and overprotective mothers.

Something was buzzing. He glanced down at his phone, strangely off balance. It was still ringing.

"Please," she said again. "I can explain."

He clicked the end button.

"Thank you." She took a deep breath. "You see, Bill… Well, Bill is a good friend of mine. He knows he isn't supposed to drive. He has someone who does that for him. But something must have happened—"

"Steve didn't show up, that's what happened." While Red had been gathering his wits, Bill Longmire had apparently decided to join them in the street, his entourage of well-wishers behind him.

Allison slipped her hand under the old man's elbow. "But when Steve is late, you're supposed to wait." She shook his arm gently. "You know that, Bill. Someone could have been hurt."

"Well, no one was." Bill winked one rheumy eye, then reached out his long finger to tap Allison's nose. "Besides, sweetheart, I couldn't wait. You only work until ten today, and no one else ever gets my omelet right."

Red frowned. Was that bony antique actually flirting with this woman who was only a third of his age? His jaw tightened, but Allison didn't seem to find it disgusting. She grinned and, sighing, let her head briefly rest on the old man's shoulder.

"Darn it, Bill," she said with affectionate exasperation. "If you're not careful, you'll be eating your eggs off a hospital tray."

"Allie's right, Bill," someone from the crowd said. A murmur of agreement rumbled through the rest of them.

Red felt his fingers close hard around his cell phone, and he realized he was seriously annoyed. Hooray that Bill Longmire, whoever he was, hadn't killed himself today. But what about Red's car? What about the whiplash he hadn't gotten, but might have?

"Still," he broke in flatly. "We need to call the police. We'll need to report this to our insurance companies."

Allison frowned. Though she lifted her head, she didn't let go of Bill's elbow, as if she were afraid he would topple over without her support. "Surely you two can work out—"

"Of course we can," Bill broke in. He extricated his arm, then dug around in his pants pocket. "I don't know how much money I'm carrying." He found a battered old leather wallet. "Let's see—"

Great. The guy probably still calculated in 1930s prices, and was going to try to placate him with a pair of limp twenty-dollar bills.

"I'm sorry," Red said, "but I'm afraid I'm going to have to get an estimate—"

As if Red hadn't said a word, Bill extended a fat wad of cash. "I've only got about five thousand on me, but if you'll take a check—"

"Bill!" Allison batted his hand down. "What are you doing, walking around with that kind of cash?"

"I'm paying the man for the damage." Bill turned his elegant smile Red's way. "I suspect the final costs will be at least twice this," he said. "Mercedes parts don't come cheap. But if you'll accept this as a down payment, Mr...."

The sentence trailed off as he waited for Red to supply his name.

Red thought a minute, then decided it didn't matter. Allison wouldn't connect his name with Victor Wigham. "Malone. Redmond Malone."

The old man nodded. "Mr. Malone. Delighted to meet you. You're not from Windsor Beach, I take it?"

Red shook his head. "San Francisco."

"Oh, yes. Lovely city." Bill extended the money again. "So, as I was saying. You can take this as a down payment, and I will write you a check for another five thousand to cover the rest."

"That's very generous, Mr. Longmire, but I'm afraid—"

"Hey, give the guy a break, why don't you?" Two burly men separated from the crowd and flanked Allison, one at each shoulder as if they were hired bodyguards. One spoke through a tight jaw. "He said he'd pay for the damages. Why do you gotta bring in the police?"

Another murmur of agreement moved through the crowd, which clearly had only one mind among them. They inched forward, closing ranks. For a minute, Red felt like the hapless stranger in a horror film who stumbles into Looneyville and spends the rest of the movie running from its spooky townsfolk.

Or…maybe he was in the middle of a very strange dream. A dream—yeah, that would be nice. Maybe he wasn't really standing here at all, negotiating with this old man, who was probably insane. Maybe Victor wasn't really dead. Maybe there was no Allison York, no baby, no danger to Victor's grieving family.

"Mr. Malone?" Allison turned her eyes toward him,

wordlessly asking for his help. More crazy dream material. Those big bedroom eyes didn't begin to match that girl-next-door face. They were gorgeous—round, dewy, lash-fringed. A clear dark honey-brown that looked strangely bottomless.

He almost found himself saying okay. *Okay, we'll do this your way.*

But that would make him crazier than the old man.

"I'm sorry," he said. He lifted his phone again, ignoring her disappointed frown, as well as the army of Windsor Beach zombies lined up behind her. "I'm afraid I'm still going to have to call the police."

By that afternoon, the story had grown even better in the retelling.

Red was pretty good with impersonations, and by the time he'd finished describing the scene to his older brother Colby, both men were laughing. Red could even picture the accordion-folded rear end on his poor Mercedes without cringing.

The best part? The Windsor Beach policeman everyone had been so afraid to call turned out to be Bill Longmire's pimple-faced great-nephew Larry, who was clearly terrified of the old man. Equally clearly, the kid also had a crush on Allison York and would have flushed his own badge down the toilet if she'd asked him to. For a minute there, Red thought he might end up getting a ticket for upsetting her.

"Hell, Red, this town sounds nuts." Colby glanced around the small store space they'd been inspecting. "Are you sure we want to open a Diamante here?"

Red shrugged. "Crazy people eat pizza, too, don't they?"

This trip to Windsor Beach was doing double duty. He'd set aside the morning to get a glimpse of Allison York, and now he could devote the afternoon to checking out the single storefront that had become available. Scouting new locations for Diamante take-out stores was Red's piece of the family business, and he'd had his eye on swanky, touristy Windsor Beach for months.

He'd been waiting to find the right spot. He thought this might be it. The strip mall was fully occupied—this vacancy was rare. He'd only found out about it because he had a friend who had a friend. The building had easy access, ample parking and about a thousand bored, hungry rich people within a three-mile radius.

"And the price is right," he said, opening the door to the storage closet. He recoiled as a cloud of vanilla-scented air wafted over him. The Bath Goddess had moved out of the space yesterday. "Damn, we'll have to do something about the stink, though."

Colby, who was the company lawyer and therefore wouldn't get really interested until he got his hands on the lease, had already wandered over to the windows, where sunset-pink was seeping into the western sky.

"Stink?" He tossed a grin over his shoulder. "Oh. I thought that was you."

Red ignored him. As the youngest of three brothers, he was used to being insulted. He poked around some more, though he'd already decided to take the store. He'd put out an SOS to Colby because, after the assault on the Mercedes, he needed a ride home. Not because he needed permission to rent this place.

It had taken him a while to find out where he fit into Diamante, but he had finally carved out his own niche. Nana Lina had long since taken the training wheels off, allowing him to make these acquisition decisions more or less alone. Turned out he had great instincts about real estate.

And he owed it all to his mentor. Victor Wigham.

Which brought him full circle to Allison York. Irritably he kicked a small net full of rose petals into the corner that was functioning as a trash can. What was he supposed to do now? What on earth was he supposed to do about Allison, the waitress with freckled cheeks, a snub nose, and Scheherazade eyes?

He'd been so sure that, once he met her, he'd be able to size her up easily. He assumed he could calculate what it would take to buy her silence, just as he could look at a property and sense what he would have to pay to acquire it, almost to the dollar.

But this situation hadn't worked that way. Instead of being a simple, money-grubbing "mistress" type, she'd turned out to be a stew of contradictions. Part kid, part sorceress. She was an unwed mother, a waitress living on tips who needed a new pair of shoes. But somehow he could sense she was also a force to be reckoned with. She could coldheartedly betray Victor's wife and kids, but she was a marshmallow for an eighty-year-old nut job.

She didn't break down into logical, predictable elements. And yet somehow he had to fix this. What a mess.

"You know—" He turned and saw Colby watching him with a worried big-brother expression in his eyes. Red straightened, scowling. *"What?"*

"Don't pretend with me," Colby said. "I know that look."

"What look?"

"The *holy shit* look. You're thinking about Allison York. You're regretting it already, aren't you?"

For a minute, Red wanted to deny it. Right from the start, Colby had told him he was a fool for agreeing to "take care of" Allison. "God, Red," he'd said. "If Victor had asked you to rope-swing naked into a snake pit, would you have promised to do that, too?"

But Red put aside his instinctive defensiveness. He wasn't a kid anymore. He was thirty-two years old, and, though Colby might occasionally revert to using a paternal tone, the three years between them hadn't really mattered for a long time.

Besides, Colby might rib him, but ultimately he had Red's back, no matter what. And, as a lawyer, he might have some good advice. Red decided to come clean. He wiped his hands on a piece of sparkling tissue paper left over from some Bath Goddess purchase, then joined Colby at the window.

"Yeah, I am. Well, not regretting it, exactly. Just not sure what to do next."

"Can't you do what you said you would do? Present the deal, and hope she takes it?"

Red took a deep breath, though it made him inhale so much potpourri he nearly choked. "It's not that simple. If it was, Victor would've sent Lewis."

"He should have."

"Yeah, maybe, but you know Lewis is bullheaded. No subtlety. I've noticed lawyers tend to be like that."

Colby couldn't have missed the joke, but he didn't allow himself to be diverted. "We're bullheaded because we know how tricky the law is. I've warned you about this before, but it's worth repeating. Private settlement agreements with confidentiality provisions are not only tricky…they're begging for trouble. You get even a *hint* of coercion, exploitation, improper influence—"

"There's no improper influence, damn it." Red felt his pulse quicken. "He simply wants to give her some money to help with the baby. In return, he wants her to promise she won't drive to Russian Hill and toss a bomb into what's left of his family. If she says no, she says no. No one's going to threaten to break her knees."

Colby shrugged. He wasn't the nagging type. He'd said his piece—said it twice, in fact, which was rare enough—and Red knew that he would back off now.

"So, anyhow, Victor didn't think Lewis could handle it. That means she's prickly?" Colby's voice was carefully neutral. "She needs to be charmed, and he thought that, as a Malone, you could charm her?"

Red turned away. The sunset was a hell of a lot easier to look at right now than Colby's face. "Charm? I don't know. Obviously he doesn't mean I should order roses and candlelit dinners. I think he hoped I could…you know…*finesse* the presentation. The last thing Victor needs is to antagonize her."

"Well, I guess today put paid to that. You got her favorite old geezer arrested. I assume you'll be handing this off to Lewis now after all?"

Red shook his head. "Victor doesn't want Lewis involved."

An awkward silence hung between them. It seemed to stretch, though it probably wasn't more than a few seconds.

"Red." Colby's voice dipped low. "You know you keep talking about Victor in the present tense."

Present tense. Of course. As opposed to past tense. Dead tense.

For a horrible second, Red wasn't sure he could answer. His throat closed up, as hot and painful as if he'd swallowed broken glass.

He clenched his jaw until it burned. He hadn't cried since he was a kid, not even when he sat in Victor's shadowed bedroom and watched him drift between the sweating clarity of pain and the terrifying morphine hallucinations.

But how the hell could he accept the fact that Victor was dead? The man had been only fifty-two, at the top of his career. So completely alive.

Victor was the closest thing to a father Red had ever known. He'd literally saved Red's life fifteen years ago, when he happened to be in the right part of the Pacific to drag a stupid, unconscious teenager and his surfboard to safety. But he'd also saved Red's life again, metaphorically, five years later, when he showed him the way to a career.

Victor's wife, Marianne, was too young to be a mother figure, but she was a good and loyal friend. And, by God, Red would do whatever was necessary to protect her.

Whether Colby approved or not.

Red might not have gotten off on the right foot with Allison York today. But today had been merely the first skirmish in a much longer campaign. Colby was right. Victor had obviously picked him for this mission because of the Malone charm. That charm might be diluted a bit, sifting its way down to him, the youngest brother. But surely he'd inherited at least enough to get the job done.

The sun had almost dipped down to the horizon, and the buildings across the street lurked in deep shadow. The electricity was still on here in the empty shop, but the fixtures had been removed, and the bare-bulb glare was depressing.

They should be getting home. The brothers always went to Nana Lina's Belvedere Cove waterfront house for dinner on Fridays, and if they didn't hurry they'd be late. It was an hour back to San Francisco, though luckily on a Friday afternoon most of the traffic would be headed into Windsor Beach, not away from it.

"Shall we hit the road?" Colby put his hand in his pocket and extracted his keys.

Red shook his head, his decision suddenly made.

"You go," he said. "I think I'll get a rental car and stay here a couple of days."

CHAPTER TWO

IT WAS 3:00 A.M., and Allison had walked at least a hundred miles. She must have worn a groove in the peach-and-green braided rug that covered the small living room. When she moved out, she'd probably have to pay her landlord a fortune to fix it.

Not that she had any hope of moving out anytime soon.

With only a full moon and the distant rays of the corner streetlight to guide her, she kept circling, humming an old Beatles song while she walked. A hundred and one. Her eyes drooped and her arms ached. So few hours between now and 8:00 a.m., when she'd have to meet the real-estate agent.

But still Eddie wouldn't go back to sleep.

With a suddenness that startled both of them, Eddie sneezed that little snicking sound of his. It was hardly a noise at all, but it was enough to jolt him awake. He widened his eyes, as if someone had insulted him. Then he arched his back, straining away from her, and let loose a furious wail.

"Shh, shh, honey, hush." She bounced him softly, holding the back of his head in her palm. He sneezed a second time, and she listened for wheezing in his lungs. If he was getting pneumonia again...

Nothing. The tension in her chest eased. So far, so good.

"Hey. Keep it down, why don't you, kid? People are trying to sleep in here."

Allison looked up to see Jimbo Stipple, her roommate, housekeeper, babysitter and best friend, standing in the hallway. He never wore a shirt to bed, and his sweatpants had so many holes in them he was barely decent. But Jimbo had lived on a navy sub for the better part of four years, and he wasn't exactly the self-conscious type.

"Do you know what time it is?" He tried to sound annoyed, but his yawn got in the way. He leaned toward the kitchen to see the stove's digital clock. "Oh. Shit. It's three in the morning."

Allison raised her eyebrows. They'd had a deal. As soon as the baby was born, Jimbo had to stop cursing.

"What?" He twisted his arm over his shoulder to scratch at the Rubik's Cube tattoo on his back. "Come on. The kid's only three months old. He doesn't know that *s-h-i-t* is a cuss word. He thinks it's an entertainment choice."

Allison managed not to laugh. Life with Jimbo had its challenges, but it was never boring.

"Sorry," she said. "His nose is stuffed up again. He can't settle."

Jimbo frowned. "Does he have a fever?" He crossed the room in three strides and put his hand gently on Eddie's forehead. Against the flawless powder-pink of the baby skin, it was almost a shock to see the knuckles tattooed with black block letters.

B-A-C-K, this hand said. The tattoos on the other hand completed the threat. *O-F-F-!*

He let his fingers absorb the warmth for about three seconds. Then his features relaxed. "He feels okay." He bent toward Eddie's red, fussy face. "Don't scare me like that, buddy."

Eddie snuffled. Then, as he always did when he stared into Jimbo's face, he broke out in a grin. He reached out to grab a fistful of the man's spiky blond hair.

"Ouch!" Jimbo complained in a cartoon voice. All drama, designed to delight Eddie, which it did. The baby giggled and pulled even harder, his discomfort forgotten for the moment.

A rush of warmth moved through Allison. Jimbo was such a good, good man. She was so lucky to have him in her life. Maybe Eddie's biological father had been a lying, cheating bastard who wasn't interested in helping walk the floor at night, but thanks to Jimbo she wasn't in this alone.

"How about I take him, and you get back to bed?" Jimbo glanced at her, his head cocked at a forty-five-degree angle so that Eddie could hold on. "You've got the closing with the agent at the crack of dawn, right?"

"Close enough. Eight."

Jimbo groaned. "Any chance you could reschedule?"

"No way." She shook her head emphatically. "I've waited too long for this day."

He nodded. She didn't have to say any more. He'd known her since she was four, lived with her since she was six. He was as close to a brother as anyone could ever be without sharing DNA. In her senior year of high school, he'd fixed her favorite tomato bisque soup while she wept over a cheating boyfriend. Five years

later, he'd fixed up another big pot the day she signed
her divorce papers and swore off men forever.

When her father died, even Jimbo's food couldn't
help. But his tattooed hand had held on tight and somehow kept her from being swept away on a river of grief.

So he knew how much owning her own restaurant
would mean to her—the security, the independence, the
focus. The dream that had already been deferred three
times. Almost ten years of disappointment could come
to an end tomorrow.

As long as she didn't sleep through the appointment.

He touched the side of her face. "Okay. Then let me
wrestle with the little demon here, and you get some
sleep."

So tempting. But guilt nipped at her. Jimbo was
tired, too. Eddie was her responsibility. But when Jimbo
held out his hands, Eddie practically leaped out of her
arms trying to get to his big, silly friend.

Laughing, she relinquished him. Her arms burned
from the sudden release. "If he starts to wheeze—"

"He won't." Jimbo propped Eddie against his shoulder with the practiced skill of a true parent. He put his
hand against Allison's back and steered her toward the
hall. "Nobody wheezes on my watch."

She smiled. The truth was, if Eddie had trouble
breathing, Jimbo would give the air out of his own
lungs, literally, to help him. The forty-year-old chef/
babysitter spoke three languages and quoted Greek
playwrights like pop songs. He knew CPR and first
aid, the doctor's number, and most of the *Merck Manual*
by heart. He could have been a surgeon, a stockbroker,
a CEO—anything he wanted.

But by some miracle he wanted to be her guardian angel. And Eddie's.

She surrendered, and, after planting a grateful kiss on his cheek, she headed down the small hall. At her doorway, she yawned and glanced once toward the living room. Jimbo stood near the window, where the streetlight shone just bright enough to let him read his new cookbook.

And Eddie the Demon was asleep.

"OHMIGOD." Allison's best waitress friend, Sue, paused with a set of silverware half-rolled in a napkin and inhaled sharply. "Look! There he is."

Allison, who was really too busy to care, glanced toward the door, which had jingled its incoming-customer melody of joy. But it was lunchtime on a sunny spring Saturday, and at least a dozen people crowded around Moira's hostess station. Allison couldn't make them all out clearly.

"Who?"

"I don't know his name. Look. Can't you see him? Tall, dark and handsome from yesterday. The one with the mangled Mercedes."

Oh. Allison felt her own breath swoop in, and she nearly dropped the order of coconut prawns she needed to deliver to table eleven, which would have been a shame, since they were regulars and big tippers.

But Sue was right. There he was. Redmond Malone. Yeah, she didn't kid herself—she remembered his name. Even here in this upscale tourist town, she didn't see many guys that sexy. A couple of inches taller than tall. Dark, wavy hair. Blue eyes so intense they looked Photoshopped.

Loose jeans and a black T-shirt that resembled the ones she bought at the superstore but probably cost more than she'd made in tips all week. Definitely an understated style. No obvious come-ons—nothing form-fitting to show off assets, either God-given or gym-acquired. No gold trinkets, no hair gel, no Armani. Actually, he looked as if the thrill of being a stud might have worn off somewhere between twenty and thirty, and he was tired of having to bat females away like flies.

Still, he had an industrial-strength level of self-confidence, and was in love with his boy-toy car. Definitely not her type.

Not that she had a type anymore. Except maybe the type that wore diapers.

Still, she wondered what he was doing here. She hoped it didn't mean more trouble for Bill. Ordinarily, Bill would have been at table eleven, with his friends. They called themselves the Old Coots Club, and they rarely missed a Saturday. But Bill was at home, pouting about yesterday's accident.

"He's looking at you," Sue said with a low growl. "Damn it. Why aren't the sexy ones ever looking at me?"

"Don't be ridiculous." Allison grabbed the Ultimate Club that Sven slid onto the shelf, added it to her tray with the coconut prawns, and headed over to eleven. She tried to give Moira the dark eye, warning her not to put Mr. Mercedes in her section. But Moira just shrugged. She really didn't have much choice. Flip, the owner, ran The Peacock Café like a military operation, and it was Allison's turn to get a table.

Oh, well. The closing on the new restaurant property had gone smoothly this morning, and nothing was going to spoil her good mood. Not even this Redmond Malone guy, who had insisted on reporting Bill's accident.

Bill already had acquired so many points that another ticket might tip the balance. They might take his license away. And though all Bill's friends worked hard to keep him from getting behind the wheel, they knew losing the license would badly damage his self-esteem. His wife's death last Christmas had hit him hard, and he desperately needed to pretend he was still completely independent.

But what was done was done. She couldn't undo it by being rude to Redmond Malone. Yesterday, he'd been the problem. Today, he was merely another customer.

As she approached eleven, Sarge Barker was returning from the restroom, whistling. She'd heard him announce earlier that he'd won the Fantasy Five last night. A whopping six bucks, but money didn't mean much to a millionaire. He simply liked winning.

She had barely set the tray down when the old man scooped her into his arms and danced her around the table.

"Sarge!" she protested, laughing, but he was almost as burly now as when he'd been in the army fifty years ago, a fact he broadcasted proudly while he loosened his belt after every meal. She couldn't pull away without making a scene. "You're going to get me fired."

"So, what? You're too good for this place." Sarge tried to get a quickstep going, but he had two left feet and it ended up a terrible galumphing mess. They barely avoided crashing into the chairs. "Marry me, and we'll dance into the sunset together."

"Sarge…"

But the rest of the Old Coot Club were clapping now, egging him on. *Damn it.* It had probably gone on only fifteen seconds, but that was an eternity for something this inappropriate. She was going to have to get tough.

Hoping she didn't throw off Sarge, who had an impressive spare tire that clearly redistributed his center of gravity, she suddenly ducked under his arms and moved backward fast to free herself.

He must have thought she was falling, because he reached out and tried to grab her shoulder. His hand caught her left breast instead. He yanked it back as if he'd touched a hot stove, and immediately lost his footing, plopping onto the table, scarcely missing the tines of a fork.

Equally startled, she took two more awkward steps backward, tangling her feet. Her rear end hit the small folding table on which she'd rested the tray, and before she could even think about righting herself, everything toppled over with a crash.

She landed in the prawns, with a broken glass of iced tea pooling in her lap, freezing her thighs. Sarge cried out, and, in a very stupid move, decided to rush over to help. He slipped on something, maybe a piece of bread slathered in mayonnaise, and landed in a heap at her feet.

Well, of course. Nothing by half measures.

Though her tailbone hurt, her hand was stinging, her dress was soaked and she was downright mortified, she suddenly had the strangest urge to laugh. Apparently, if you went far enough beyond awful, you reached ridiculous.

"Are you all right?"

She looked up. Redmond Malone squatted beside her, looking her over with an expression she couldn't quite interpret. She wondered whether he, too, might be trying not to laugh.

"I'm fine," she said, hoping she didn't have any parsley in her hair. She plucked ice off her skirt and plunked it into one of the unbroken glasses. "We've almost got it, don't you think? Next stop...*Dancing with the Stars.*"

"Well." He gathered the largest chunks of glass and set them on the tray carefully. "You might want to work on the dismount."

"Allie! I'm so sorry, honey." The others had helped Sarge to his feet, and he held out a hand to help Allison up. Unfortunately, it was covered in mayonnaise. "Bring Flip out here. I'll explain that it wasn't your fault."

She didn't want to hurt the old guy's feelings, but if she took Sarge's slippery hand, she'd end up right back on her rear end. She glanced around for something more stable to hold on to.

Redmond, who still squatted only inches away, didn't waste any time. He placed the last shard of glass in a safe place, then turned to her and held out both his hands. She glanced at those shoulders, then down at the lean, strong thighs. He could definitely support her. She put her hands in his.

She didn't even have to use her own strength. In one fluid motion she was on her feet, tilting ever so slightly toward that soft black T-shirt. She got close enough to tell that he didn't wear cologne and smelled only of fresh cotton and soap and something they ought to bottle and call Raw Sex Appeal.

Then, because she had a highly evolved sense of self-preservation, she held her breath and angled her head away from him. What the hell was she doing smelling this stranger's T-shirt?

For that matter, why was she standing here at all, staring into his electric blue eyes, like a deer frozen before an oncoming car? She had things to do. She had to get a redo on that order into the kitchen, stat. She had to get the floor cleaned up, new drinks delivered.

She glanced down, and to her horror she realized she was still holding the man's hands, as if she still hadn't quite found her equilibrium. She pulled her fingers free and rubbed them nervously on her damp skirt. "Thanks," she said. "I—"

"Gotcha covered, girlfriend." Sue winked as she and Moira joined the crowd. Within seconds the two of them had efficiently cleared the food off the floor and carted it away. Teddy, the busboy, headed toward them with a mop.

The Old Coots Club had mobilized, too, and brought their silverware and salad plates to order. They clustered around her, fussing over her wet skirt, making sure the broken shards hadn't cut her hand.

"I'll make it right, Allie." Sarge had washed his hands somehow, probably in his water glass. He put his arm around her shoulder. "I'll talk to Flip and make sure he doesn't dock you for the food. Don't you worry."

"I'm not worried," she said honestly. Flip wasn't here today, but he'd believe her version of the story. He knew what the Old Coots were like. Now and then, they'd break into a barbershop quartet version of some sad old song, like "Apple Blossom Time," or "Sixteen Tons," which would enchant the other customers, at least until Dickey O'Connor started crying. And last week Bill and Stuart Phipps had brawled up one end of the café and down the other, all because Bill had insulted Elizabeth Taylor.

Flip said they were like a free floor show. Plus, they were great customers. Every one of them an eccentric, well-to-do widower who hated eating alone at home. Mostly, though, Flip put up with them because, like everyone else who lived year-round in Windsor Beach, he loved the goofy old guys.

"Hey. Allie. Over here." For some reason, Dickey O'Connor was talking out of one side of his mouth. Only five feet tall, and a hundred pounds soaking wet, he was a wonderful storyteller, but he was a little too fond of drama. He frequently created cloak-and-dagger mysteries out of thin air.

Maybe he was going to warn her that her fall had been orchestrated by the evil conspirators of Shadowland. But she'd play along. Dickey was probably the closest of all the Old Coots to a nursing home, though it broke her heart to think of it.

"Psst. Allie."

She glanced once at Redmond, who seemed to be watching the whole thing with a strangely analytical interest, as if he were an anthropologist studying some indigenous tribe. Then she joined Dickey at the side of the table.

"Here, honey," he said under his breath, sounding more like a gangster than the honest, retired Irish boatbuilder he was. He had something hidden in his hand, which he held stiffly at his side. He gestured jerkily, trying to get her attention. *"Here."*

She put her own hand out, low and sneaky, as obviously was required.

He nodded, satisfied. "You don't need anything from Sarge," he said. "This'll make it right." He flicked his hand and dropped something in hers. Then, laying one finger aside his nose, he glided smoothly away, pretending it hadn't happened.

She turned her back to him, and opened her hand. Glittering against her palm was a very large, very beautiful, but very fake diamond. *Oh, Dickey.*

Sighing hard, she clamped her fingers shut over her palm, then slid the diamond into her pocket. As if she didn't have enough to do…

She felt suddenly prickly, as though someone were staring at her. She glanced up. Redmond was only a few feet away, watching her intently. The expression on his face had changed dramatically in the past few minutes.

His eyes were cold. His mouth, which had looked quite nice in a smile, was tight, utterly unyielding. He flicked a glance at her pocket, then returned his gaze to her face without blinking.

She tilted her head, confused.

In response, he casually tossed some bills on the table. "Sorry," he said. He smiled, but his voice was cool under the surface friendliness. "I'm afraid I won't be able to stay after all."

Then he turned and walked away. Within seconds he had simply exited the restaurant without ordering a single thing.

What on earth?

For a minute, the strange attitude stung her. She stared stupidly at the door. Had he received a call… some emergency? No…his attitude had felt almost hostile. And oddly personal.

Had he watched the weird interlude with Dickey?

Did he think she was doing something criminal? Or was simply greedy? Her cheeks flushed. Was he daring to pass judgment on her for accepting the diamond?

What the hell did he know about Dickey, about her... about anything?

Then she forced herself to turn away, brushing the feeling aside. Redmond Malone was nothing to her. A total stranger. A stranger she didn't even like very much. The fact that he had an overabundance of sex appeal only made him that much less desirable, at least in her life.

So good riddance, Mr. Mercedes. She wouldn't waste another minute worrying about it. As a single mother, she'd fought too long and too hard to get where she was today. She'd had to eliminate old, deeply ingrained patterns. To keep herself focused, she'd created a both a Do list and a Don't list.

The Do list included saving money, working hard, keeping a positive attitude, opening her restaurant. Creating a good, secure life for her little boy.

The Don't list was simpler still.

Men.

CHAPTER THREE

RED KNEW HER HOME ADDRESS, of course. Lewis had provided it in the packet of contracts and other legal odds and ends. It was a small second-floor apartment in a white concrete block building. Nice porch from which you might, if you were about ten feet tall, catch a postage stamp–size glimpse of the Pacific in the distance.

The landlord didn't exactly kill himself with the yard care, letting a few rock gardens and one stringy hibiscus suffice as landscaping. But he seemed to keep up with the paint and repairs pretty well, which helped.

It wasn't a crummy address, but of course it was on the "wrong" side of town, which meant not on the water. Windsor was a small pocket beach about an hour south of San Francisco, one of the few little towns that didn't even try to be artsy. The low bluffs, sandy beach and warm water had originally attracted the retirees who wanted to be left alone, and now the old guys were constantly at war with the Chamber of Commerce, which wanted to attract more paying tourists.

Two categories of people lived in Windsor Beach year-round. One—those retired, relaxed rich people. And two—the housekeepers, waiters, shop owners and repairmen who facilitated their cushy existence. About twenty-five hundred people, all told.

Red had been waiting across the street for the past hour. He hoped Bill Longmire wouldn't be stopping by tonight, but he'd bought all the extra coverage the rental agency offered, in case.

The western sky had taken on a deep pink tinge before Allison finally drove up in her Honda. As soon as she parked on the tiny asphalt driveway, he opened his own door and called her name.

She didn't seem to hear him. She got out slowly, stuffing her sneakers into her purse and taking a minute to rub and flex her arches. She still had on her striped uniform. She must have worked all day. No wonder her feet hurt.

She put her purse on the hood, then crossed to the passenger side of the backseat and leaned in. *Oh. Right.* He really wasn't thinking very clearly about this whole thing, was he? He'd forgotten she probably would have the baby with her.

Victor's son. The birth certificate listed the baby's name as Edward James York. Mother, Allison Rowena York. Father, a blank line.

As she pulled the lumpy bundle out of its car seat, Red steeled himself not to react. He'd been around enough kids to know it wasn't likely he'd recognize Victor's features in the face of a three-month-old. His brother Matt's little girl was the spitting image of her mom, Belle. But that hadn't happened until she was… maybe two. His friend David Gerard's son, same thing. At three months, babies all still looked as if they'd been hastily molded out of Play-Doh.

He called her name again, and she turned, tucking the baby's blanket under her chin so that she could see.

What was left of the fading light was right behind him, and she squinted, trying to make him out.

After a fraction of a second, she stiffened. He'd expected that. If he had asked for her phone number while she was serving him a sandwich at the café, she might have refused to give it, but she wouldn't have been freaked out. Probably happened to her all the time.

But a customer showing up out of nowhere, clearly having tracked her to her home…that was stalker territory. He had decided to risk it because he suspected she wouldn't agree to talk to him if she knew who he was. Still, he hoped she didn't have pepper spray and an impulsive trigger finger.

"Hey," he said. "I'm sorry to bother you at home, but I was hoping to get a chance to talk to you privately. I'm Red Malone. I'm the guy who—"

"I know who you are." Frowning, she pressed the bundle of baby closer to her chest. The kid whimpered, as if she held on too tightly. "What do you want? Is it about Bill?"

"No." He smiled. "No, our insurance companies are handling that fine. My car's already been towed to San Francisco and put on the lift. I'm actually here about something else."

"Really?" She still looked suspicious. "What?"

He glanced around. The street wasn't exactly crowded, but the April weather was balmy, the kind that made people open all the windows to let the breeze blow through. Anyone could be listening. "It is personal. Is there somewhere we might talk privately?"

Her eyebrows drove together, and she took a step backward. She clearly thought that was pushy as hell.

"I don't think so, Mr. Malone. I'm not sure how

you got my address, or what you think we have to talk about. But I don't know you. I certainly am not going to invite you into my home."

"Please, call me Red," he said. "I'm sorry. I know it seems strange, but I promise you I'm not some creep who followed you home from the café. I'm here on behalf of a mutual friend. It's important."

At that her eyes widened. The setting sun lit their honey-brown depths. It also pinked her freckled cheeks and full lips. The effect was amazing, and he felt a purely male reaction that he clamped down on instantly. Panting like a pervert wouldn't be at all helpful in the I-am-not-a-creep department.

"A mutual friend?" Her voice sounded tight, as if her breathing had accelerated. Her nostrils flared subtly. It looked a little like anger. He wondered who she thought he meant. Was it possible she'd already begun to suspect the truth?

The baby began to fuss and wriggle, as if he reacted to his mother's emotions. She dropped a kiss on top of the blanket to soothe him, then looked at Red. "What are you talking about? What mutual friend?"

Okay, moment of truth. He met her gaze squarely. "Victor Wigham."

She lifted her chin, but not before he saw the contempt that flickered behind her eyes. "Victor Wigham is not my friend."

"Okay. That might be the wrong word." Red tried to remember that he'd been chosen for this task because he supposedly understood how to be diplomatic. "But, as I understand it, he was the father of your child."

She didn't even blink. "And since that fact doesn't

seem to interest Victor in the least, I'm afraid I don't see how it could possibly interest you, either, Mr. Malone."

Red hesitated. She was using present tense when she mentioned Victor, just as he sometimes found himself doing. But why? He was struggling with grief, but clearly she had no affection for the man who had fathered her child.

Which had to mean…she didn't realize Victor had died.

Hell. That complicated things. For some reason, he'd taken it for granted that she knew. But how? The Wighams owned a vacation house here in Windsor Beach, but they kept it rented out, so they wouldn't be considered locals. His obituary wouldn't even have made it into the back pages of the *Windsor Beach Bulletin.*

And obviously the "other woman" wasn't likely to be mentioned in the will. So unless she kept tabs on him via the internet, how would she have found out?

The baby sneezed. She pulled the blanket up, covering the last inch of downy forehead that had still been visible. "I'm afraid I need to get Eddie inside. It's too chilly for him. So if you don't mind—"

"Allison." He decided to say it. "Victor died two months ago."

Her body froze in place, but a dozen different microexpressions swept across her face. Surprise, definitely. And…could that have been fear? Anger? Something negative…but it all happened too fast. He would have loved to capture the display in slow motion, so that he could decipher even half of them.

When the baby began to cry, she blinked, and all visible emotions disappeared.

"I see," she said. She picked up her purse with her free hand and gestured toward the stairs. "Then I guess you'd better come in."

HALF AN HOUR LATER, Allison still hadn't recovered from the shock. She had gone through the motions of playing hostess, getting Red a cup of coffee—two sugars, no cream—and inviting him to sit while she changed Eddie and put him in bed.

Thankfully, Eddie was exhausted and fell right asleep. Afterward, she stood at her bedroom door for a couple of frozen seconds, still numb and reluctant to emerge. Her mind wasn't working. She couldn't think where to begin.

She wasn't sure why the idea of Victor's death bothered her in the first place. She'd long since accepted that he wouldn't be a father to Eddie. But obviously somewhere, buried very deep, the hope had lingered that someday he might wonder what he'd missed. That he might find his son and try to make up for lost time.

But now her son truly did not have a father. And never would.

She had to go out there. She could see enough of the living room to know that Red had picked up a magazine. He leaned back, comfortable and relaxed on the scratchy plaid sofa.

That kind—the completely confident kind—always claimed their personal space with ease. Victor had looked equally at home on that sofa. Fat lot that had meant, in the end.

She couldn't stall forever, though. So she straightened her spine and walked down the hall.

"Sorry to keep you waiting."

"No problem." He half stood, maybe because his mom had raised him right, and maybe only to set down the magazine on the coffee table. "I learned a lot about fat-free casseroles."

She bought some time by circling the living room, turning on the lights to banish the twilight gloom. Then she sat on the opposite sofa and folded her hands in her lap.

"So, what happened?" she asked. "To Victor."

Red leaned forward, his hands dangling near his knees. He looked sober, but under complete control. She couldn't tell from his manner how close he and Victor might have been.

"Throat cancer. He was diagnosed about a year ago, more or less. He didn't tell any of us until about six months ago." He seemed to be watching her closely. "I take it he didn't tell you, either?"

"Victor and I haven't spoken for at least that long," she said. "But, no. He didn't tell me he was sick."

She worked to keep her expression neutral, too. They were like two poker players, neither willing to give the other an iota of advantage.

But her mind was racing. About a year ago...that would have been close to the time she met Victor. He'd been a regular at her dad's restaurant. He'd clearly been sad—a bad divorce, he'd told her. And she had been keeping a death vigil on the restaurant. On the night she closed the restaurant doors for good, she and Victor had finally made love.

She wondered whether he had known about the cancer then. She wondered whether his sickness had anything to do with his leaving her.

Not that it was an excuse. Sick or not, he shouldn't

have walked away without a word. Their relationship had lasted about five weeks. They hadn't been in love— they'd both known that. They were good friends who had helped each other through some tough times.

But you're never too sick to call and tell a friend goodbye.

Besides, he'd sounded fine four months later, when she called to tell him about the baby. He'd sounded quite normal as he explained that he hadn't been entirely truthful with her.

Not entirely truthful? *Yeah. You might say that.*

He was a married man with two children.

He'd apologized, of course. And he'd instructed his lawyer to send her a check. Not a huge one—enough to pay for the abortion he'd earnestly advised her to seek, and then a little cushion for "emotional distress."

She'd torn up the check the day Eddie was born. And then she'd done the one thing she was truly ashamed of in this whole mess. She'd found Victor's address and mailed the pieces back to him, along with a picture of Eddie. No note.

She'd never heard from him again.

So what was his emissary doing here now?

She was suddenly exhausted. She'd been up since six, after only three hours sleep. And Eddie had been waking up every couple of hours lately, as if he still didn't feel quite right.

So whatever Red Malone wanted, he needed to get to the point.

"Victor made it clear that he wanted nothing to do with me, or with Eddie," she said. "So I have to admit I'm a little confused. Why are you here?"

He moved forward. The light from the end-table

lamp tilted the shadows, hiding one side of his face. "Because he asked me to come. He was—" He seemed to search for the correct word. "He was worried about you. He wanted me to give you something."

"What?"

"This." Red had been wearing a windbreaker, which he'd folded beside him on the sofa. He reached into the front breast pocket and pulled out a long, thin brown envelope. He opened it and pulled out a small, rectangular piece of paper.

"It's a check," he said unnecessarily, holding it out for her to take. "For you and your son."

She accepted it without comment and took a moment to look it over. The amount surprised her. Twenty-five thousand dollars. That was a lot of money. Five times what he'd offered her to get rid of Eddie in the first place. But Victor's name was nowhere on it.

"This is your check," she said, holding it out for Red to reclaim. "Not Victor's."

He held up his hand, forestalling her. "It's Victor's money, though. He gave it to me with the understanding that I would give it to you."

She smiled, though she could feel her pulse beating in her throat. "So you laundered it for him. How sweet. The two of you must have been very close."

He understood how she felt now, she could see that. His eyebrows lowered over his blue eyes. "Yes," he said. "It would be difficult to overstate Victor's importance in my life. I'm close to his family, as well. His wife. His son and daughter."

He waited a minute, as if to let that sink in, as if she might not have realized Victor had another family.

"Yes," she agreed. "Cherry and Dylan."

Red's eyebrows went up. But he shouldn't have been surprised. Victor had told her their names, the day she called about the baby. He'd told her all about them. Cherry was much older, beautiful, ambitious and good at math. Dylan, who was starting to play soccer, was going through a difficult phase. Victor had wanted to make Allison understand. He'd been so sure she would see that his beloved legitimate children were far more important than any bastard child she might be carrying.

"Yes, Cherry and Dylan," Red repeated. "They're grieving right now. Obviously Victor didn't want them to be hurt further by any…disturbing revelations. But he also wanted you and your son to be remembered. So yes, I was happy to help make sure no one got hurt unnecessarily."

Clearly he wasn't going to take the check back from her. She laid it gently on the coffee table between them. Then she folded her hands in her lap. She clenched them so tightly her knuckles went white.

"Twenty-five thousand dollars is a lot of money," he said coolly, still watching her with that appraising look. "And yet, you don't seem particularly impressed."

"I'm not."

He waited, apparently unfazed. She tried not to reach across the table and slap that smug arrogance from his face. He was so sure, wasn't he? So sure he had her number. And that number, he assumed, was twenty-five thousand.

"Apparently you haven't ever looked up the average cost of raising a child from birth to age eighteen, Mr. Malone. I have. Would you like to know what it is?"

He smiled. "About ten times that."

"Exactly." She sat back in her chair, though she didn't allow her spine to touch the fabric. "So you're correct. I'm unimpressed."

He raised one brow. "You want more?"

"No, actually. I want *less*." With effort, she kept her voice down, so that she wouldn't wake Eddie. But God, she was mad. She was so hot, blazing angry. "I want less ingratiating B.S. I want less of your insulting, patronizing arrogance. This check isn't a bequest, or a gift. This is a payment."

"A payment?"

"Yes. Or rather, a pay*off*. I'm not an idiot, Mr. Malone. Victor never felt the urge to toss this kind of money my way before. Why now? What does he want? I'd be willing to bet the answer is in that nice envelope you're holding. So why don't you show me?"

The look he gave her now was odd—part contempt and part grudging admiration, as if she'd turned out to be a worthier opponent than he'd expected. She could feel his scorn, but in a strange way she was glad the poker faces were gone. The cards were on the table now, and the game was almost done.

With a cool smile, he opened the envelope and unfolded a sheaf of papers. He flattened them so that they could be more easily read, then extended them to her.

"It's a confidentiality agreement. In a nutshell, he would like you to agree that you will not disclose to anyone that he is the father of your child. If you sign, you'll also be agreeing to renounce any interest in the estate and relinquish any claim you may have to it."

She took it. She gave it a cursory look, though the black squiggles didn't even seem to form words in front of her fury-glazed stare.

Then she leaned over and picked up the check. She folded the check inside the papers, neatly. With an almost tender care.

And then she tore it all into pieces.

"Ms. York, I think you might want—"

As if it had been rehearsed, Jimbo chose that moment to come home.

He opened the door with his own key and blundered in, singing. His gorgeous, toned body was barely covered by his yoga pants, which rode low on his hips. He wore no shirt at all, displaying his colorful tattoos. At chest level, he held a pile of take-out boxes so high that only the spiky blond tips of his hair could be seen above the cartons.

"Hey, sugar lips. Lookee what Daddy brought home from Mamma Loo's!"

Red Malone stared for a split second, and then, running his fingers through his hair, he began to chuckle darkly. "I see. The new meal ticket, I presume?"

"Hey." Jimbo cocked his head around the food. He clearly didn't like the tone. "Who the hell are you?"

"I'm nobody. I'm gone." Still smiling, Red stood. "No. Really." He put his hand out to prevent Allison from rising. "Don't bother. I can find my own way out."

CHAPTER FOUR

ATTORNEY LEWIS PORTERFIELD, who usually ate his lunch in lonely, Gothic splendor, obviously wasn't happy to have Red as his guest today.

Well, too bad. Red wouldn't say he was having the time of his life, either. The firm's impressive, mahogany-walled conference room had obviously been decorated by a mortician. The lighting was as dim as what you'd get from candle sconces in an underground tomb.

Room was cold as a crypt, too, though that sensation might have been coming from Lewis.

The lawyer's small, pasty form was almost invisible in the high-backed armchair at the head of the table. He could be located primarily by watching the ghostly glisten of his boiled calamari as he rhythmically lifted one forkful after another to his lips.

Red had often wondered why on earth Victor used this guy. Sure, Lewis could write a contract so tight even Houdini couldn't wriggle out of it. But so could Colby, and probably a thousand other lawyers in the San Francisco Bay area alone. And they could do it without giving everyone the dead-eye creeps.

"So, tell me again." Lewis took a sip of water, the only beverage Red had ever seen him drink. "In your estimation, is Ms. York saying no because she means no? Or because she is holding out for a larger payment?"

"I can't be sure." Red had said this five times now, but apparently Lewis planned to keep asking until he got an answer he liked. "I got the impression she really meant it. But it's hard to be sure. She's…complicated."

The calamari hovered a few inches from Lewis's lips. "Complicated how?"

Red shrugged. "I don't know. She looks like the girl next door. And she lives simply, almost…" He thought of the squeaky clean, threadbare apartment. "Well, let's just say that if she's a gold digger, she's not a very good one. Plus, you can't help sensing that there's this sweet quality in her personality, in spite of the situation. But she's got a backbone. She's far from weak."

He wondered suddenly what Nana Lina would think about Allison. His grandmother was the shrewdest judge of character Red had ever met. She liked women who had what she called "starch."

Lewis tapped his cloth napkin to his lips, three times, as always. "Is she beautiful?"

Beautiful? With that short nose and those freckled cheeks? All skin and bones, and wash-and-dry hair? Hardly.

But Red had hesitated a moment too long. Victor set down his fork with a ring of sterling against fine china. "Ah. She is, then. Is that why she's complicated? Your mind can't process her properly because she's simultaneously a beauty *and* a tramp?"

Red's shoulders twitched. God, what a judgmental— He knew this was merely how Lewis talked, but still. Red needed to get out of this room. He needed to breathe fresh air and eat something that didn't look like boiled slime.

A whole hour of this crazy Victorian scenario was too much. Red sometimes wondered whether Lewis put it all on, for fun. Maybe at home Lewis wore a Giants cap and Nikes and burped up his beer while he watched *American Idol*.

Hell, the guy was only about fifty, Victor's age. Maybe Lewis had a girlfriend, too. One who—

But no. That was taking even a comedic fantasy too far. If there was a female out there who would date Lewis Porterfield, Red didn't want to meet her.

"I think *tramp* might be a little extreme, don't you?" Red was proud of his restraint. "For all we know, she was deeply in love with Victor."

Lewis raised one eyebrow. "There's already a new man in her house. Besides, you said she hated Victor."

"Love can turn to hate pretty quickly." Red tapped the table irritably. "But I'm not saying she did love him. I'm only saying we don't know."

Pause. Then Lewis's mouth twisted in something that might have been a smile. "And, of course, there's the fact that she's...*complicated*."

Oh, great. Sarcasm. That was the annoying part about Lewis. He might look like a caricature of a Victorian lawyer, but his brain was sharp and relentless.

Red shoved his plate of calamari away, untouched. "Okay, look. If I had to commit one way or another, I'd say she's not going to take Victor's money, no matter how high the offer goes. She needs it, but there was a kind of, I don't know, steel behind her eyes. She said no, and I think she meant it."

"Very well. Unfortunately, it doesn't really matter because we have to follow Victor's wishes, in any case."

"What do you mean? I thought Victor's wishes were for me to make that offer, and—"

"That was plan A."

Oh, hell. "And what is plan B?"

"We wait a week. If she hasn't accepted the offer by then, we go back, and we'll offer her fifty thousand."

"No." Red shook his head. "That's the worst thing you could do. Victor's main concern was that Marianne and the kids wouldn't have to find out. I'm telling you, Allison York doesn't seem like the tattling type. I'd bet my life that, unless we antagonize her, she'll leave well enough alone."

Lewis stared at Red a long time before answering. Finally, after another sip of water and three more taps with the napkin, he cleared his throat. "But it isn't your life that's in jeopardy here, is it? It isn't your family. It isn't your legacy."

"No, but—"

"We cannot substitute our judgment for Victor's. He said he wanted us to wait a week, then double the offer. That's exactly what we'll do."

"Big mistake. She's offended by the idea that we want to buy her silence. Besides, the offer itself is offensive. It's too low, Lewis, even if it's doubled. Tripled. Given what she's up against—"

"What she's *up against?*" Lewis tilted his head, which, with his hooked nose, made him look oddly like a vulture. The plate of glistening, wormy squiggles in front of him didn't help. "Sounds as if you feel sorry for the woman."

"Not really. I simply see the reality of her situation. Being a single mother can't be easy."

"Immoral behavior leads to difficult situations." Lewis sniffed. "She should have thought of that."

Red's shoulders tensed. "God, Porterfield. I was thinking this room looked a little Victorian. An attitude like that fits right in."

Lewis smiled again. "Are you defending her? Interesting. I'm curious about this excess of sympathy. In fact, Redmond, I'm wondering if you might be a touch compromised here."

"Really? Well, I'm wondering if you might be a touch *reptilian.* Putting basic human sympathy off-limits is a little cold-blooded, don't you think?"

Lewis steepled his fingers and stared at Red over the tips. He spoke in a contemplative voice, almost as if he were alone, mulling over a thorny point of law. "Actually, I am not particularly surprised. I told Victor it was risky, sending a man like you to do a job like this."

Red's jaw felt tight. "A man like me?"

"Yes. A man with a…shall we say a *fondness* for a certain kind of young woman? Shall we say a certain *vulnerability* to their charms?"

Without realizing how it happened, Red was suddenly on his feet. "Shall we say *bullcrap?*"

Though Red was three times Lewis's size, the lawyer didn't show a hint of fear. He lifted one pointed shoulder. "You may call it whatever you want, but I call it a problem. I think perhaps I'd better be the one to deliver the next offer."

"No."

"No? Why?"

"Because—" Red caught himself right before he

could say the words, *because you're an arrogant jack-ass, and you'll piss her off so much she'll tell Marianne everything just to spit in your eye.*

That was what the whole ugly mess always boiled down to, of course. Protecting Marianne. And Dylan. At twenty-eight, Cherry was probably mature enough, and far enough outside the fray, to handle the truth, but Dylan was already messed up as hell. He and Marianne needed some peace. They needed time to heal.

And Red had promised to help make sure they got it.

"Because I'm the fool who vowed to fix this," he said, pushing his chair in and preparing to get out of this oppressive room. "And I'm going to do exactly that."

THE MEETING WITH Lewis had left a bad taste in his mouth—and it wasn't only the thought of that revolting calamari, either. Red went to the Diamante office, hoping to lose himself in some paperwork. The city council had sent over traffic figures for three of the new locations he was considering. They looked good, but he wanted to analyze them carefully.

For once, though, work didn't help. The numbers ended up running together, like crazy hieroglyphics on the computer screen. So by three o'clock he turned off the computer and decided to leave early.

The Malone brothers hadn't ever been brooders. Nana Lina had always said there was no case of the blues that a good sweat wouldn't cure. Consequently, they worked hard and they played hard, and that didn't leave time for the sulks.

Work had failed. Time to try play.

Matt and Belle were out of town on their sixth honeymoon in four years, so he was no help. On the way out, Red checked Colby's office. A good heated game of handball would be perfect, and Colby was ahead in their lifetime stats.

His brother wasn't there, but Nana Lina had commandeered his desk. When she saw Red, she smiled and motioned him in.

He plopped in the chair opposite her and got comfortable. A dose of Nana Lina was always good for what ailed you.

"So, did you finally get wise and fire Colby?" He grinned. "I always said the guy was overrated."

Nana Lina never bothered to laugh at stupid jokes. If they got lucky and said something genuinely witty, her eyes could twinkle with true appreciation, but after living around three boys so long, she was immune to the daily exchange of cheap sarcasm.

She looked at a spreadsheet she apparently had been studying. "He's out at Half Moon Bay, number three. We got word that the drawer's not right again. Sixth time this week."

Red frowned. "Since when did the company attorney have to count the pennies in the cash register? Don't we have a decent manager out there?"

"You know Colby." Nana Lina raised one graceful pewter eyebrow, as if mildly amused. "They think it's the Mathison kid they hired last month."

Red groaned, finally understanding. Colby took these things so hard. The oldest Malone brother, Colby talked tough, but he was a hopeless idealist at heart. He never could quite believe that, when they gave summer jobs to the sons of their friends, the kids would rob them blind.

"What is it about rich kids?" He laced his fingers behind his head, stretched and yawned. "No work ethic. Not paragons of industry and virtue like me."

Nana Lina made a disapproving sound between her teeth. Then, finally, she smiled. "If you boys were half as useless as you pretend to be, I'd have to get out the switch."

"Ooh. The switch." This had been Grandpa Colm's running joke. No one, neither their parents nor their grandparents, had ever laid a violent finger on any of them, but Grandpa Colm had loved to refer to the mythical switch as if he beat them daily.

Every now and then, when she was feeling particularly affectionate, Nana Lina would borrow the jest. It gave Red a warm feeling now, remembering his vibrant grandfather and the musical Irish lilt he'd never dropped, no matter how many years he'd been in the United States.

No, no one had ever whipped the Malone boys. No one had needed to. Their parents had been intelligent, calm, loving. And the three brothers had never been bad kids, though of course they'd had their defiant moments. Red had been slap in the middle of his worst adolescent prickliness when their parents died.

But after the accident—one of those freak automobile catastrophes that happened a few miles from their own home—the rebellious attitude dropped from the boys like magic. Once they got a glimpse of true tragedy, they never again confused it with the little annoyances, like curfew or chores. No more mountains out of molehills.

"I wish Dylan Wigham had someone like you to turn to right now," Red said thoughtfully. "He's been having a rough time since Victor died."

Nana Lina nodded. She knew the family well, as they all did. Victor hadn't been her favorite person, but they were in the same social set and ended up at many of the same functions. And, of course, Red's friendship with the Wighams meant that they got invited to most of the Malone/Diamante events.

She might not know all the details of Dylan's struggles, but she knew that the boy had been in a rehab clinic for the past several weeks. "When is he getting out?"

"I'm not sure. Soon, I hope. Marianne needs him at home, I think. She's pretty lonely."

"Yes," Nana Lina agreed, though her voice remained crisp. She wasn't a fan of extravagant mourning. Though Red knew she missed Grandpa Colm every day of her life, she had turned to work to give her life meaning. Work and her grandsons.

Predictably, she thought everyone should do the same.

She gave Red a straight look. "I hope you're not planning to try to fill that void yourself."

"I spend as much time with her as I can," he said. "But if you're asking whether I'm romancing her, the answer is no. Of course. Victor's only been gone two months, but even if it had been two years, Marianne and I are just friends."

"Good." Nana Lina never leaned back in her chair, but Red thought he saw a slight relaxation in her shoulders. "She's not right for you."

He laughed. "She hasn't got enough starch?"

Nana Lina had said this about the brothers' girl-friends so often it had become the code word for her disapproval. Conversely, when she said a woman did have starch, they knew it meant a world of respect. The first time they'd heard her say it, she'd been talking about their own mother. For in-laws, those two women had had an amazingly solid and close relationship.

"No, actually, she hasn't," Nana Lina said tartly. "She was probably born with starch. You can glimpse it, sometimes, underneath the silliness and the insecurity. But marrying Victor was probably the worst thing she could do. He valued her looks, but he didn't value the qualities she possessed that were far more worth-while. Consequently, she lost respect for them, too. So all she's left with is a pretty face, which won't hold anyone up in a crisis."

Actually, Red thought that was a perceptive evalu-ation. And Nana Lina should know. She was still one of the most beautiful women he knew, with her silky waves of gorgeous silver hair and her lively, intelligent blue eyes set in a heart-shaped face. In pictures, he'd seen what a stunner she'd been as a young woman.

But she'd never let vanity control her. She worked as hard as any of the Malones, male or female, young or old. He'd seen her mussed and covered in flour, pull-ing all-nighters in the kitchen before Diamante took off enough to pay someone else to do all that. He'd seen her sweating and splashed with paint, or potting soil or sawdust. And she always looked amazing, vibrant and intelligent and in love with her life.

"I wish you could adopt Marianne," he said. "I bet you could straighten her out in no time."

Nana Lina laughed. "I've got my hands full, I'm

afraid. But you don't need me. You know how to help her. Tell her to spend less time picking out earrings and more time being genuinely productive. Get a job. Or, if that's beneath a Wigham, she should do a Google search on the word *volunteer*. Or *charity*."

To Red's surprise, Nana Lina's voice sounded sharper than usual. He gave her a more careful look. Was she a little pale? Just the other day, Colby had said he thought she looked tired.

"Okay. I'll do that." He tried to sound casual. "So, enough about Marianne. How are things going for you? Everything okay?"

She frowned and shook her head. "Everything is fine," she said, "except that people keep coming in and distracting me, so that I'm never going to get this report analyzed. Don't you have somewhere to be? Some property to buy, some widow to console?"

He stood, smiling. "Yes, ma'am," he said. But he made a mental note to ask Colby what he thought. No way they were going to let Nana Lina get sick, even if it meant they had to get out the switch.

WHEN RED GOT OUTSIDE, squinting against the bright sun after hours in the artificial light, he saw a rectangular piece of paper hooked under his windshield wiper, and his sour mood turned even nastier. God. A ticket?

But it wasn't. When he yanked it out, the wiper bouncing, he saw that it was a flyer for the Splash Camp kickoff, which was being held today at Baker Country Day School in Russian Hill.

Marianne Wigham must have put it there. She was volunteering at the kickoff. *Damn it*. How could he have forgotten? This was the first time she'd done anything official or public since Victor's death. And since by now everyone at the Baker School knew about her son's problems, this was bound to be a stressful day.

In fact, though she hadn't exactly asked Red to come, she'd made very sure he knew exactly what time her shift was, and which tent she'd be staffing. She clearly hoped he would show up for moral support.

Not a far-fetched hope. For the past two months, he'd stopped by at least three times a week. He'd brought flowers and food. He'd visited Dylan in rehab. He'd offered a shoulder to cry on, and a hand to hold.

And now, because of the mess with Allison York, he'd almost let Marianne down on this one.

He looked at his watch. Just three-fifteen. If he hurried, he'd be fine.

The traffic was with him, so he made it to the school with time to spare. He parked in a space left by some early departure, then climbed the emerald-green lawn toward the solid Normanesque buildings that housed the school.

Only the best of the best got into Baker. In spite of his crazy-high IQ and his good address, Dylan almost hadn't made it. Victor's family tree had the right kind of roots, but Marianne was officially a nobody. She'd been a nineteen-year-old cosmetics model when Victor married her, which made the older Baker moms shiver politely and made the younger ones jealous as hell.

She'd had an extra strike against her simply because she was not Erna, Victor's beloved first wife, who had succumbed to a heart attack.

The grounds looked serene, daffodils swaying in the breeze and birds wheeling high in the blue sky. Most of the action was out back, where the Olympic-size swimming pool and field houses were found. But a few hospitality tents had been set up out front, and Marianne was in the one farthest west, out where the school grounds began to slope toward a thick, shadowy greensward.

It wasn't an accident, of course, them putting her in the hinterlands. Red felt a surge of annoyance at the snobs who couldn't see that she was better than all of them.

Or maybe they did see it. Maybe that was, in the end, Marianne's unforgivable sin.

He found the tent easily. She was apparently dispensing water bottles, though hardly anyone had ventured out this far. Just a crying little kid who had clearly been brought out here for a time-out, and a couple of late-teens eyeing the woods as if they needed a few minutes alone.

"Hey, there," he said as he got close enough to be heard. "Word is this booth has the best water in town."

Fiddling with a cooler, she had her back to him and hadn't seen him approach. She wore a crisp white dress that looked like a long shirt. It was belted around her tiny waist with some kind of turquoise cloth. Her hair lay on her shoulders like a yard of the most expensive gold satin. She always looked fantastic, though he could have told her she'd score more points if, just once, she showed up looking frumpy.

The minute she turned her face to him, he knew it had been a rough afternoon.

"Hi," she said, and he heard the relief that made the syllable heavy and thick. Her round blue eyes were red-rimmed, as if she'd been crying. "I thought you might not be able to make it."

"I almost didn't," he admitted, finding it impossible to lie to those eyes. "I've had a junky couple of days, and I almost forgot."

"That's okay," she said hurriedly.

"No, it's not," he said. He touched her shoulder to stop the apologies he knew were coming. "But I'm here now. Tell me about it."

She opened her mouth, that perfect rosebud that had sold a million tubes of lipstick. But then she shut it again and shook her head. "It's nothing. Tell me about your junky days. What went wrong?"

Oh, no. That was one conversation he wasn't going to have.

"Junky days are best forgotten," he said. He came around the side of the booth and picked up the cooler of water bottles. He plopped it on the cloth-covered table and then propped open the lid. In the unlikely event that anyone showed up thirsty, they could help themselves.

"Come with me," he said. "You need to get off your feet."

He would have taken her hand, except that somewhere, no doubt, a snobby Baker School mother's radar was twitching, and within seconds the grapevine would be humming with the gossip. No one cared that he and Marianne had been friends for fifteen years, or that the two of them had lost someone very dear.

Hell, even Nana Lina had wondered how far his stalwart-friend, shoulder-to-cry-on role might take him.

So he led her to a nearby bench. He swept a few leaves and strawberry crepe myrtle petals from its stony surface, and then they both sat.

For a few seconds, she twisted the fringed ends of her blue cloth belt in her lap and wouldn't meet his gaze. She sniffed a couple of times, and he knew she was trying to pull herself together.

"So," he observed mildly. "You look pretty done in. I hope you aren't letting the snarling blue-blood bitches get you down."

As he'd anticipated, the straightforward approach surprised her, and actually made her smile. "No," she said. Then she shrugged. "Not much, anyhow. Maybe a little."

He shook his head. That was the difference between the two of them. They both failed the sniff test when the social bloodhounds came around. Marianne cringed and tried to hide her background—the foster parents and the GED and the self-made career.

Red, on the other hand, was irrepressibly proud of being an immigrant's grandson. In fact, sometimes, when he knew he was going to one of the snobs' black-tie events, he'd hang out in the Diamante kitchens for a while so he would delicately stink of pepperoni. He loved watching the snobs flare their nostrils a bit, then try to pretend they hadn't noticed.

"To hell with them," he said. He glanced at the school. The late-afternoon sun was intense and pinkish-gold behind the columns, and the granite twinkled. Pretty, but he knew what went on in there.

"You know," he said without thinking, "it might do Dylan a world of good to get out of this place. Go to a real school for a while. Meet real people, with real problems."

"Don't say that," she said. "You know how important it was to Victor that Dylan get in."

Red nodded. He hadn't understood it, but he knew it was true.

"That's part of what went wrong today, actually. When I arrived, Gwen Anderton told me the board had scheduled a hearing about the…the party. Dylan's party."

Crap. Red pulled out his BlackBerry. This was one date he wasn't going to let himself forget. She couldn't possibly face down these barracudas, not without Victor. She had tried so hard to make her husband proud, to fit in his world. But the hopeless struggle to live up to someone else's superficial expectations had left her with a completely irrational sense of inferiority, as if these people had the right to pass judgment over her.

"When will it be?"

"I think she said next month. She said they sent a registered letter, so I guess that will be waiting for me when I get home."

He put his arm around her shoulder. To hell with the gossips. "I'll be there," he said. "We'll bring Colby, if you think we'll need that kind of ammunition. It'll be fine."

"Will it, Red? Will it really be fine? Sometimes I think nothing will ever be fine again." She lifted her face toward his, and her eyes were sparkling again, as if she were losing the fight to hold back the tears.

"It will. I promise."

He hoped he was right. If the board had called a hearing, they were taking Dylan's transgressions pretty seriously.

The boy, who had recently turned fifteen, had pulled a few pranks in his time—mostly innocent stuff, like spray painting the back fence of a cranky neighbor. Nothing his dad couldn't buy him out of.

But his father's death had hit him hard. Abnormally hard. He'd become uncommunicative, surly, difficult for Marianne to control. Red had spent a lot of time trying to help. He'd known Dylan since he was a baby, and Red seemed to be the only person the boy didn't hate right now.

But apparently even "Uncle" Red wasn't enough. About a month after Victor's death, Dylan had been caught at a friend's "pharm party," half out of his mind on the concoction of prescription drugs the kids had gathered from their parents' medicine cabinets. A neighbor had called the police, and all the teenagers had spent a few terrifying hours at the local jail. Several of them, like Dylan, had been taken straight to the hospital. By the time the dust settled, most of the kids had landed in high-priced, in-patient rehab.

At first Marianne had been horrified, dead set against the idea of rehab. She believed Dylan to be a good kid, underneath all the acting out. But after Red had visited the rehab center a couple of times and talked to Dylan privately, he'd understood it was necessary. This hadn't been Dylan's first pharm party, not by a long shot. The boy was lucky to be alive.

"He wasn't the only Baker kid at that party," Red reminded Marianne now. "If they kick them all out, how will the trustees pay their country-club dues next year?"

She smiled weakly, but she didn't say anything, and he couldn't tell whether she believed him. She bit her lower lip and tortured the ends of the belt some more.

Then, abruptly, she lifted her head and said, "Dylan comes home next week."

The minute the words were out of her mouth, tears

began to stream down her cheeks. With a small sound, she lifted her hands to her face as if she thought she could catch them.

His heart twisted. No wonder she was so fragile—ricocheting between her grief over her husband and her anxiety about her son. *Damn it, Dylan.* Why didn't the boy see that his wasn't the only broken heart in the family? Why didn't he give his mom a little support, instead of becoming another burden?

But Red knew that wasn't fair. At fifteen, you didn't understand a single thing. The world confused the hell out of you. Red had been fifteen when his own parents died. If it hadn't been for Grandpa Colm and Nana Lina, God only knew what would have become of him. Of course, he'd also been lucky enough to have two older brothers who had no intention of letting their obnoxious younger sibling sink, no matter how much of a pain in their ass he was.

Dylan hadn't had all that. He had one half sister, Cherry, who was a solid ally and a delightfully spunky person. But Cherry had moved out years ago, and had a life in Los Angeles now. After Victor died, Dylan had been left with only one frightened, forlorn mother who loved him but didn't have a clue how to handle him.

And he had Red. He would always have Red.

He tried to nudge a smile out of her now. "Come on, Mari. Don't cry. Isn't being released a good thing?"

"I guess so. Dr. Packard says he thinks Dylan will make more progress if he's at home, where he won't feel so isolated."

"Well, then. That's enough to convince me." Red gave her shoulder a brief squeeze. "You know how strict

Dr. Packard is. It's not as if Dylan can wheedle him into believing he's doing better than he really is."

"Yes, I know. I'm sure Dr. Packard is right. If he says Dylan's ready, he's ready." She turned her blood-shot gaze to Red. "But what about me?"

"What do you mean?"

"I mean…am I ready?"

"Of course you are."

"I'm not so sure." She forced her hands into her lap and braided them together. The knuckles were white with tension. "I feel so inadequate. He's so angry…with me, with his father, with everyone. When I visit him, it's as if we're strangers. I don't even feel as if I know him anymore. When he was little, we were so close. But lately…"

"That's part of being a teenager," Red assured her. "Adolescent boys are always trying on new attitudes. Deep inside, we're still the same stupid little dweebs we always were."

She smiled, a fleeting sunbeam of thanks for his attempt to cheer her. But he could see that it hadn't really helped much. "Maybe. But…I'm such a mess myself. Half the time I forget what I was supposed to be doing. I'll open the freezer to take the casserole out for dinner, and then I'll realize I've stood there crying for twenty minutes, and everything is melting. How does a basket case like that take care of anyone? What if I do something wrong? What if I can't protect him?"

"You'll do fine. You're not a basket case. You're hurting. Give yourself a little slack, Marianne. It's only been two months."

"Fifty-seven days." Her voice caught. "It's so strange. Sometimes, when I wake up, it seems like Victor must surely be in the next room. I can almost hear him breathing. But then, other times, it seems like he's been gone forever. Or as if he never really existed in the first place. As if he was only a dream I had."

Red didn't know what to say. Platitudes were useless here. Her grief was so real it shimmered darkly around her, like a terrible halo. He wondered what it must be like to love someone that much.

It must be terrifying.

They sat in silence a couple of minutes, watching the trees stretch olive shadows across the bright green grass. They heard children laughing and splashing in the distance, from behind the administration building. It must be nearly five. The breeze had cooled, and the streaky pink clouds hinted at gold to come.

"You know what I think sometimes?" Marianne's sudden words were clear in the crisp air. "Sometimes I think Victor was taken away from us because I didn't deserve him."

"What?" He frowned, but she held up her hand quickly.

"I know how absurd that sounds. Even egotistical. Not even the cruelest fates would take a father away from his children to punish his wife, would they? No matter how unworthy she was."

Though he'd vowed he would respect her feelings, whatever they were, Red couldn't let this nonsense pass. "That comment certainly is absurd—on so many levels. For starters, what on earth would make you think you didn't deserve him?"

She lifted one tired shoulder. "I didn't."

"Mari. That's ridiculous."

"It's not, though. At least for the past two years, I've

been a crummy wife. Always nagging. Always complaining."

He shook his head. "I don't believe it."

She gazed at him, but with eyes slightly unfocused, as if she stood at a great distance and could hardly make out his details. "That's because you are so easygoing, Red. You never demand too much of other people. I do, or at least I demanded too much of Victor. He was everything to me, but I was only one piece of his life. I resented how hard he worked. I resented that he wasn't at home with us. I—"

He waited, and finally her limpid gaze fell. She stared at her hands, her cheeks reddening. "I wanted to have another child. When it didn't happen, I was so disappointed. So angry. I blamed his work, especially, because it took him away so much. We fought all the time."

Clearly she expected Red to be shocked.

And, until a couple of months ago, he would have been. Until Victor had told him about Allison and the secret baby, Red had considered the Wigham marriage to be idyllic. Everyone did. The elegant town house on Russian Hill had seemed to hum with peace and tranquility. He'd envied Victor his loving family. How lucky was a guy to find true love not once, but twice?

But under the serene veneer, apparently the same pain and confusion that complicated other lives had roiled at the Wigham house, too. Marianne had been dissatisfied, unhappy. Dylan had been escaping into recreational drugs. Victor had found himself in Windsor Beach, in the arms of a stranger.

What part had Marianne's unhappiness played in all that?

But in all their discussions, Victor had never once blamed Marianne. To his credit, he'd never uttered the clichéd words *she just didn't understand me,* never subtly hinted that his wife had been cold and critical, driving him into another woman's arms. He had taken full responsibility for his adultery, had spoken of it as an unforgivable, selfish act. He had clearly been eaten up with shame.

Red could still feel the bone-cracking grip with which Victor had clutched his hand that last hour of his life. "She must never know," he'd whispered. "Never. Promise me, Red. It would break her heart. She doesn't deserve that."

He glanced at Victor's widow now. "I'm sure you weren't as bad as—"

"I was." She drew her eyebrows together, as if girding herself to remember everything. "By the time I found out he was sick, we were hardly speaking. Can you imagine how I felt? Dylan knew. He hated me for it. He probably hates me still, for driving his father away."

"But you didn't drive him away. Married couples fight. All of them. It doesn't mean anything. If Dylan doesn't see that now, he will see it eventually. You didn't drive him away."

She was hardly listening, he realized. She kept talking. "The disease claimed him so fast. We had so little time. A few months, that was all, to make it up. To make him know I had always loved him, no matter how terrible I acted."

The tears were falling freely now, trailing silver down her cheeks and then disappearing over the roundness of her chin.

"Over and over, I ask myself whether he believed me.

Whether he still loved me, even though I'd been so..."
She swallowed hard. "His love was the best thing that
ever happened to me, Red. If I killed it, how can I ever
look our son in the eyes again? If I killed it—"

"You didn't." He put his hands on either side of her
face. "You couldn't. There aren't many things I'm sure
about in this crazy world, Marianne Wigham, but I'm
completely sure about that."

He had a momentary mental flash of a dark haired
young waitress, a baby in her arms and her golden eyes
fiery with fury. He pushed the vision away. He didn't
understand what had happened between Victor and Allison York. He probably never would understand.

But somehow he knew that, whatever it had been, it
didn't change what he was about to say now.

"From the moment he laid eyes on you, until the
moment he took his last breath, your husband loved
you with all his heart."

CHAPTER FIVE

ALLISON YAWNED AS SHE PICKED up a sweet potato and perched it atop all the other vegetables in her canvas bag. The yawn came from deep in her soul and went on forever, too wide and heartfelt to hide behind her hand.

"Excuse me," she said, laughing. She reached for another potato.

"No!" Jimbo barked from behind her. He reached into her bag and pulled the yam out again. "No, no, no. Too stringy. We want only the fat ones. I told you this was a bad idea. I saw that yawn. Apparently you're too tired to know a decent vegetable from a runt."

She was tired, definitely. But they'd had this battle, or one like it, every Saturday for months. She loved the farmer's market, adored strolling through the sun-dappled dirt lot with Eddie nestled against her in his sling pouch.

Jimbo, however, would have preferred that she stay home. He was the kind of chef who liked to hand-pick every ingredient, trusting no one's judgment but his own. Before they checked out, he always pawed through her choices and put half of them back.

The attitude made her laugh. The restaurant would be hers, at least on paper—which meant the payments would come out of her checkbook. But Jimbo's heart was every bit as invested as hers. If Summer Moon failed, it wouldn't be for lack of love.

It might, however, be for lack of money. She had spent a couple of hours this morning with a rep from the food distributor, and his estimate had taken her breath away. A quarter higher, at least, than she'd planned for.

Against her will, her thoughts darted to Red Malone's check, the one he'd dangled in front of her the other day, the same way she might shake a ring of plastic keys in front of Eddie to distract and amuse him. The arrogant bastard. Red had so clearly sized up her apartment and concluded that she'd be easy to buy off. She needed the money too much to afford the luxury of pride.

She wasn't fooling herself. The money would come in handy in about a million different ways. She could do so many things for Eddie. For the restaurant. For Jimbo. It would be a safety net that would help her sleep a lot better every night.

But accepting that check would have been impossible. Did Red think she'd slept with Victor because he had money, and she hoped he'd sprinkle a little of it on her? She hadn't even really known Victor was wealthy. He had presented himself as just a guy taking a solitary vacation to clear his head. He'd needed couple of weeks away from a bad divorce, he said. He found himself enjoying the anonymity of a little resort hotel, and the good food and good company of a small, family-owned restaurant.

She'd had no idea he had some swanky town house in San Francisco. Much less that he had a wife and children living there.

And why on earth would Red Malone believe she would ever consider signing away Eddie's right to his biological father's family? Allison had no way to predict what challenges life would hold. Suppose…suppose Eddie needed a transfusion, a bone marrow transplant, a kidney? None of that would ever happen, of course, but what kind of fool would give up the right to ask for help, if disaster did strike someday?

But…she picked over a small crate of blueberries, trying to be honest with herself. All those rationales were true, but the bottom line was that she had been deeply humiliated by Red's offer. She'd rejected it because, if she took it, her self-respect would never recover.

Jimbo was in front of her now, glaring at a bright red row of strawberries. She put her palm over Eddie's head, not so much to calm him as to steady her own nerves.

"Do you think Summer Moon ought to be dinner only for a while?" She spoke to Jimbo's back. "Just until we can put a little more money away? We could add lunch later…"

He didn't even turn around. With those huge, tattooed fingers, he picked out a plump red berry and popped it into his mouth. Eyes shut, he chewed with the intense concentration of a wine connoisseur checking out a Château Lafite. He waited, then swallowed.

Then he made a rude sound. "Local?" He waved his hand over the display. "I don't think so."

Allison was glad the stall's owner wasn't within earshot. She shoved Jimbo with her hip to move him along before he started a brawl. "Hey. Did you even hear my question?"

He tossed a patient smile over his shoulder. "Of course I heard it. I didn't answer because it wasn't a real question. You know we can't change the game plan now. You're locked into a budget that requires serving lunch and dinner."

As his words sank in, she fell behind, watching his broad shoulders move through the crowd toward a booth stacked high with melons. He was right, of course. That fateful morning three months ago, when she submitted her detailed business plan with her loan application, she'd committed herself absolutely to the dream. When the loan was approved, she had moved ahead full steam. She bought the property, hired a restaurant designer, ordered equipment, created entrées, printed menus, wrote Grand Opening ads, memorized safety codes and food temperatures, and even interviewed waiters and busboys and dishwashers and hostesses and managers.

The opening was still four weeks away, but she was already so far in hock there was no turning back now. It was like when they clicked the safety bar into place on the roller coaster, and you felt the car jerk into motion. After that, all you could do was hold on and hope for the best.

She feathered the soft petals of a multicolored bouquet of daisies from the flower stall beside her and breathed deeply, her hand back on Eddie's head. Yes, it was a lot like that. The same sick feeling, the same nervous urge to jump off, the same sizzle of fear mixed with excitement.

She was scared, all right, but she was also thrilled. She loved roller coasters.

Bored by the lack of motion, Eddie made a small

sound and kicked out his feet restlessly. She began to walk again, her exhaustion miraculously disappearing.

She caught up with Jimbo, who must finally have found a vendor he approved of. He was sniffing the stem end of a cantaloupe, dragging in a breath so deep she thought he might blow up like a cartoon character.

"Now this is what I'm *talking* about," he raved to the woman behind the table. "This is a cantaloupe."

She looked pleased, though Allison couldn't tell whether it was because of the compliment, or because this fabulously handsome man had appeared out of nowhere. Allison, who deeply believed that Jimbo needed to be in love, checked the woman out. Loving her produce was a good start. Any chance the feeling could transfer to the farmer?

Hmm… Maybe. The woman looked smart, mid-thirties, cute in a healthy, outdoorsy way—which was the only style that could ever appeal to Jimbo.

He'd blow a gasket, of course, if he knew what Allison was thinking. They had a deal. No meddling, no matchmaking. But she hated the idea that he was giving so much of himself to Eddie that he couldn't ever find time for a romance of his own. He hadn't given up women, officially—certainly he wasn't as determined as she was to remain single. However, he clearly felt that she needed him right now, and he didn't want to be distracted from that mission.

But he couldn't stop her from making contacts with people who might help Summer Moon. So, Allison moved forward and held out her hand.

"Hi, I'm Allison York. I'm opening a new restaurant next month, and I'm hoping to work with the very best local farmers. If Jimbo's face is any yardstick, your fruit must be pretty special. Do you have a card?"

The woman smiled. Her handshake was firm. "Nice to meet you, Allison," she said in a well-modulated alto. She produced a business card from under the table. "I'm Meg Bretton."

Allison handed her own across the melons and then glanced at the card. Simple and professional—name, telephone number and website. Well done. And, of course, she got a bonus point for not stammering in the face of Jimbo's sex appeal.

"I don't remember seeing you here before," Allison ventured casually, pretending to inspect the honeydew, which looked exquisite. The globes were, she realized suddenly, the exact color she wanted for the main seating area. She put one in her bag, and she noticed that Jimbo didn't object. "Are you new to the area?"

"No. We've had a booth here for almost two years. It's just that my ex-husband used to man it." Meg's gaze glittered. "Well, I don't know that *man* is the right word. He used to *run* it, anyhow."

Allison was slow. She had to replay the sentences twice before she understood the joke, and by then Jimbo was already chuckling.

Ah. So that explained the immunity to Jimbo's charm. Meg was coming down from a bitter divorce, and she wasn't in the mood to be wowed by any man. Well, Allison knew all about that.

As usual, Eddie found immobility boring. He wriggled against the silk of his sling and began to make the noises that Jimbo called his "countdown to blastoff." About ten seconds, and he was going to let loose a wail that would take the tops off the trees.

Jimbo was still investigating the fruit and seemed to have no intention of moving on yet. So Allison pulled Eddie out of the pouch and held him in the crook of her elbow, face forward, to let him watch the bustle around them. He thrust his feet out ecstatically, clearly elated by the freedom, and, fastening his gaze on Meg, babbled something fast and exuberant.

"Is that so?" The woman grinned at Eddie, then reached out and tweaked his toe, which sent him into squeals of amusement. She glanced at Allison, and her gaze had turned wistful. "Your little boy is darling," she said.

"Thanks." Allison wondered whether Meg and her husband had any children. Custody arrangements could be so unfair....

Something caught her eye. A few yards away, near the parking lot and the small kids' playground, two men were talking...no, not just talking. Though it was restrained and careful, they were definitely arguing. That alone wasn't enough to be startling—although fights at a farmers' market were admittedly pretty rare. She wondered what had given her this sudden edgy feeling.

The man facing her was smallish, and pale, and older. She didn't know him. Both men were in suits, which was a little strange for this place, but it happened. The other man was—

She inhaled hard. The other man was Red Malone.

Without a word to anyone, she stalked across the patchy dirt-and-beaten-grass area until she was a few feet away from the men. She was so furious she wanted to yell, cuss and wave her hands, driving them out of here the way her dad used to drive wild dogs out of his chicken coop.

But she knew almost everyone at this market, both vendor and buyer. This was her town. Dealing with these farmers was now her business, her livelihood. She couldn't afford to stage a scene in front of everyone.

But damn it. *Damn* it!

How *dare* they?

She was about a yard away when the older man, who could see her approach, realized something was wrong. He straightened and threw his chest out, which suddenly made him seem bigger and younger—as if the puny, insignificant old guy look had been camouflage.

"I'm going to give you two minutes to get out of here," she said in a low tone that thrummed with fury. "And then I'm going to call the police."

Red turned at the sound of her voice. "Allison," he began. "This is Lewis Porterfield, Victor's lawyer, and—"

The older guy raised one eyebrow. "Call the police? And tell them what?"

"That you're stalking me. Harassing me." She was so heated she felt herself stumbling over the syllables. "You're the lawyer. You know what the right word is. I just know that I'm sick of turning around and seeing you there. And if you don't stop it, I'm going to get a restraining order."

"Technically, this is the first time you've seen me," Porterfield observed calmly. "Even so, you could ask for a civil harassment order, I suppose. But you'd have to prove substantial emotional distress. Even more difficult, you'd have to show that our visits serve no legitimate purpose. I don't think it would hold up, given that we're trying to carry out a dead man's instructions and give you a quite sizable check, but you're certainly welcome to try."

She blinked, rendered almost speechless by his robotlike monotone. Some distant, observing part of her mind recognized that this unemotional neutrality probably was an asset in a court case, but it was damned infuriating right here, right now.

"Listen, mister—"

"God, Lewis." Red Malone sounded as annoyed with the lawyer as Allison was. He turned to her, his features arranged in an expression that almost looked apologetic. "I tried to stop him from coming here. I know it must seem as if we're pushing too hard—"

"You're dead right it does," she said, pulling back Eddie's hand, which the baby had stretched out toward Red's shiny watch. She didn't want Eddie to touch these people. "It *seems* as if you're a couple of nervy sleazeballs who are going to follow me around and badger me until I sign some contract relinquishing God only know what rights—"

"The only right you're asked to relinquish is your right to destroy a dead man's legacy." The pale-faced lawyer angled his head to scrutinize her more thoroughly. "You don't really want to do that, do you, Ms. York? Whatever I might think of your moral code—"

"Lewis." Red sounded so angry Allison wondered whether he might punch the older man. "You seriously need to shut up. If you're trying to help Victor here, just shut up."

But it had no more effect on the lawyer than if he really had been a robot. He continued to scrape Allison with that appraising look. "Perhaps, while Victor was alive, you harbored hopes of breaking up his marriage and wedding him yourself. But now that he's dead, telling his widow could accomplish nothing. Quite the contrary. To ensure that she doesn't find out, we're prepared to offer you—"

"Get out of here." Allison's voice shook, and Eddie began to whimper, sensing her turmoil. "Just get out of here."

The lawyer frowned. "Ms. York, you haven't heard how much—"

"I don't care how much." Eddie had begun to cry, but softly, as if the tension in the air frightened him. She lifted the baby to her shoulder and tried to pat him comfortingly, but her hand was shaking, too.

Red was staring at Eddie, a strangely wistful expression in his dark fringed blue eyes. Another act? Did he think sentiment might appeal to her where bribery had failed? If he told her Eddie reminded him of Victor, she was going to smack him, audience or not.

She angled herself so that Red couldn't see the baby's face.

"I had a pretty crummy opinion of Victor before I met you two snakes," she said. "And I think even less of him now. If I could erase his DNA from my son's blood, I'd do it, so you can rest assured that I have very little interest in introducing him to the rest of the Wigham family."

The lawyer's eyes lit up, and he began digging around in his pocket. "Then surely you won't mind signing—"

"I don't think you understand me. I'm signing nothing. Nothing." She thought she might still hear a wavering in her voice, and she tightened her throat. She would not show weakness in front of these bastards. "I have no intention of contacting Victor's family now. But if the day ever comes when it's in my son's best interests for me to tell the Wighams about his existence, I'll do it without even blinking."

"Allison." Red gently touched her arm. "Let me apologize for Lewis. He doesn't always put things—"

"Don't call me Allison." She wheeled on him and shook off his fingers. "You're not my friend. You're prettier than he is, and slicker, but you don't fool me for a minute. You're a hyena, too—under the skin, the both of you are exactly the same."

Red's face registered something, but she didn't know him well enough to identify the emotion. Within a split second, his expression was as neutral and bland as the other man's.

She glanced toward the melon booth. Jimbo had finally noticed that she was gone. She could see him walking this way now, his shoulders rolled slightly forward, which meant he was ready for trouble, just in case. She needed to finish this before he came within earshot.

"You've got your answer," she said to the two men. "Now get out of here."

Red nodded. He gestured toward the other man. "Porterfield. Give it up. It's over."

The lawyer started to move, then halted in his tracks. "Fifty thousand," he said very fast, as if she could prevent the words from exiting his lips. "Fifty thousand dollars. That's what the offer is."

Jimbo had reached them in time to hear the number. He made a low noise of confused surprise. "Alli?"

But Allison was too angry to explain, or even to register anything logically. She stepped forward three hard paces, until her face was right up against the lawyer's. She could smell his breath. He smelled...antiseptic. Cold.

Between their bodies, Eddie squirmed anxiously and continued to fret.

"Listen carefully," she said, articulating every syllable, "because I'm only going to say this one more time. Victor Wigham doesn't *have* enough money to make me sign that contract. Throw in everything you and your friend here own, and there still isn't enough. So get out of here, Mr. Porterfield. I don't ever want to see either one of you weasels again."

CHAPTER SIX

THE DAY AFTER DYLAN CAME HOME from rehab, Red picked the boy up for lunch. Just the two of them, no mom around. Red knew Marianne was still emotionally fragile, and nothing was guaranteed to get a fifteen-year-old to clam up like a hovering, fretful mother who always seemed to be on the knife-edge of tears.

He thought about taking Dylan to Diamante, which had always been one of the boy's favorite restaurants. But they would be bombarded with friends and family there, and the whole welcome-back spotlight might be too much for a first outing. So instead he chose Banditos, a casual Mexican place across the street from Diamante where they could be more or less anonymous.

They got a corner table next to the windows, the closest thing to privacy Banditos could offer. For the first few minutes, while they read their menus, Red watched Dylan carefully. On the drive there, the kid's mood had seemed fairly stable. And not that weird, emotionless equilibrium achieved only by drugs. He'd acted pretty normal, actually.

"I think I want a number twelve." Dylan frowned at his tall menu, which had been covered in plastic to keep a thousand salsa splashes from spoiling it. "But can we start with chips and queso?"

Red nodded, unsurprised even though the number

twelve was a heaping platter of practically everything Banditos offered. Dylan always had been a bottomless pit for food. "Sure. Whatever looks good."

"Thank goodness. I'm starving. I'm so sick of rehab food I could puke." Dylan patted his stomach, his blue eyes grinning from under his mop of fair hair. The rehab center hadn't let him keep the hair as long as he usually liked it, but he'd managed to hang on to some silky, side-swept bangs. If he was still fighting to be a teenage heartthrob, his spirit couldn't have been completely crushed.

Red breathed a subtle sigh of relief. Plenty of work still remained to be done, but at least Dylan had emerged from this ordeal more or less intact.

They ordered. Dylan told a few funny stories about the other kids at rehab. Apparently two of his dorm mates had been Baker School friends—Philip and Brock, two of the snottiest kids at the school. Red had always found them obnoxious, but Dylan said they were cool, and acted as if he were lucky to have been deemed worthy to be their friend.

Once again, hearing how Philip and Brock had deviled the rehab counselors, Red wished Marianne would take Dylan out of that private school and give him a chance to taste real life in a regular school. He'd quickly learn that he was neither at the top of the totem pole nor at the bottom. He was just average, and that was okay.

As wealthy as the Wighams were, they couldn't compete with the serious bigwigs at Baker, so Dylan felt irrationally inferior. He wasn't tough, like his dad and his half sister, Cherry. He was emotional and vulnerable, with low self-esteem, like Marianne.

He craved acceptance so badly he'd do whatever the

cool kids suggested. Once, when he was only about ten, the other boys had asked him to slip his fingers into Brock's dad's weight machine and try to free a stuck pin. Eager to please, Dylan had agreed. At the worst possible moment, the weights had slammed down, crushing two of the fingers on Dylan's left hand.

Victor had been so disdainful, reprimanding his son for letting Philip and Brock talk him into doing something they themselves were too smart to try. The boy had cried harder over his father's lecture than he had over his broken fingers. He clearly wanted his father to admire him, but he hadn't understood the lesson his father was trying to convey.

"Dylan, do you remember that time you got your fingers smashed?" Red didn't try to make it sound casual. Dylan might not be confident, but he was smart, and he'd know the attitude was fake.

"Yeah." The boy's face closed in slightly. "Of course I do." He put his left hand in his lap, under the table. The fingernail of his index finger had never quite grown back normally.

"Well, I've always thought maybe you didn't understand why your dad was so upset about that."

"Sure I did. He thought I was an idiot. He wanted me to be more like Philip and Brock."

"No, see, that's where I think you got it wrong. He didn't think you were an idiot. He thought you were smart, a lot smarter than Philip and Brock. He believed you knew what was right. He knew you'd be fine if you started thinking for yourself."

Dylan stared down at his chips, as if they were suddenly unappetizing. "Well, I guess he was wrong. I'm not smart. I don't know what's right. When Brock says something is fun—or Philip—I believe them. It's not until later, when I start feeling weird, or the cops come, that I finally realize they might be full of crap."

"Are you sure?"

"Sure about what?" Dylan frowned.

"That you don't know, right from the start, that they're full of crap." Red settled back in his chair. "I think maybe you do. Believe me, with two older brothers I got talked into a lot of stupid things. I let them persuade me because I wanted Colby and Matt to think I was cool. But I always knew, deep down inside, when I was being played. It may have been a little wriggle of discomfort, just a hint. But it was always there."

Dylan lifted one shoulder and shoveled his biggest tortilla chip through the cheese dip. He filled his mouth, obviously so that he wouldn't have to answer. While he chewed, he focused on finding another big chip and starting the process over.

Doggedly, Red kept trying. "And you know when they finally started to respect me?"

Dylan didn't answer. He kept eating, pretending that he was bored, only partly listening.

Red watched, trying not to let his frustration show. He sure didn't seem to be having much luck these days, did he? Not with anything he tackled. So much for the infamous Malone charisma. First Allison, now Dylan.

But, though he could give up on Victor's mistress, he bloody well wasn't going to give up on Victor's son.

"They started respecting me when I started saying no. As long as I played their pet monkey, always dancing to their tune, they treated me like a monkey. They didn't treat me like an equal until I told them to take their ridiculous ideas and shove 'em."

Dylan shot him a knowing glance. As Red had observed earlier, the boy was no fool. He knew exactly what Red was trying to say.

"Yeah, well, so what?" Dylan's mouth was still full of chips, but his eyes were brilliant, like hard, hot marbles. "Your little life lesson isn't worth much to me. Philip and Brock aren't Colby and Matt. And, in case you've forgotten, Red, you're not my father."

"GOD, RED, WHAT'S WRONG with you tonight?" Matt's voice rang out across the restaurant stage, where the men were lined up like Rockettes for the Diamante dance contest. "You hula like a girl!"

"Yeah, but he sure does rock that grass skirt," a female voice called out, followed by a round of enthusiastic wolf whistles.

Red grinned and gave the ladies a little extra hip action, then offered his brother a smug smile. Matt matched it with a swivel of his own, and the room erupted in laughter.

Red loved specialty practice night at Diamante. Held after an early close on the last Sunday evening of each month, specialty practice was everyone's favorite event. Officially it was designed to familiarize the employees with the new specialty pizza and matching drinks that would create the month's new theme. But in reality it was a chance for the family to mingle with the staff, put loud music on the sound system and have a grand time making fools of themselves.

The women, under Nana Lina's direction, always organized the party and the games. In May, the specialty pizza would be Hawaiian, so tonight's festivities included a hula contest—for the men. Matt, Red, Colby and their good friend David Gerard had already vowed that next month was payback time, and the ladies had better watch out.

Not that anyone in the Malone clan, male or female, was particularly easy to embarrass. The crazier things got, the happier they were. Right now, for instance, Belle, Matt's wife, was alternating between egging Matt on to greater hula madness and trying to throw the limbo contest so that one of the waitresses could win. Kitty, David's wife, stood behind the bar showing the staff bartenders her personal nonalcoholic version of the Tropical Itch.

Colby and Red were the only unmarried guys in the room. Colby had brought a date—some new smoking-hot gal whose name Red couldn't remember. Ginny, maybe? Jenny? No, Jenny had been last month's date. Colby changed girlfriends as often as Diamante changed specialty pizzas.

Red had come alone. He wasn't sure why. For most of the women the Malones dated, getting invited to the specialty practice was like snagging the brass ring. Not only was it fun, with fabulous food, but for that evening they got to be practically family. It was much harder to get in on the casual intimacy of a specialty practice than it was to score an invite to one of Nana Lina's elegant parties out at Belvedere Cove.

He'd thought about bringing Marianne, but she wasn't up to this kind of revelry yet. It would only make her feel even more isolated. And none of his other regular female friends seemed quite right, either. He'd thumbed his contact list on his phone, scrolling almost too fast to see the names. *Nope, nope, nope.*

He'd closed his phone eventually, accepting the inevitable. He wasn't in the mood for any of them. He didn't fret over it or try to figure out the subtext. He had a feeling that, if he did, a freckled face with furious, honey-brown eyes might present itself, and he didn't want to think about all that yet.

So he simply came alone. And after the first Mai Tai—which didn't even have any rum in it—he didn't give the whole date thing another thought. It felt too good to leave all the Wigham drama behind and have a little uncomplicated fun.

After letting Harriet Alban bestow the first-place hula contest lei around his neck, he straightened. He scanned the crowd, looking for Matt. Just like the guy to disappear right when Red wanted to rub it in. Oh, there he was. Somebody had put "Blue Hawaii" on the sound system, and Matt and Belle, who had returned from a trip to Hawaii, were slow dancing under the colored lights like a couple of teenagers.

They looked ridiculous. Belle had a neon-blue, foamy drink in each hand, having scooped them from behind the bar with no chance to set them down. And Matt still had on his grass skirt.

And yet, they looked so happy, so much in love, that Red found his laughter trailing off. A few feet away, Colby had frozen as he picked up a tray of Hawaiian pizzas, and was staring at Matt and Belle, too. The expression on his big brother's face startled Red. Colby didn't give a damn about any woman, everyone knew that. And yet that look was as raw as anything Red had ever seen. It was pure, undisguised grief.

Colby might as well have been openly weeping. That look said *loss, heartbreak, regret, pain.* But what pain?

And suddenly, like a thunderbolt, Red remembered. That look said *Hayley.*

Colby had been about eighteen when his girlfriend Hayley Watson moved away, which meant Red had been only about fifteen. Not long after their parents died. No one told the youngest brother anything, so he didn't know many details, merely that everyone had acted weird for a while, and then she was gone. He knew that Colby's official line at the time had been *good riddance.* But Red also knew that the official line was baloney.

Colby turned, and rather than let him suspect he'd been seen, Red turned, too. He faced the front door, as if he had been looking in that direction all along. And when he did, he saw a brown-haired woman standing there, half in, half out. Her body language was tentative, holding the door open with one hand and peering into the restaurant, as if trying to figure out whether the place was open or not.

Shoot. It had been his chore to make sure the front doors were locked. Had he forgotten—

Then the woman turned, and the colored lights of the party found her face.

It was Allison.

He jumped down from the stage and moved toward her as fast as the crowd would allow. He waved away trays of pineapple pizza slices and umbrella-decorated drinks. He accepted a couple of congratulations, shook a couple of hands and still managed to get to the door about the same time one of the waiters did.

"I'm sorry, miss," the waiter was saying. "We're actually closed tonight. This is a…" He seemed a little uncertain what to call it. "A training session."

Allison frowned, but finally Red had made his way close enough to speak.

"That's okay, Wally," he said, putting his hand on the young man's shoulder. "She's a friend of mine."

"Oh. Oh, I'm sorry, Mr.——Red," the waiter said, seeming to remember belatedly that everyone was on a first-name basis here. He was a very nice kid, brand new to Diamante, and he turned beet-red at the edges of his cheekbones. He faced Allison. "I'm sorry, miss."

"No problem," she said politely. And that was Red's first sign that perhaps she'd come in peace. Surely if she'd come to bawl Red out some more, or arrest him for harassment, she wouldn't be so meek with the kid. She probably would have made a stink about his using the word *friend,* too.

Was it possible she'd come to accept the money, after all?

When the waiter left, Red smiled. "Hello," he said.

She looked uncomfortable. She licked her lips. "Hi."

"I have to admit I'm surprised to see you." No point pretending this was merely a casual visit, or that she'd been in the neighborhood. He wondered where the baby was.

She nodded, admitting that his comment was fair. She bit on her lower lip for a second or two, as if she had something to say but couldn't find the right words. It made her look more young and innocent than ever.

He decided to keep the tone light, at least until he knew what she was here for. "Maybe I was being overly sensitive," he said with a one-sided smile. "But I got the impression you weren't exactly keen on running into me again."

The joke seemed to surprise her. She didn't know

him, of course, so she couldn't know that his family joked about everything. And it had been a gamble, since he didn't know her, either. He didn't know whether she had even a shred of a sense of humor.

But after a few seconds, he saw the tension around her eyes relax a little. She seemed to really look at him for the first time. She noticed the blue lei around his neck, and then her eyes dropped, taking in the grass skirt, which was shimmying foolishly in the breeze from the still-open door.

She raised her eyebrows. "It looks as if I might be interrupting…something."

He jiggled his skirt. "No, not at all. This is your average Sunday night at Diamante. Want to come in? There's plenty of pizza, if you haven't had dinner yet."

"No." She shook her head, and her glossy brown hair bounced around her chin. "I really came to apologize. For…for losing my temper like that yesterday. I was angry, but mostly it was because of—" She bit her lip again. "Well, your friend was—"

"Obnoxious?" Red sighed. "Yeah. Lewis has that effect on most people. I had tried to keep him from getting in on this at all. I knew he wouldn't handle it well."

She twisted her mouth. "That's an understatement."

"I'm sorry about that. And I'm sorry that we showed up there, on the weekend, when you were living your private life. I had tried to stop him, but when I couldn't I thought maybe I could at least do a little damage control. I'm not sure it helped much, though."

"No. It did. You probably kept me from strangling him." She took a deep breath. "That's why I wanted to apologize. I treated both of you the same way, but he was the one…the one who really made me furious. I said things that I probably shouldn't have."

The music had switched to "Tiny Bubbles," and someone—probably Kitty—had organized a sing-along. The voices, mostly off-key, swelled behind him until he almost couldn't hear himself think.

"I've got an idea," he said. "How about we go some-where quieter and have a cup of coffee? I promise I won't mention the check, or the contract, or any of that. I get that the answer is no. I'd just like to leave things between us on a…a happier note."

She hesitated.

"Please," he said. "Look at me. You'd be doing me a favor to get me away from here." He did a figure eight with his hips, setting the grass skirt swaying. "Ten min-utes, tops, before someone drags out the coconut bras."

She glanced past him at the rowdy crowd. He could only imagine what was going through her mind. She probably wouldn't believe that Nana Lina didn't allow alcohol at these practice parties, and everyone was merely drunk on camaraderie.

"Okay," she said. "As long as we don't mention that contract." Her lips tilted up in what might have been the shadow of a smile. "And as long as you take off that skirt."

CHAPTER SEVEN

ALLISON WONDERED WHERE he planned to go, this late on a Sunday night. She'd been in San Francisco for hours, but it had taken so long for her to scrounge up her courage that she'd arrived at Diamante well after nine.

Obviously he knew the area well. A little coffee shop a couple of streets over was still open. Joey's. A yellow neon cup gleamed from the storefront's hanging sign, its curling spiral tube of white steam blinking on and off invitingly against the black night.

The place was clean, well lit and completely empty, except for the two of them and a guy watching a muted baseball game on a TV behind the counter. The man waved at Red as they entered, but he didn't seem able to take his gaze from the screen.

"Wait…wait…*wait for it*…no…no…back up, you idiot, back up…*back up*…" The man groaned, slapping his hand against the counter. "You moron. For fifteen million dollars, my dead grandmother could have caught that ball."

Sighing, he turned to his customers. "Hey, Red. Sorry. Just had to get my nightly dream crushing. Two? Leaded or un?"

Red glanced at Allison.

"Thanks," she said. "Decaffeinated, please."

The guy behind the counter nodded, unsmiling, still

muttering at the television. Something about how their only runs were in their panty hose, a lovely pun that Allison understood only because Jimbo, too, screamed at baseball games on TV two or three times a week.

Red staked out a window booth, with the classic red-and-white-checkered plastic cloth on the table. They'd barely sat on the vinyl benches when the coffee arrived, steaming like the neon sign and smelling fantastic. The guy might not have great people skills, but he knew how to make coffee. Allison lifted her chin to see if she could glimpse what kind of machine he used, or even what beans. But all she could see was the guy, who had gone back to glowering at the TV.

An awkward moment of silence followed, which Allison foolishly tried to fill by sipping her coffee. It was still black, which she hated, but even worse, it was far too hot and she burned the roof of her mouth. She tried to keep her face straight, but Red grimaced, clearly feeling her pain.

"Sorry," he said. "I should have warned you. Joey's only temperature is scalding hot."

She shook her head to minimize the importance. But *ouch*. She was going to remember that for a while.

She was starting to feel she shouldn't have come. This was too awkward, and there was no way to unsay the horrible things they'd each said.

But she had driven all the way into the city to offer this apology, and she wasn't going to go away without trying. Ever since she'd seen him at the farmers' market yesterday, she'd been wrestling with her conscience. She'd been replaying the encounter over in her mind, and by about the fourth time she had realized that she'd probably come across as a raging shrew. Every single objectionable comment had been uttered by the lawyer, not Red, and yet she'd called them both…was it weasels or hyenas?

She flushed, remembering. Not either/or.

Both.

"Look," she said, "I may have made a mistake in coming here. I don't want you to get the wrong idea. I'm still…very uncomfortable talking to you, or anyone connected to Victor."

"I understand."

"And I'm not here because I've changed my mind. About the money or the contract."

He smiled. "What contract?"

She couldn't help smiling back, but she gave it a wry twist, so that he would know she was on to slick guys like him. He'd promised he wouldn't talk about the contract, and he wouldn't—at least until he thought he had her softened up. He wasn't a fool. But neither was she.

"But the truth is…" She spooned half a packet of sugar into the coffee. "I got the impression that you really cared about Victor, that the two of you were close. And that you might be sincerely concerned about the welfare of his family."

He nodded. His face was guarded, now, less slick but no less handsome. That great bone structure and that dramatic Black Irish coloring weren't dependent on a twinkle or a grin. As she poured the thick cream into her cup and stirred the beige swirls into the black liquid, she found herself wondering whether he was married, or engaged…or even, like Victor, a daddy by mistake.

Then she told herself to stop wondering things like that.

"You're right," he said. "Outside of family, Victor was my closest friend. He was my mentor, in fact. I'm like an uncle to his kids—well, at least his son. So when I came to see you, my object wasn't to hassle you. It was to protect them."

He shifted his cup in its saucer. "To protect everyone, actually, if that was possible. Your son is Victor's child, too. I wouldn't want to think that he was unhappy in any way, either."

Her throat closed up unexpectedly, and she was forced to lower her gaze. That was the first time anyone had ever stated the fact straight out. *Eddie was Victor's child, too.* The acknowledgment shouldn't matter so much, but it did. If only Victor had ever said those words…

Instead of the words he did say. *Damn it, Allison. There's still time to get rid of it, isn't there?*

Remembering that awful moment could still make her emotional. She cleared her throat. "Yes. Well. I appreciate that, from the start, you've taken a relatively respectful attitude, given the circumstances. That's why I wanted to apologize. I still have a lot of animosity toward Victor, and I have to admit I'm not crazy about your friend Porterfield, either. It wasn't fair, though, for me to take it out on you. The truth was, when I looked up and saw you at the farmers' market—"

He ran his hand through his hair, as if the memory made him self-conscious. "I know. It was insane. I knew it would freak you out, but Lewis…well, Lewis likes to play lawyer games. He thought if you were surprised, you'd be at a disadvantage."

"And you agreed?"

"No. But he plays games with me, too. He didn't

even tell me he was heading to Windsor Beach until he thought it was too late for me to head him off. If I hadn't already been checking on a property at Half Moon Bay when I got his message, he would have been right. As it was, I showed up as he did."

"But...how did he know where I'd be?" This was one of the elements that had haunted her. How did they find her so easily? Her work, her home...even her weekend outings. She felt like Dorothy in *The Wizard of Oz,* whose every move was monitored in the wicked witch's crystal ball.

Did that lawyer have someone following her? If she tried to drive up to Victor's house tomorrow, would men in black spring out of the bushes and block her way? It was unnerving—downright creepy. How far would these people actually go?

"I suspect he found out the same way I did." Red stirred his coffee. "I went to your apartment first. The downstairs neighbor told me you always shopped at the farmers' market on Saturday mornings."

Oh. That was possible. Hector was a sweetheart, but he was a talker. At eighty-nine, he'd outlived his own children and was very lonely. If he'd thought it would stretch the conversation a single second, he'd have been happy to share everything he knew about Allison with anyone.

For some reason, having another explanation made her feel slightly less tense. She really hadn't liked the idea of spending the rest of her life watching her rear-view mirror for a tail. She was a farm girl from Iowa who wanted to make chicken marsala for her friends. She didn't know anything about a *noir* kind of life.

"I guess I could ask how *you* found *me* tonight," he

said with a small smile. "Except I'm pretty easy to find. If you knew about Diamante, you undoubtedly knew it was a good place to start."

Of course she had known about Diamante. She'd looked him up. The Malones made the news a lot. The family was tailor-made for TV—one elegant matriarch and her three preposterously glamorous and witty young grandsons. Two of them bachelors. The press ate them up, and they played it for all it was worth, generating PR for their franchises.

She read the articles about their pizza chain with real interest. She had no aspirations for Summer Moon to branch out to multiple locations—heck, she'd have to beat the odds even to make the one location profitable. But it wouldn't hurt to learn a few things about getting the word out.

"Yes," she said. "I'd been in the city this afternoon for some other errands. Stopping by Diamante was an impulse. If you hadn't been there, I probably would have gone on home."

No need to mention that her errand had been to look at some used ranges and ice makers at a wholesale place. He probably knew everything about her, including the fact that she was opening her own restaurant, but if by some miracle that one piece of information was still private, she intended to keep it that way.

She blew on her coffee and took another sip. "This is wonderful," she said.

But she didn't know where to take the conversation from there. Twenty-four hours ago, she'd called him a weasel and practically spit in his eye. How did she transition from that to détente?

And was she sure she was ready to? They were both

trying to be civilized, but the atmosphere had a wary feeling. Though the cease-fire had been declared, neither side was sure it was safe to put down their weapons.

She took another sip and decided not to bother. This wasn't a date, or a social occasion of any kind, really. Besides, he was the slick one. Let him handle the rest of the conversation, until it was polite for her to get up and leave.

Of course, good as he was, he jumped in without missing a beat.

"It is fantastic, isn't it? Joey is a genius with coffee." For a few minutes, he rambled comfortably about the coffee shop, and its owner's love-hate relationship with the Giants. Apparently he and Joey went way back, to when their families had both been new restaurant owners in this neighborhood.

Gradually, she relaxed enough to lean against the pillowed vinyl back of the booth. She drained her coffee cup, wishing she'd asked for caffeinated, because she suddenly felt too relaxed, almost mesmerized.

Lightly, easily, he kept talking, plying that famous Malone charm on her. Before long, he was telling a funny story about how, the year the Giants won the World Series, Red and some friends had come into Joey's and found him prostrate in front of the TV, twitching and speaking in tongues. And before she knew it, she was laughing. Really laughing.

Then he moved on to explain why he'd been wearing a hula skirt, and from there to his amazing grandmother....

Suddenly she realized that his face looked different. Shadowy, sexy, the blue eyes darkened to a shade between cobalt and black. At the same time, she came out of her spell long enough to register a lulling drumming sound on the roof.

She glanced at the window beside them and realized it no longer looked out onto a dark, quiet street. Instead, the glass was opaque, and all streaking, liquid gray, with smudges of yellow and blinking halos of white from the neon sign.

Oh, lord. It was raining. Hard.

She looked at her watch, which reflected the watery mess of the picture window. It was almost ten-thirty. She rubbed her eyes, as if she truly had been hypnotized and was just waking up from the dream, back into reality.

And what a reality it was. The world seemed unreliable, ever changing, completely formed of liquid. Something dark and spiky, like a small tree branch, skittered down the sidewalk, accompanied by silver needles of rain. She hated driving in a storm. Her beat-up little car had a hard time handling the rain. Something was always shorting out. And ever since some tourist had dented her front bumper last year, the hood didn't make a tight seal.

She prayed that her battery would stay dry enough to start.

Plus, she knew San Francisco weather. After the rain came the fog. The fog was dreadful to drive in, too. Her headlights were already slightly cross-eyed—she kept meaning to have them aimed but since Eddie was born she so rarely drove at night. And she hadn't had fog lights for years.

"I should go. I should have gone an hour ago, in fact. I never like driving the beach road in the rain."

He was surprised. She could see it on his face. Well, of course—he thought he'd been doing so well. He'd been warming up, and probably expected to have her eating out of his hand by midnight. That was a laugh. He wasn't used to dating women with infants, obviously, or he'd have known he couldn't go that slowly. By midnight, she'd be keeled over on this booth, dead with exhaustion, no matter how scintillating he was.

He glanced out the window. "It does look pretty nasty." His voice was carefully casual. "Maybe it'll blow over."

"I can't afford to wait and see," she said, slipping her purse strap over her shoulder. "I need to get home. Jimbo has to work early tomorrow, and Eddie hasn't been sleeping through the night yet."

His friendly, no-pressure manner suddenly tightened. He almost said something. She could see his jaw muscles work for a split second, then stop. This, the existence of Jimbo, was what bothered him. What was it he had called Jimbo that first night? *The new meal ticket.*

Her hackles rose slightly, remembering the contempt in his voice. So, actually, lawyer Lewis Porterfield hadn't been responsible for *all* the nasty comments, had he?

"You want to know who Jimbo is," she said flatly. She didn't make it a question.

He hesitated one more fraction of a second. And then he nodded.

"Look," he said, putting his hands on the table. "Your private life is none of my business. I get that. Victor's offer, the money—none of that is contingent on your remaining…single. It's just that…clearly you're leaving the baby with this guy. How can you be sure that's safe? I mean, how long can you have known him?"

"Long enough," she said. She felt her back go very rigid. "I am trying to give you the benefit of the doubt here. You cared about Victor, so perhaps I can believe you also care about Victor's son, even the illegitimate one. But are you suggesting that you care *more than I do?*"

He drew his head back slightly, obviously surprised by the change in her tone. "I don't think I understand you."

"I'm saying Eddie is my son. My only son. Do you think I need you to remind me to protect him?"

"No. Of course not. It's just that, after Victor—I mean, you were with Victor a year ago. So this guy must be fairly new in your life and—"

"Must he?" She narrowed her eyes. She had come here to make peace, but something in his snap judgments about her, about Jimbo, brought out her fighting instincts. She knew how his narrow-minded snob logic worked. She had become pregnant out of wedlock, ergo she must be a fool or a tramp or both. Jimbo wore cheap clothes and had tattoos, hence he was definitely shady, and probably a perv.

"Can you hear all the assumptions you're making, Mr. Malone? Why must he be new in my life? Why couldn't I have been sleeping with him at the *same time* I was sleeping with Victor?"

Red was too sophisticated to show any shock, though his gaze on her sharpened slightly. "Were you?"

"No." She squeezed the canvas strap of her purse so hard the fabric dug into the pads of her palm. "Because, you see, there's another way your assumptions could be dead wrong. You forgot to ask the real question, which is…am I sleeping with him at all?"

"All right." His eyebrows lifted. "Are you?"

"No."

"Oh. I see."

"Jimbo is my brother. Not by blood, but every other way. My father took Jimbo into our home when I was only six. He's been my closest friend ever since. He is brilliant, and good, and generous. He has been there for me at every difficult moment of my life. And he's been there for Eddie, too. He has never, ever let us down."

She shoved herself out of the booth and stood. "Which, as I think you know, is more than I can say for Victor Wigham."

It would have made such an excellent exit line. She knew she'd have to stride out into the rain and walk two blocks to her car, but it would have been worth it.

Except that…at that very moment, her phone rang.

She glanced at the number. It was Jimbo. But he wasn't calling from the apartment, where he should have been right now. He was calling from his cell.

What was he doing out in the night, in the storm? Why did he have to call from his cell?

Her heart pounding, she ignored Red's quizzical look and answered the phone.

"Jimbo? Is everything all right?"

"It's going to be fine," he said in that calming voice he used whenever he knew she was going to be very, very frightened. "But I think you should come home. It's Eddie."

"Eddie?" Her voice was only a whisper. She could hear him crying in the background. Crying that ran through her like a branding iron, scorching her nerve endings. She forced herself to be logical. Crying was good, really. Crying wasn't weak. Crying wasn't blue.

"Yeah. I'm sure it's going to be fine," Jimbo said again. "It's just that…Eddie's breathing sounded hinky. We're heading to the E.R. now. I think you'd better meet us there."

She tightened her hand on the phone. "I'll get there as fast as I can."

When she clicked off the call, she slipped the phone into her pocket rather than her purse, for easier access in case Jimbo called. Her heart was beating so fast she wasn't sure she could speak.

"I'm sorry," she said. "I'm going to have to go."

Red stood, obviously aware that her news couldn't have been good. "My car is right out front. I couldn't get a spot close to Diamante tonight. Let me drive you to yours."

She wanted to say no, but her glance darted once to the wet, pearly world outside the window. She'd get to the car faster, and drier, if he took her. It wasn't a time for false pride.

"Thank you," she said, already moving toward the coffee shop door. "I'd appreciate that."

He took off his jacket and held it over her head as they dashed through the driving rain, their feet landing in puddles with little explosions like tossed water balloons. Fat drops splashed against her face, and she had to squint to see where she was going.

Luckily, his car was only feet away. Something big and expensive, that much was obvious even though the rain obscured the details, including the color. The lights blinked once, and he pulled open the passenger door.

When she got in, he swept away the wet jacket and tossed it onto the backseat.

Her mind was so jangled she couldn't, for a minute, remember exactly where she'd parked. When she first got to Diamante, she'd driven around awhile, waiting for something to open up, and she was disoriented now, coming from a different direction. She had never been to this neighborhood before, and knew no landmarks. Besides, everything looked different in the rainy gloom.

He was wonderfully patient about it. He had a little of Jimbo's extreme calm that seemed to spread itself over a crisis like a soft, soothing blanket. She described her car for him, so that he could look, too, and finally they found it. The whole thing had probably taken less than three minutes, but it seemed like a lifetime.

"Are you sure you wouldn't like me to drive you? This is a sturdy, sensible rental, a comfortable sedan that still makes good time." He faced her, his eyes shadowy in the dark. "You seem upset, and the weather really is terrible."

"Thanks. But I think I'll be fine."

"Is there anything at all I can do?"

"No. Thank you. No." She appreciated his solicitude, but she already had her fingers on the door handle, ready to push. Every second mattered.

"Wait—I'll be right there." He dug a small travel umbrella from between the seats, and darted around the car to open her door. He stood beside her, holding the umbrella above her head, until she got the wonky lock on her little Civic to open and slid in.

"Allison," he said, his voice hard to hear over the noise of the rain beating on the car roof.

She looked up. He was frowning, eyeing the banged-up Civic as if the very look of it made him uncomfortable.

"What?"

"Just…" He angled the umbrella so that the rain didn't pool and drip from her partly open door. "Just drive carefully."

"Thanks," she said, nodding. "I will." She shut the door, then jammed the key into the ignition. It had grown bitterly cold with the storm, and her fingers felt slightly numb. At first the key wouldn't turn, but then, while she muttered a prayer under her breath, it did.

The engine struggled, struggled… It always took a while. She knew how to baby it, though she wished Red weren't still standing there, watching. Finally, her coaxing paid off, and the engine flared to life.

Yes. She leaned her head against the headrest and let her eyes drift shut for a second.

But then, as she hooked her fingers around the gear to shift into Drive, she felt an ominously familiar vibration. The engine shuddered, then made a noise that fell somewhere between a cough and a hiccup.

And then, though she was moving her lips in a silent plea, begging it to hang in there, it gave up the ghost and died.

CHAPTER EIGHT

APPARENTLY, RED DISCOVERED after he'd finally persuaded Allison to let him drive her to meet Jimbo and
the baby, Windsor Bay residents had to travel a little
north of Half Moon Bay to get to a medical center with
E.R. services. That would be a thirty-five, forty-minute
drive from Diamante on a good night, which meant
nearly an hour on a night like this. Highway 280 wasn't
horrible, but once Red peeled away to the southwest
and caught CA 1, it got murky as hell, and he had to
slow down.

Allison was a surprisingly calm passenger, and she
never badgered him to go faster. She was clearly panicked—he could see that from the way she gripped her
own elbows, as if she were afraid she might come apart
at the seams. But she kept all that on the inside. Out-
wardly, she was completely silent, except for occasional
calls she took from Jimbo, as he relayed updates and
directions.

Of course Red couldn't avoid hearing those brief
conversations, and eventually he gathered some details
about what had happened. Jimbo and Eddie had arrived
at the medical center but seemed to be still in the waiting room. Red gathered that Eddie had battled pneumonia once before in his young life, and while he was

babysitting tonight, Jimbo had heard a rattle that he didn't care to take a risk on.

But there seemed to be some hitch about insurance. Or, more accurately, the lack of it. Red knew the doctors wouldn't, in the end, refuse to treat a sick baby, but it looked as though they were trying to squeeze all the up-front money that they possibly could.

"Did you bring one of my checkbooks?" Allison's voice was level as she posed the question to the man on the phone, but the sound was as tight as a bowstring. "Well, I have my debit card. Tell them I'll pay as soon as I get there."

A pause, then a restless twitch. "They'll get whatever they want. I don't care what the amount is. Tell them to take care of Eddie and stop wasting time. I'll be there in—"

She glanced at Red. He glanced down at the GPS.

"Twenty minutes," he said.

"Twenty minutes," she repeated into the phone. "They'll get whatever they want in twenty minutes."

She didn't care what the amount was? For a minute, Red's mind flashed to the moment when the old geezer at the restaurant had surreptitiously slipped a diamond into her palm. Was it possible that, though she lived simply, she was actually sitting on a comfortable cushion of "gifts" from the old men she befriended?

But then…the cheap apartment and the beat-up wheels would have to be…what? Part of some elaborate con? The thought almost made him laugh. Even considering the possibility that she was posing as little orphan Annie to scam the senile old men of Windsor Beach required cynicism more suited to the Lewis Porterfields of the world.

He cut a glance toward the passenger seat. She had opened her purse and pulled out her checkbook. Bending her head forward to see in the dim light, she ran her finger down the numbers of the register, clearly doing some math. Wordlessly, he flicked on the overhead bulb.

It shone directly on her face. It caught the silver gleam of a tear track down one freckled cheek.

He had to tighten his hands on the steering wheel to keep from reaching over and wiping the tear away. She was clearly going to give them every penny she had in the world, in exchange for the safety of her little boy.

He wondered how many pennies that was. He wondered what she'd do if she didn't have enough. What she'd do *without*.

When she finished, she closed the checkbook softly, and he flicked off the overhead light. And they drove on through the night in silence.

Luckily, traffic was thin, and the storm was finally passing. It was closer to fifteen minutes later that he slipped the rental car into the covered admitting area in front of the brightly lit E.R. entrance, with its gleaming red letters. She opened her door a split second before he brought the car to a complete standstill.

She slipped out, then stuck her head back in briefly. "Thank you," she said. "I'll—"

"Go on in," he said. "I'll park the car. We can talk after you see what's happening."

THE E.R. WAS SO PACKED Red had hardly been able to find anywhere to sit. People with arms in makeshift slings, hands wrapped in bloody towels and heads bent over plastic barf buckets lined all four walls and whispered softly to each other while they waited. He wasn't particularly disturbed. Coming from a family of three athletic boys, he'd spent so much time in emergency rooms, they'd come to seem like his home away from home.

Allison and Jimbo were nowhere in sight, which must mean the doctors had finally summoned Eddie to an examining room. Good. Red had already been sorting through which of his brothers he'd call to bail him out of jail if he had to knock some sense into the doctors' heads.

God only knew how long it would be, though, and he had no intention of leaving until he learned how the baby was doing. So he found a comfortable chair next to one of the bleeders—at least that wasn't contagious—and killed the time reading his email. Occasionally he'd find his attention wandering, wondering what was happening in that room. But worry didn't help anyone, so he forced himself to focus on reading through Colby's boring lawyer notes about the new Windsor Beach lease.

After nearly an hour, he sensed commotion in the hall, and suddenly Jimbo came through the doorway, his spiked blond hair looking even messier than Red remembered it. He was more conservatively dressed, too. Boots, jeans and a polo shirt that had to stretch to cover the notable lumps of his arm muscles.

Red checked out Jimbo's face for clues to Eddie's condition. The man looked tired, and older than Red had originally thought. Maybe in his forties. But he didn't look racked with despair.

Nothing unspeakable had happened, then. Nothing

the baby wouldn't recover from. Something inside Red relaxed.

Jimbo's gaze raked the room, starting with the opposite wall and moving from one patient to the next. He was clearly looking for Red, and when he found him, his eyebrows lowered over his dark, hollowed eyes. He moved with heavy deliberation to Red's side of the room and stared at the bleeding young woman next to him.

"I'm sorry," Jimbo said without inflection, "but that's my seat."

The woman opened her mouth. She knew it wasn't, but she didn't have the courage to call the big man on it. She secured her bloody towel, gathered up her purse, and moved.

Red had to give him points for guts. How many people would be willing walk right up to a woman who had probably stuck her finger in a food processer, and roust her from her chair?

He closed his email program as the woman scurried away to the farthest empty spot in the room. Then he waited, watching Jimbo try to settle his muscular body into the small chair.

"Red Malone, I assume? I want to talk to you," Jimbo said. This time the voice was far from toneless. It sounded a little like John Wayne at the O.K. Corral. It told Red volumes about the man's relationship to Allison.

"Okay." Red angled in his own seat, so that he could see the other man's face a little better. "First, though, tell me what the doctor said."

Jimbo stared at Red a minute, as if trying to decide whether he had the right to the information. Seen up close, Jimbo's eyes surprised Red. They didn't match the overdeveloped muscles or the tattoos. They didn't even match the John Wayne voice. They were... Red couldn't think of a word that quite summed it up.

Smart. Those eyes were smart as hell.

Smart enough to get the baby to the E.R. before anything unspeakable could happen. Though he hadn't even been aware he was still coiled, Red felt himself relax even more.

Jimbo seemed to finish his calculations of Red. He leaned back with a grunt that was hard to interpret. "The doctor said it's pneumonia again. Bacterial. Probably from strep. He's prescribed Tylenol, antibiotics and fluids. Eddie's fever was about a hundred and one when we got here, but it's down below a hundred already, and they say he'll be fine. They want to send him home, but Alli's back there trying to make them admit him. She wants IV fluids, and I think she's right. Last time he had it, he got dehydrated pretty fast."

When the man finished speaking, Red still had questions, but none of them were urgent. Jimbo had given him a sensible summary. All the important details, with a minimum of words.

"Good," he said. "I'm glad to hear it."

"Me, too." Jimbo's face was still grim. "Now you tell me things."

"Okay. Like what?"

"Like what is going on between you and Allison."

Red considered that. "Maybe she should be the one to tell you," he suggested. "Some of it is fairly personal, and only she can say how much she wants to share, and with whom."

Jimbo waved that off with a set of tattooed knuckles.

"I forgot more than you'll ever know about that girl," he said. "But if you're feeling squeamish about mentioning Eddie's dad, don't be. I've already heard that you came to Windsor Beach as a lackey for that snake Victor Wigham."

Red narrowed his eyes. "Victor was a friend of mine. And he's dead."

Jimbo made a sound that was an evil first cousin to a laugh. "Pardon me. That *dead* snake Victor Wigham."

Well, no sugarcoating there. Definitely no mistaking his true feelings. The contempt rolled off Jimbo in waves. Red frowned, wondering what Allison had told him.

"Okay," he said. "So you know about Victor, and you know why I came to see Allison the other day. In that case, I'm afraid I don't quite see what else you want to know."

Jimbo obviously didn't like Red's tone. He gave him the time-honored macho stare down. Red met the man's steely gaze without blinking. He'd been willing to come in here and take on any doctor who refused to treat a sick baby, and he'd take on this rude jerk, too, if he had to. He looked at the size of the guy's arms, though, and almost laughed. He should have spent a little more time at the gym, and a little less time surfing and dancing at Diamante.

Oh, well, as the youngest brother he was used to getting his ass kicked. And when Jimbo made mincemeat of him, at least he was in the right place to get the medical attention he'd undoubtedly need.

"What I want to *know*," Jimbo said slowly, as if he were still trying to decide whether he would rather ask Red questions or punch him out, "what I want to *know* is why on Saturday she tells me you're an arrogant weasel, and on Sunday the two of you are chitchatting over coffee. I want to know why, when she says she hates your guts, she's driving up to the emergency room in your car."

"Probably because her car—"

But Jimbo wasn't listening anymore. His face changing abruptly, he clambered to his feet, almost bringing the too-small waiting room chair with him as he stood. "Alli."

She stood in the entryway to the hall. Her clothes were rumpled, and she looked exhausted. Her freckles stood out on her pale cheeks as if they'd been applied with a child's crayon. Dark shadows rimmed her eyes.

"He finally fell asleep," she said.

Jimbo put his arm around her shoulders. "How did it go?"

To Red's surprise, she didn't relax into his embrace. She didn't even really appear to be made of normal flesh and bone, but something stiffer and more unyielding.

"They're finding a room for him." Her voice was monotone. She sounded…the best word Red could think of was *numb*. "It was a fight, but finally they saw reason. Because it's the second time he…"

"You go, girl," Jimbo said. "You make them do right by that kid."

"I will," she said. Her eyebrows drew together and her jaw tightened. "I will."

Red stood, too—if only to remind them that he was here. When Allison saw him rise, she turned to him immediately.

"Oh, good. You're still here. Thank God."

"Yes. I told you I'd stay until we could talk. We probably should make arrangements to get your car—"

"Forget the car," she said. Her voice was strained. Low and intense. She didn't sound like herself. "Can I talk to you privately, please?"

He glanced at Jimbo, who obviously didn't like this one bit. He was surprised that the big man didn't protest. But apparently Allison called her own shots. Without speaking, the two of them walked away a few feet, and Jimbo stayed where he was.

"I can arrange for someone to bring the car here," Red said when they stopped and stared at one another for a long second. Anything to bridge the gap. "One of the Diamante employees can drive—"

"Thank you, but we can handle that. And the car's not important right now. What's important is…"

He waited.

"What's important is Eddie, and the insurance… and…"

With a sound of inarticulate frustration, she ran both her hands through her hair. She seemed to be having trouble swallowing. The whole time she was in there, waiting for news about her baby, she'd probably been holding back a lump of tears that had finally grown too big to choke down.

"Allison," he began.

She held up her hand to make him stop. "What's important is Victor's offer. The money. The contract. I've changed my mind, Red. I don't care what I have to promise. If the offer still stands, I'll take it."

THREE DAYS LATER, Red stood in the spacious upstairs sitting room of Marianne and Victor's Russian Hill town house, helping Marianne pack away Victor's clothes—a chore they'd both been dreading. But she'd finally decided that all the fine things shouldn't gather dust in the closet when they could be doing good for someone. She'd identified a charity, and today she'd said she was ready to do the deed.

Unfortunately, less than half an hour into the task, she had come across a ticket stub in one of the pockets. It was for the last concert she and Victor had ever attended together.

And she had fallen apart.

For the past hour, Red had been working alone, while Marianne, curled up on the yellow silk sofa, wept quietly into a tissue. She had Victor's dresser valet next to her, and was slowly looking through that, but she wasn't making much progress.

He didn't really mind. In fact, he'd expected it. But he did wish she'd turn off that damned depressing music she'd put on the CD player. It sounded like some classical composer's requiem, which in his opinion was like pouring salt into a wound.

At the Malone house, wallowing in grief was considered an insult to the lost loved one. They never even mentioned anniversaries of death days. But every time Grandpa Colm's birthday rolled around, the whole family went out to the boathouse he'd built with his own hands and sang songs and laughed so hard they cried, and cried so hard they laughed.

But then, they were half-Irish. And as Nana Lina— the Italian side of the family—always said, the Irish were crazy.

And, of course, everyone grieved differently.

"How's Dylan settling in?" Red asked. He really

wanted to know, naturally. The lunch the other day hadn't gone particularly well, and he hoped there hadn't been any aftereffects.

But also he wondered whether, if he gently reminded her that someone else was in the house, someone fragile, she might turn off the funereal music.

"He seems much better," she said, perking up a little bit. "We had a good talk last night before he went to bed. A real talk. I wanted him to know we would be giving Victor's clothes away today. I wanted to be sure he was all right with it."

"Good." It wasn't as if Dylan was likely to want any of the clothes. The closets of a fifty-year-old man and a fifteen-year-old boy couldn't have had less in common. But seeing this closet empty, thinking of someone else putting on the clothes that still smelled like Victor… That might be rough, if he hadn't been warned.

"Did he say much about rehab?"

"No." She sighed. "He said he doesn't want to talk about it yet. Except that it was like being in prison."

Red smiled. Probably had felt that way, given the luxury the boy was used to.

Red surveyed Victor's shelves of shoes, his next section to box up. Two or three dozen pairs, at least. And Victor hadn't been particularly obsessed with fashion. That was simply how much discretionary money floated around this household.

The pretty pair of diamond stud earrings Marianne was wearing right now, for instance, would have paid little Eddie York's hospital bill for a week.

Odd, uncomfortable thoughts like that had been occurring to Red all morning. Every time he opened a drawer and found another wad of cash Victor had tossed down and forgotten. Every time he pulled another soft-as-butter suit off its mahogany hanger. Hell, even as Marianne lifted her hand to brush away a tear, and her gold charm bracelet gleamed in the sunshine that poured through the leaded-glass French doors, he'd think...

If Allison had a piece of jewelry like that, she could sell it to get her car fixed.

And, even more disloyally, when he heard Marianne sniffle, collapsed there on her elegant sofa, in his mind's eye he'd see Allison York taking off her sneakers and massaging the arch of her slim foot, hoping she could make the pain go away before she had to climb the steep steps to her apartment.

He tried not to. He knew it wasn't fair, comparing one woman to another. They were different people, with different backgrounds, different struggles, different strengths.

Plus, it felt a little hypocritical. They weren't exactly eating cat food at any of the Malone houses, either.

"So did you get the letter about the hearing?" He filled a box with shoes, taped it shut, then started filling a second one. "The one Gwen Anderton warned you was coming?"

She nodded. "I set it aside, downstairs on the hall table. I couldn't bear to read it yet."

And again, those disloyal thoughts. All this fearful avoidance and denial... If Allison got a threatening letter saying something unkind about her son, she would be more likely to track down its sender and claw his eyes out with her bare hands.

Or she might call him an arrogant weasel.

For some reason, the memory made him feel like

grinning. She really was a holy terror when she felt threatened. If only she could give Marianne a tiny shot of that fire and grit.

Maybe then Marianne would turn off that godforsaken melancholy music.

Suddenly, the sitting room door flew open. Dylan stormed in, his eyes wild with anger and red with tears.

"For God's sake, Mom! What the hell are you trying to do?" He stomped to the CD system without looking right or left. "Turn that crap off before we all slit our wrists!"

Marianne froze, a tissue halfway between her lap and her eyes. Dylan punched the off button so hard the cabinet rocked against the wall.

Though in his heart Red couldn't agree more, it fell to him to haul the kid up short. "Hey," he barked. "Don't talk to your mom like that."

"Yeah," a voice from the door chimed in heartily. "Don't talk to your mom like that, brat."

Red glanced over and felt a whoop of delight. The cavalry had arrived. And in the nick of time.

In the doorway stood Cherry Wigham, Victor's twenty-eight-year-old daughter from his first marriage. As usual, she was dressed in the final word of Los Angeles fashion, with her black curls springing everywhere, and her green eyes sparkling with life and drive.

Just a few years ago, Dylan would have launched himself into his sister's embrace, so thrilled to see her that he didn't care who knew it. But a lot had changed. Except for a few sickbed visits and the funeral itself, Cherry had been in L.A. for three years now. While she had been gone, Dylan had hit the age when image was everything.

And, of course, the one man who had tied them together, the only person whose blood ran in both their veins, had died.

Still, Red could see a change in the boy's expression, a lightening of the anger and attitude. Even Marianne was smiling.

"What? No kiss?" Cherry growled playfully, and then stalked across the room and whisked Dylan into her arms. "Very annoying for you to grow up so fast, imp. And unacceptable for you to think you're too big to kiss your sister."

She leaned down and planted one right on the boy's cheek. She was too smart to ask him to acknowledge or return it. She simply rose gracefully, smoothed out her pencil-thin, ultra-sophisticated navy blue suit, and made her way, high heels clicking, toward Marianne.

She hugged her stepmother warmly, then plucked the box of tissues from the sofa and tossed them on the beautiful inlaid table a few feet away. The box landed there with a soft thud, unceremoniously on its side.

"No more crying," she said. "You can cry after I'm gone, if you like, but not while I'm here. I can only stay a week or two, and I don't want to waste a minute."

Finally, she looked at Red. "And you, you disgustingly handsome piece of studly wonder…are you going to refuse to kiss me, too?"

God, he'd forgotten how much he missed Cherry. "Just waiting my turn, sweetheart," he said with a smile. He opened his arms, and she moved into them comfortably, planting a big, noisy kiss on the side of his mouth, expertly missing his lips by a fraction of an inch.

Once, for an intoxicating but very brief moment ten

years ago, he and Cherry had dated. She'd wanted to get serious, and had sort of, almost, talked him into agreeing to be engaged-to-be-engaged. He blew that sky high in short order, of course. He'd been just out of college and far from ready to settle down. He'd accidentally let her find him on the *MacGregor*—the Malone family's boat—with another woman in his lap.

Probably that was when he first understood Freud's contention that there are no accidents. He'd wanted to get caught. They hadn't really been in love, and neither one of them had been ready for marriage. He'd apologized, and eventually she'd forgiven him. So had Victor, who knew his little girl's heart hadn't really been broken.

Still, since that day she'd never once kissed Red on the lips, though they always met with a genuine, comfortably demonstrative affection.

Guess she was still paying him back. He smiled at her as she made her way across the room. She dropped down next to Marianne on the sofa, and, without asking permission or requiring explanation, simply began helping her stepmother separate cuff links and tie tacks to be packed away in the charity boxes.

What a tiger she was. Within about two minutes, she even managed to get Marianne smiling. She had been the sunshine of her father's heart, and Victor had been her rock. But she was too tough to crumble. She was one strong lady.

Too bad, he thought, in another of those strange, stray moments, that she could never meet Allison. The two women had a lot in common, under the surface. For starters, both of them refused to put up with any crap from Red.

He gave himself a mental shake. Why did everything keep leading him back to Allison? He hadn't seen her for a few days. Before he left the hospital that night, her friend Jimbo had assured him he would help Allison retrieve her car. And sure enough, the next day when Red arrived for work at the offices above Diamante, the beaten-up old Honda was gone.

The next day, he'd heard from Lewis. A lawyer representing Allison had called and arranged for her to sign the contract at his office in Windsor Beach. Once that was finished, the money had been wired into her account, the notarized contract had been stashed away in Lewis's safe and the whole episode was officially concluded.

Literally signed, sealed and delivered. Even Red's Mercedes had come back from the body shop, purring like a kitten and looking none the worse for wear.

So. Case closed. He turned to Cherry, wondering what she was doing for dinner tonight. It might be fun to catch up with an old friend. Cherry was witty, and she always had funny stories about the loonies who bought mansions in L.A.

It would be distracting, if nothing else. And he needed distraction.

If he was smart, Allison York's name would never cross his lips—or his mind—again.

CHAPTER NINE

ALLISON WAS SO EXCITED about her new refrigerator you'd think it was filled with diamonds, which, if she opened its doors, would come spilling out to roll across the kitchen floor.

It wasn't, of course. For now, the huge metal box was completely empty. But she'd learned from her father that the refrigerator was the most important piece of equipment in any restaurant. It must be big enough, reliable enough, and energy efficient enough to hold and protect a cargo as precious as gemstones—her food.

This one, which had been delivered this morning, was perfect. She'd bought the biggest and best model she could afford. Wide and substantial, six feet tall, divided into thirds. One third had a glass front, and the other two thirds had solid doors.

Eddie had been especially fascinated by the digital display, which glowed against the shiny aluminum, sophisticated enough to launch a spaceship. It would always tell her the temperature—the most crucial element of any food storage.

Even Allison couldn't stop staring at the big, hulking beauty. She couldn't believe it really was hers.

She and Eddie had been hanging out here in Summer Moon all day—or rather in the building that soon would become Summer Moon. To the untrained eye, the space probably looked chaotic and disorganized, with boxes everywhere, and half-assembled furniture lying on its side across the seating-area floor.

But Allison knew, hour by hour, exactly how much progress had been made. And, though she'd been working her heart out, and hiring out whatever she could, the progress wasn't enough.

Way back at the beginning, she'd spent hours with city hall and the health department, making sure she was following every fire code, health code, building code to the letter. Then she'd hired a designer to help her lay out her space efficiently. After that, for months she had worked all day, then stayed up half the night, poring over plans and menus and catalogues.

By the time the equipment and furnishings started showing up in delivery trucks, she'd known every square inch of her unborn restaurant, had seen it in her head as clearly as if it already existed.

And now that she'd worked her last shift at the Peacock Café, and could devote every minute to Summer Moon, things would start to move at warp speed.

"Three weeks." She picked Eddie up out of his carrier and hugged him tightly, which made him wiggle and coo. "Just three more weeks, Eddie, until our dream comes true! Wouldn't your granddaddy be proud?"

"I told you we'd find her here." Jimbo and Bill Longmire came sauntering in through the alley door. "The woman doesn't know the meaning of the word *relax*."

When Eddie heard Jimbo's voice, he turned and, using Allison's stomach as a takeoff pad, stretched his entire body out, reaching for his favorite friend. Jimbo laughed, obviously flattered.

"That's right, big fella," he said as he took him out

of Allison's arms. "Time for a little male bonding. A guy can't stay in the kitchen with the girls all day."

Allison stuck her tongue out, but she knew Jimbo didn't have a chauvinistic bone in his body. Plus, since he was the one who would be living in this kitchen, not Allison, there was little danger that Eddie would grow up believing that cooking was for girls.

Bill watched the baby, who lay in the crook of Jimbo's arm, completely contented, mesmerizing himself by wiggling his own fingers while Jimbo investigated the new refrigerator.

"He looks great," Bill said, his voice sounding relieved. This was the first time he'd seen Eddie since the pneumonia. "You'd never know he was sick at all. God, to heal that fast."

"Absolutely." Allison smiled at the pair, then gave Bill a pat on the arm. "He's good as new. He only stayed in the hospital the one night, to be sure he was hydrated. After that, the antibiotics really cleared things up in a hurry."

She didn't mention that, though Eddie had recovered within a few days, she was still feeling the aftereffects of fear. She still woke about ten times a night to check on his breathing. She still looked up infant pneumonia compulsively on the internet, trying to figure out why he'd come down with it twice. She still wondered whether it meant he had a weakness in his lungs, his immune system, his diet. Was there something more she should have done, something she should do differently in the future?

"Yep, this'll do," Jimbo said with a sound of immense satisfaction in his voice. He looked at Allison as he shut the refrigerator door. "You picked a good one. I think we can do some business with this baby."

Allison nodded, pleased. They'd briefly considered buying used equipment, to save some money, but they'd decided it was a false economy.

Jimbo came over and handed Eddie to her. "Okay, now you go home."

"What? No. I'd planned to stay another couple of hours. There's still so much to do, and I'm running out of time. I wanted to unpack the utensils. The rack came today, and—"

"Tomorrow. Tonight you rest." Jimbo scowled. "I wish there were a mirror in here, so you could see the bags under your eyes. Bill and I will play with the ladles and meat cleavers after we get the lights hung. Sue said she'd try to get by to help, too, if Flip didn't keep her late at the café. And—" He stopped short, his face changing ever so slightly. He rotated his left shoulder, then pulled on his ear, both sure signs that he was feeling self-conscious.

"What?" she said suspiciously.

"Nothing. Don't go grilling me and reading into things that don't mean anything."

Allison grinned. "Eloquently put."

Jimbo rolled his eyes. "I'm just saying. You do that. Anyhow, the thing is, Meg Bretton said she might stop by tonight, too. We talked about maybe using her melons, you remember. She thought she might come see the restaurant, talk it over."

Allison smiled, but kept it mild. If she made too big a deal of it, he might call Meg and tell her not to come.

"Okay," she said blandly.

"Don't go looking like that, damn it," he said. "It's nothing personal. She just has nice melons."

Bill laughed, but when Jimbo wheeled on him, he widened his eyes.

"Sorry," Bill said quickly. "It's just that, in my day, when you said a woman had—"

"I know what you're laughing at!" Jimbo's scowl deepened. He picked up an unopened box and let it drop on the newly installed prep table. He pulled out his pocketknife and slit the tape. "But it's purely business with Meg. If anybody is guilty of getting distracted by the opposite sex, it's Allie here, not me."

Bill's wide eyes began to twinkle. "Really? You've got a new fellow? Do tell."

Allison shook her head. "No. No fellow, new or any other kind. Don't listen to Jimbo. He believes that old adage that the best defense is a good offense."

"Oh, too bad," Bill said, his mouth drooping. "You need a man, Allie. Just because your marriage to Chuck didn't work out, that doesn't mean you have to join a convent, you know."

"Ha! Chuck." Jimbo made a rude noise, which didn't surprise her. He'd hated Chuck from the moment he met him, back when Allison was only fifteen.

He'd known, long before Allison did, that Chuck was nothing but a good-looking, easygoing con artist who wasn't ever going to buckle down and help her pursue her dream of owning her own restaurant. Chuck wouldn't even show up for work on time when he worked for Allison's dad. But she'd been bewitched by his green eyes and his big plans, and the minute they graduated from high school, she married him.

Over the next six years, he'd tried one get-rich

scheme after another, growing more embittered and angry when each one failed. For the last one, a land deal in Florida, he'd asked her to kick in her restaurant seed money—money she'd been setting aside since she was twelve and had her first babysitting job.

Because she couldn't imagine herself giving up on her wedding vows—even though his green eyes didn't look quite so enchanting now that they were hungry and sour—she had said yes. She'd given him every cent.

And he'd lost it. That was what Chuck did.

She'd even tried to keep the marriage together for a year or two after that. But eventually, he'd found another girl, one who still worshipped him and believed in his grand schemes. And then he'd asked Allison for a divorce.

So Allison definitely understood why Jimbo said Chuck's name as if it carried a nasty smell. She'd forgiven him, but Jimbo wasn't the forgiving kind, not if someone hurt her that badly.

His feelings toward Victor were even worse. They went beyond civilized words.

Bill, who might have heard a few rumors but didn't know the whole story, looked annoyed. "I'm serious. Having one bad marriage doesn't mean she can't ever fall in love again."

"Maybe not," Jimbo retorted. "But it definitely means she shouldn't fall in love again until she acquires better taste in men."

"Jimbo—"

"It's true, and you know it. Chuck was a loser, and Victor was a skunk." He waved the pocketknife for emphasis, then turned to Bill. "Maybe she gets a pass with Chuck, because they were in high school, and she

didn't know any better. How could she know he'd rob
her blind? And maybe you can even cut her some slack
on Victor, because her dad had died, and the restaurant
was failing."

Bill turned sad puppy-dog eyes Allison's way. "Aw,
honey," he began.

"But this time she's got no excuse," Jimbo cut in.
"Supposedly, she's sworn off men. She's going to con-
centrate on the restaurant. But where do I find her last
Sunday night? In a coffee shop in San Francisco, play-
ing footsie with some self-satisfied playboy named Red.
Red. What kind of name is that?"

Bill looked surprised. "Red Malone? The boy with
the wrecked Mercedes?"

"Right. And a friend of Victor's, no less. Can you
imagine anything dumber?"

Bill's brow suddenly seemed to have twice as many
creases. "I do think that boy may be wrong for you,
honey," he said earnestly. "Sarge and I were talking
about him, when he first showed up in town. The Old
Coots are always looking out for someone who might
make you happy, you know, and this Malone is a pretty
good-looking fellow. Got money, too, unless he stole
that Mercedes. But he looks…well, he looks as if he
might be the love 'em and leave 'em type. And you
don't need any more of that."

Allison groaned under her breath. Eddie reared back
a couple of inches, to see where the noise had come
from. He grabbed her cheeks with both little starfish
hands, and lowered his wet mouth to check out what
he'd found.

As always, he lightened her spirit and rebalanced her

Send For
2 FREE BOOKS
Today!

I accept your offer!

Please send me two free Harlequin® Superromance® novels and two mystery gifts (gifts worth about $10). I understand that these books are completely free—even the shipping and handling will be paid—and I am under no obligation to purchase anything, ever, as explained on the back of this card.

❏ I prefer the regular-print edition
135/336 HDL FJGQ

❏ I prefer the larger-print edition
139/339 HDL FJGQ

Please Print

FIRST NAME

LAST NAME

ADDRESS

APT.#   CITY

STATE/PROV.   ZIP/POSTAL CODE

Visit us online at www.ReaderService.com

mood. She rubbed noses lightly, and they exchanged their silly, private cooing noise.

Then, still smiling, she turned to the other men.

"Listen, you two. I don't care if Red Malone breaks every heart in California, because, in spite of Jimbo's fantasies, I am not interested in him. I'm not interested in anyone. I appreciate your matchmaking efforts, Bill, but I hope you and Sarge and Mickey will take a break."

Bill laughed. "Oh, Mickey isn't trying to find a man for you. He still thinks he can marry you himself. We tell him it just proves how bloody senile he is, but—"

Allison began to laugh. Mickey did ask her to marry him almost every day. Sometimes, though, she wasn't sure who he thought she was. She wondered whether he might think she was his wife, who had died many years ago.

"Enough." She held up her free hand. "Congratulations, gentlemen. You two have accomplished in nine minutes what nine hours of hard physical labor couldn't do. You've made me tired enough to give up and go home."

BECAUSE THE FAMILY had decided it was important to take advantage of the summer tourist business, Red had hired a crew of twelve men to transform the Windsor Beach Bath Goddess site into a classic Diamante takeout store as fast as was humanly possible.

Consequently, less than ten days after signing the lease, Nana Lina had sent over a manager from corporate to begin hiring and training the staff and drivers. The store could open in three days, assuming the vendors made their deliveries on time.

They already had ads in the local handyman flyers,

and coupons on the cars in every apartment parking lot within driving distance. One of their generic TV spots would be running on local channels tomorrow.

Though Red had driven over to Windsor Beach four times in those ten days, he was proud of the fact that he hadn't once called Allison. Not even to ask how Eddie was. He hadn't eaten breakfast at the Peacock Café, though it was only a couple of blocks away. He hadn't driven by her apartment.

He'd heard plenty of gossip as he stopped at other restaurants around the little town, diners for lunch, or a family spot for a quick dinner before driving to the city. He heard that Allison was in the process of opening a restaurant of her own. The community seemed to be looking forward to it. Turned out her father used to own a restaurant, too, which had closed only because a prolonged construction/zoning battle had been waged on the street where his restaurant was located. And because he got sick, and had spent the last of his savings paying doctors to tell him he was dying.

Red didn't ask questions, not wanting to draw attention to himself. But he listened. Summer Moon, that was her new restaurant's name. It was over at the corner of Smith and Princeton. A good location, high visibility and easy access. He'd considered the spot for Diamante some months ago, but had ultimately decided the building had more space than he needed for a take-out operation. Besides, the owners wanted to sell, not rent.

He couldn't help being curious. He'd grown up in the restaurant world, and all its facets interested him. But he was proud of his restraint. He hadn't even driven by to check it out. He focused on his own business, which was plenty hectic enough to keep him occupied. The labor pool in a town this small wasn't exactly deep, so the manager was struggling to find enough experienced staff. Diamante corporate might have to offer a transfer to some of the younger people in the city who were mobile and might be attracted by the lure of the beach.

Yes. He was focused. If his mind wandered now and then, well, he was only human.

On his last night, though, he ate a quick dinner at a beachside bar, listening to a guy sing Jimmy Buffett songs and drinking enough coffee to keep him alert on the ride home. Halfway through his sandwich, he noticed a woman sitting at one of the other tables, eating alone.

His pulse quickened. The woman had her back to him, but she looked mid-twenties. Her hair was glossy, chin-length chestnut. And she had a baby propped in a carrier on the table next to her.

He stood. Restraint was all well and good, but if fate had placed Allison York right here, a mere ten feet away...

He walked to her table, arranging a careful, polite smile so that he didn't appear overeager. "Allison?"

The woman turned, and his smile fell so fast he could almost feel a thud as it hit the ground. It wasn't Allison.

The woman smiled at him, her even teeth the kind of sparkling white you got only from veneers. Her eyes were bright blue, her skin tan, her body full of curves.

She was very pretty. Prettier than Allison, strictly speaking.

"No, I'm sorry." Dimples formed at the edges of her lips. "I'm Tania."

He apologized, ignoring the dimples. He chatted

a few seconds, because she clearly wanted to, but he didn't follow up on the subtle invitation to bring over his sandwich and share the table. He went back to his bar stool and stared at the breeze-blown water. Its ripples fractured the sunset into a thousand flecks of softly colored light, like an Impressionist painting.

Something restless stirred inside him. Even thinking he had seen her…something had stirred inside him.

A dangerous something.

He should get in the car and go home, before he did something stupid. Better still, he should call Cherry now, as he'd been promising himself for days he would.

Probably his restlessness came from working too hard, playing too little. He needed some fun. He should definitely call Cherry. She probably wondered why he hadn't. Hell, *he* wondered why he hadn't. He should see if she wanted to go to a club. Cherry loved to dance, and she was good at it. It would be fun.

But no matter how hard he sold the idea to himself, he simply wasn't buying.

He summoned the waiter and paid the bill. Then he got in his car and dialed Allison's home number.

No answer. He tried her cell. Still no answer.

He scrolled down, to where he found the name *Cherry.* His finger hovered over the number, a fraction of an inch away from hitting Call. *Come on,* he told himself. It would be the smart thing to do. Besides, it would be fun.

But he didn't do it. He clicked off the phone and headed for the corner of Smith and Princeton.

CHAPTER TEN

IT WAS SUNDAY, and it was after eight, so most of the stores here in Windsor Beach were closed up tight, windows black and signs unlit. That visual silence made Summer Moon stand out more.

It was a quaint stand-alone building, with a faint Cape Cod feel in its pale green shingle siding, hunter-green shutters and two fake gables perched like eyes in its steepled roofline. Its sheets of uncurtained windows blazed with so much illumination that he could have counted every chair in the place from across the street.

Allison obviously didn't mind letting everyone see the place in disarray. And boy, was it in disarray. He tried to remember how soon they'd said she planned to open. Unless she had a big crew, she was nowhere close.

Boxes rested on every surface, flaps gaping and bright white foam popcorn spilling like confetti from the sides. A broom tilted against one table, and on another a food processor lay in unassembled pieces.

But Allison herself was nowhere to be seen.

Red parked in front and rapped on the door. No answer. He tested it, and it swung open easily.

"Hello?" he called into the empty room.

"Oh, thank God!" It was unmistakably her voice, but

she sounded frazzled. "Why haven't you been answering your phone? Hurry! We're drowning back here."

Drowning? He moved quickly, pushing through the mess of cartons, chairs with no legs and tables arranged like children's forts. Bare wires dangled like snakes descending from the ceiling. Someday, the snakes would undoubtedly be attached to the Tiffany-like hanging lamps he saw stacked along the far wall.

She must be in the back. It was a fairly spacious restaurant, but not so big that the kitchen was hard to find. Especially since, once he got within a few feet, he spotted water seeping along the floor, a shimmering tentacle of clear liquid that was reaching out and spreading fast.

As he rounded the corner, he saw the problem. Allison stood at the far side of the kitchen, over by the main stainless-steel sink, from which a geyser of water spurted in every direction. The floor around her feet looked more like a running brook, at least half an inch deep.

Allison herself was soaked and clearly furious, with the broken faucet splattering her in the face. She looked as if she'd been swimming, her hair glistening, dripping and molded to her head. Her jeans sagged with water weight, and her white T-shirt was so thoroughly plastered to her skin it had become damn near invisible.

God, what a mess. Eddie was crying, which made Red's shoulders tighten briefly. Where was the baby? But then he saw the carrier. Allison had put Eddie up on the highest table, where obviously he was safe. No matter how much water flooded the kitchen, it would all run through the restaurant and hit the gutter before it ever came close to the top of that table.

So...next order of business, turn the water off. He darted one glance around, found a silver metal bucket and grabbed it. He approached the faucet quickly and thrust the bucket over the spitting, high-arch spigot. It didn't stop the water, of course, but it at least directed it down, so that it began to fill the sink.

He turned to Allison. "Have you tried closing the main valve?"

Her mouth had fallen open the minute he appeared in the doorway, and she hadn't shut it yet. She stared at him with those water-spangled eyelashes blinking, and didn't seem to be able to say a word.

"Allison. The main valve. Where is it?"

"I already tried that," she said, finally snapping to. She wiped a hank of brown hair away from her forehead, then flicked her fingers to shake off the water. "I tried that first. It's faulty somehow. It just spins, and nothing happens."

He didn't doubt her, and he didn't waste time rechecking the valve. "There has to be one out by the street, too," he said. "I'll see if I can find it. Have you called a plumber?"

"I called Jimbo," she said. "He can fix it. Or I can. Surely it's not that big a deal. A plumber will charge a fortune on a Sunday night."

"But Jimbo's not answering his phone, right?"

"No. But if I can get the water off, I'm sure I can—"

"Okay." He heard the anxiety in her voice. Money problems again? What about the fifty thousand dollars she'd received from Victor's estate last week? "You stay here with Eddie, and don't let that bucket shoot off and hit something. Let me see if I can find the main valve."

It took longer than he would have liked, given how

dark it had grown, and how little illumination the access alley had on a Sunday night. But finally he found the shut-off and, though he didn't have the right tools, somehow he managed to screw it far enough that the little water meter stopped spinning madly and settled down in one stationary place.

When he got inside, Allison had moved Eddie's carrier down to the prep table, and was unbuckling him. She seemed to have found one of the light green kitchen towels he'd seen stacked by the dozens in the main seating area. She'd draped it across her shoulder to protect Eddie from her wet shirt. He was still crying, still damp and red-faced and furious. But he might be a shade less strident.

"I'm sorry," Allison mouthed to Red. "I've got to…"

He nodded. "It's okay."

He'd often watched Matt struggling with Sarah, who had been a placid baby most of the time, but could be a screaming hurricane when the mood struck. At times like these, he knew, pacifying the baby came before anything. Otherwise, no one could think.

So Red didn't say anything further to Allison, not sure whether a strange male voice might agitate the already anxious infant. Instead, while she patted Eddie's back, and hummed, and paced the wet floor trying to calm him, Red poked around and found a storage closet. He was in luck. She'd already stocked it well with cleaning items, including a couple of industrial-strength mops.

He wasn't sure what kind of flooring Allison had out there in the seating area, but it probably wouldn't take well to being marinated in sink water. He gathered up all the towels he could find and laid them at the threshold to the kitchen, like sandbags piled high against a flood.

And then he began to mop. He soaked up as much as he could, then wrung the mop out in the sink. Then he went back, and did it all again.

After a couple of minutes, he realized that Eddie was quiet, except for some small whimpers that had begun to sound sleepy. Red glanced up, and found Allison watching him, a strange expression on her face. She paused in her pacing and seemed to try to think of something to say. "Red, I—"

Almost instantly, as her rhythmic movements ceased, Eddie protested. He lifted his head, though because he was sleepy his neck wobbled adorably. His eyes weren't fully focused. He clearly wanted to sleep. They were almost home free, if he didn't start crying and stir himself up again.

Red smiled, and twirled his fingers to say *keep moving*. And, though she hesitated, she did resume her pacing in time. The baby hiccupped, made one last fussy noise and slowly let his head drop to Allison's shoulder. He put two fingers in his mouth, sucked softly and then, finally, he was asleep.

She waited a few minutes, obviously reluctant to push her luck. Finally, she laid the baby in his carrier, buckled him in and turned to Red.

"I don't know what to say." Her voice was very soft, almost a whisper, but still she glanced toward Eddie, to be sure it wasn't going to wake him. "I was so surprised to see you. I thought you were Jimbo."

"Sorry," he said. He smiled. "But I might be the next best thing. I'm a guy with years of experience cleaning up restaurant kitchens."

She flushed and, reaching out, she put her hand on the handle of his mop, stilling it. "You don't have to do that. I can take over now."

He gently moved her hand away. "I think this may call for all hands on deck." He pointed toward the closet. "I noticed you have two mops, so why don't we each take one? You don't want this soaking in anywhere and starting a mold problem. Take it from me, that's a mess you do not want to step into."

"I can't—" She looked miserable. She shoved at her wet hair again, trying to keep it off her face. "I can't ask you to do this."

"You didn't. I offered." Honestly, when she was wet and bedraggled like this, she didn't look old enough to be a mother. She looked like a little kid who'd gotten caught playing with the hose.

Except for the lacy blue bra he could see so clearly through the wet shirt. He imagined the matching panties, soaked under those jeans until they stuck to her pale skin. Nothing childish about any of that.

And nothing appropriate about thoughts like that, either. To play it safe, he refused to let his gaze descend lower than her cute, pointed chin.

"Come on," he said. "At a moment like this, two mops are definitely better than one."

Though she still seemed self-conscious, she obviously couldn't argue with his logic. With a small shake of her head, she grabbed the other mop and went to work.

Getting the floor dry took a long time, and the water weight made the mops heavy as boat anchors. He wondered how she kept going. Her arms and shoulders must be aching. But she matched him swipe for swipe.

They didn't talk much. A few practical comments about what to move where, which section to tackle next, where to add towels or sponges. He asked her if she had overhead fans and she told him she did, and a few on stands, as well, that they could put out later to make sure everything dried out thoroughly.

Thankfully, through it all, Eddie slept on.

After about an hour, he suggested they take a break. He needed it, and so did she. He could tell by the sheen of perspiration that had broken out on her collarbone, and the pink on her cheeks from heavy breathing, that she was pooped. But she was a gritty woman. She probably would have keeled over before she let herself be the first one to cry uncle.

They rested the soggy mops against the gleaming prep table, and then, with belly-deep sighs, propped their own tired bodies against it, too.

He felt a simmering burn in his palms that told him he was going to have blisters tomorrow. Damn. He was too soft these days, too white-collar and clean. Handball and tennis passed for exercise in his cushy life, but nothing matched the kind of sweaty, real-life labor he used to do in high school. Today Diamante was so big they hired all the dirty work out, but back then all the brothers had constantly been on call as Diamante handymen.

"I want you to know how grateful I am," she said in that same half-whispering voice. "I don't know where Jimbo is—I would have expected him here by now. I'm so sorry you got tangled up in this mess. I bet you're sorry you decided to get anywhere near this place to-night."

He didn't answer for a minute, trying to sort out exactly how he did feel. He was wet and uncomfortable. He was tired.

But sorry?

Not one bit.

"No," he settled for saying. "I don't regret it at all. In fact, I can't think of anything I'd rather be doing."

She almost laughed out loud at that, but she glanced at Eddie and bit her lower lip to clamp back the sound.

"Nothing you'd rather be doing," she repeated skeptically, "than mopping up the lake I used to call my kitchen?"

He shook his head. "Nothing."

For a minute she let her gaze explore his face, as if she needed answers and hoped she might find them there. She must not have seen what she needed, because finally her eyebrows drew together, as if she were bewildered.

"Why?" she asked.

He didn't have an answer for that, so he told the truth. "I don't know."

He looked at her, wishing he did understand all this better. Of all the people in the world he should never, ever be attracted to, Allison York was at the top of the list. He was undoubtedly at the top of her list, too. And yet...something about this woman had started to burrow deep under his skin.

She obviously wasn't coming on to him. Given the situation, she shouldn't possibly have had an ounce of appeal in her tonight. She was wet, exhausted, embarrassed and confused.

She looked, in fact, like a half-drowned kitten.

And yet, when she whispered to him this way, the

sound touched him like warm fingertips, and then it went deeper, as if it could move past the barrier of skin. He could feel his body stirring in response.

And if he weren't careful, these wet jeans of his would reveal a whole lot more than he had any interest in sharing.

Their faces were inches apart. He'd told himself it was because of Eddie. They couldn't afford to yell across empty spaces. He'd told himself they were being cautious, sensible.

But the truth was more selfish than that. He whispered because it brought him close enough to kiss her.

Because a kiss was what he wanted. What he craved…

Bad move, a voice inside his head said sternly. *Be quiet,* the hungry, fired-up part of him answered back. *Just kiss her.*

Her lips were full, parted slightly, pink and waiting.

"Allison…" He lowered his head an inch or two, enough to signal his intentions. Enough to give her time to stop him.

Her brown eyes widened. At the last possible moment, when there was barely enough room left between them that they could still pretend it hadn't happened, she pulled back. She blinked. Then she shifted a couple of inches away, casually, as though she hadn't noticed anything strange.

A small needle of disappointment stung him. But he had no choice other than to accept it. He tried to tell himself it was for the best. The ramifications of kissing Allison were…

Too complicated to predict.

The first second or two after were awkward. He watched her while she toyed with the tip of her mop handle. Finally she glanced at him from under a sheltering black fringe of lashes. "So, why *are* you here, Red?"

He tried to laugh it off. "It's not more stalking, I promise. I called you first—both at your apartment and on your cell. I got no answer. But everyone's been talking about your new restaurant, so I thought I'd come take a look as I headed back to the city."

She looked skeptical. "No, really. Does it have something to do with Victor?" She met his gaze squarely. "I signed the papers, you know. Last week. I thought that would be the end of it."

It should have been. It should have been The End, in capital letters, like the last word in the book, the last frame of the film. He had no legitimate reason for coming to see her.

"It's got nothing to do with Victor," he said. "I wanted to say hello. When I left you at the hospital, things felt...unfinished. I know Lewis took care of the paperwork, but I wanted... I wanted to see how Eddie was doing."

He paused, knowing that last line probably sounded every bit as dishonest as it was. "I wanted to know how *you* were doing," he added, more truthfully.

His candor seemed to reduce her tension. She let go of the mop and breathed evenly for the first time since she realized he wanted to kiss her.

"Eddie's fine," she said. "And I'm fine." She glanced around and lifted her shoulders wearily. "Or rather I will be if I can get the restaurant ready on time."

Glad for neutral conversational ground, he jumped on the topic. "It looks great. I can see that there's still a lot to do, but—"

She laughed. "That's an understatement. I planned so carefully, and I thought I'd anticipated every single detail. But new problems keep cropping up. I'm starting to wonder whether I can be ready in time."

Red knew exactly what she meant. Opening a restaurant was like launching a war. So much at stake. So many things that could, and did, go wrong.

Most people who thought they wanted to run a restaurant knew nothing about the nitty gritty hard work involved. They pictured themselves floating among their guests, dispensing wine to go with the beautifully garnished lamb chops, which in their fantasies somehow appeared out of thin air. If Marianne, for instance, tried to start a restaurant, she'd hire Le Cordon Bleu cooks, forget to order fresh lettuce and be forced to close up shop within the week.

But Allison, with her firm jaw, her no-nonsense gaze, and her willingness to meet her problems head on, seemed much more grounded than that. The sad truth was, odds were against all new restaurant enterprises. But he just might bet on hers.

He looked around the kitchen, mentally inventorying the equipment. She had most of the big pieces, and she'd bought well. He recognized the brands. The shiny aluminum surfaces, still reflecting both the splattered water and the bright overhead lighting, said she'd bought new.

The layout was efficient, but several large empty spaces spoke to some missing basics. No range yet. No freezer. No dishwasher.

And of course there was the muddled mess out in the front. He wondered where she stood on hiring, and paperwork, and contracts with suppliers.

"When do you plan to open?"

"A soft opening, just for friends, in ten days," she said, lifting her thumb to her mouth and biting the nail nervously as she gazed around. "Two weeks till the real deal. No wiggle room, really. The word's already been put out, and besides, if I don't start bringing in money instead of spending it, things are going to get scary in a hurry."

Didn't sound as if she had much of a cushion. He hated to bring up anything touchy, but he couldn't help himself. "What about Victor's check? Doesn't that buy you a little safety net?"

"Victor's money is for Eddie." She frowned and tilted her head back slightly, as if she found the question insulting. "I'll use it for his medical care, if we have an emergency, but that's all. The restaurant must pay for itself."

He thought of a dozen responses to that—all the truisms about how the first six months were rough, about how no new business could be expected to draw a profit right away, maybe even for a couple of years. He could even say, quite sincerely, that the success of the restaurant would be important for Eddie's future, too.

But when he looked at her, with that resolute brow knitted intently, he just couldn't say any of those things.

"Is there any way I could help?" He knew it was unlikely that she'd accept, but he wanted to offer. He wanted to make things easier for her. "Diamante is opening a take-out and delivery store over on Shorefront, and we've got a pretty big crew there. I was just about to let some of the men go. I could send them over here to lend a hand."

She flushed. "Thank you, but I really can't afford to

hire anyone else. My budget is pretty much carved in stone."

"No, I didn't mean you'd have to pay for them. We've already—"

"No."

He stopped. Having grown up in a restaurant family, she was too smart, of course, to buy any kind of lie. He should have known he couldn't spin some well-intentioned deception and hope she'd accept it, glossing over the inconsistencies and lapses of logic.

Besides, she wasn't the type who wanted her facts sugar-coated. She swallowed the bitter truths straight.

"Thank you," she said again. "But really, I want to handle this myself."

He nodded. They had forgotten to whisper, and Eddie started to whimper in his carrier, though his eyes were still shut fast. His mouth moved in small pouting shapes, and even childless as he was, Red knew that meant the baby was hungry.

His time alone with Allison was running out.

Allison had noticed, too. She tucked the blanket around Eddie's feet, then flicked off the light switch to the overhead fixture that had shone directly over him, as if to buy a few more minutes before he awoke.

Then she turned to Red. Her eyes glimmered darkly in the new, more indirect illumination. "I think I should tell you something," she said quietly. "Something important. At least to me."

"Okay."

"I'm not interested in bashing Victor," she said. "I know he was your friend, and you thought the world of him. I never imagined we'd talk about this, but here you are and—"

He knew what she meant. Here he was, and they'd come within an inch of kissing.

"And somehow I want to set the record straight."

"Okay," he said again.

He heard her take a deep breath. "I don't know what Victor told you. But I want you to know that I had no idea he was married. I knew he wasn't in love with me. I wasn't in love with him, either. But we were— I thought we were friends. And it was a time in my life when I very badly needed a friend. My father had just died, and I was losing his restaurant, which he'd worked so hard to save."

This was the same story the others had told him. Her father dying, the restaurant failing. A horrible one-two punch.

"He was very sweet to me. He was working through a bad divorce, he said, and hiding out in Windsor Beach to be alone for a while. I thought we were both in a bad place, and maybe we could help each other. So, for a few weeks—though I knew it wouldn't ever be permanent—we were lovers. Jimbo was out of town. He does work with disabled vets, and sometimes they go on short trips. So we were able to go to my apartment, instead of his hotel."

His hotel? Red knew that Victor had a glamorous, beach-front house on the outskirts of Windsor Beach. He wondered why Victor hadn't romanced Allison there. And then he understood. The beach house was filled with pictures of Marianne and Dylan and Cherry. His bedroom closet would have been filled with women's clothes, his bathroom lined with perfumes and skin creams that screamed wife.

"It went on, as I said, for only a couple of weeks. He

stopped showing up. Stopped calling. I had absolutely no idea about his wife and children until I called him to tell him I was pregnant."

For a minute, Red tried not to believe it. Victor deliberately misleading this woman, hiding the very fact of his marriage, his family—even his house? It was impossible. Victor was the definition of a family man. He would no more deny their existence than he would...

Pay off his pregnant mistress to hide their child from the world?

Any way Red looked at this whole fiasco, Victor had done something it should have been impossible for him to do.

"I understand if you don't believe me," Allison went on. "It doesn't really matter, anyhow. It's just that, for some reason, I wanted to tell you, and—"

"I believe you," he said. To his surprise, he really did. There was something about this woman. He knew she wasn't a liar, the same way he knew Nana Lina wasn't a liar. Or Belle, or Kitty, or any of the women who had become part of the Malone family. This was Nana Lina's famous quality of starch. The ability to tell even hard truths with so much authority and courage that everyone heard it for what it was.

She nodded slowly. "Thank you. But there's something else I need to say, too. It's about—" She turned her head and began playing with a small pool of water that lay on the prep table. She brushed it across the slippery, silver surface, using the heel of her hand, until it slid over the edge and sank onto the damp strands of her mop. It left a sheen of rapidly disappearing wetness on the table.

"It's about what almost happened earlier. When we almost—you almost—"

"When I wanted to kiss you?" Strangely, he was glad she'd mentioned it. It felt good to get it out in the open. "I'm sorry about that. I know I don't have the right."

"It's okay," she said. "But that's what I want to tell you. I can't…I don't want to have any complications in my life right now. Especially complications with men. I've made a lot of mistakes in the past few years. Before Victor, I had a marriage that ended badly. So, as you can probably imagine, I want to stay away from all that for a while. I want to concentrate on Eddie. And my restaurant."

She looked up again, a half smile playing at her lips. "I'm not suggesting you wanted to get involved with me. A kiss is just a kiss, and all that. And that wasn't even a kiss. Still. I wanted to explain where I stand before…before things could spiral out of control."

"All right," he said. "I get it. You don't want complications. But how about a friend? Is a friend too complicated? Because I'd like very much to be your friend, maybe help out now and then. Maybe see Eddie now and then."

She hesitated. "A friend…"

"Yes. Not a friend like Victor. More like…your buddy Bill Longmire." He smiled. "Only with better driving skills."

She shook her head slowly. And then he heard the low, melodic sound of her laughter. "Like Bill Longmire. Yeah. Right. Anyone less like Bill Longmire…"

But her laughter was the final intrusion on the baby's dreams. Eddie's eyes blinked a few times, then stayed open. He wriggled unhappily, twisting his body until he could see his mother's face. Then he began to cry in earnest.

She tilted her head ruefully. "He's hungry," she said. "I guess I'd better—"

"Okay. I should get to the city, anyhow." He held out his hand. "So…friends, then?"

For a split second, her gaze raked his face. Then, with only a hint of reluctance, she accepted his handshake. Her hand was cool and small, but he could feel tiny calluses on the pads of the palms, and on the side of her thumb. God help him, even those signs of work and worry charmed him.

"Friends," she echoed softly.

CHAPTER ELEVEN

WHEN ALLISON AGREED to be friends with Red Malone, she'd assumed it wasn't a particularly dangerous promise. In her experience, that kind of guy—the charismatic, self-assured playboy type—didn't really have female friends. He merely had women who were still lined up in the relationship queue, waiting their turn to take a spin on the Red Malone love machine.

Once the possibility of progressing to sex was off-limits, he'd lose interest in a hurry. So when she didn't hear from him over the next three days, she wasn't surprised.

She assured herself she wasn't disappointed, either. They'd left their temporary association in a good place, considering how rocky their early meetings had been. When Red came to the restaurant the night the plumbing went wacky, he had clearly been looking for a way to close things amicably. Which was not to say she didn't appreciate his help. He'd been a godsend, especially considering Jimbo didn't return her SOS until midnight.

So Red had kept the boat from sinking. And on that chivalrous note, he could leave with a clear conscience. Now he could return to his real life, and his real women. He could go back to hanging out at the country club with Victor's "real" family.

And she could once again focus on the business at hand. Which, right now, was an entrée-tasting session with Jimbo and Meg Bretton, the farmers' market find who was quickly becoming a good friend. Allison sat at a small table in Summer Moon's kitchen, waiting, while the two foodies worked side by side at the newly installed range, concocting marvels and dueling for Allison's approval.

Eddie was staying with Sue for the afternoon. What with hot burners and spitting oil, with knives flying, cleavers hacking through melons and ten-inch blades spinning through vegetables, this competitive kitchen was no place for a baby.

"Here you go. Pork chops with melon salsa." With a flourish, Meg set a plate in front of Allison. The scent rose invitingly to her nostrils. If this were a cartoon, Allison thought as her mouth watered, the steam would consolidate into a hand, with a bent finger beckoning her in.

"Don't fill up on that," Jimbo cautioned from the stove. "I've got a salmon skewer coming next...same salsa."

"*My* salsa." Meg's smile was smug. She tossed her shoulder-length blond hair triumphantly. "Remember how you predicted it would taste like bilge water?"

He grumbled something inarticulate, then turned his focus to the stovetop. "Okay," he said grudgingly. "I admit it. The salsa isn't terrible. In fact, Alli, we need to get her under contract right now. Exclusive contract." He seemed to notice Meg's triumphant grin, and rolled his eyes. "Not that anyone else is exactly beating down her door."

"Really?" Meg gazed at him, one hand on her hip, her expression arch. "And you would know that...how?"

Allison covered her smile with a forkful of pork chops. If Jimbo and Meg had already progressed to affectionate insults, the intimacy was developing even faster than she could have hoped. Jimbo's insults were reserved for two groups—the people he couldn't stand and the people he was crazy about.

"If you've got salmon coming, too, I'm going to need some help," Allison said as she ate another piece of pork. This was the fifth entrée so far. With the others, she'd been sensible, simply tasting, then moving on to the next delight. But this one was too good. "Meg. Get a fork and save me from myself."

After the salmon, Jimbo had created every dish on today's list and could finally join in. He grabbed a beer from the refrigerator and ran his thumb along the rim, his version of washing the lid. He started to pop the tab, but he froze midmotion. He twisted up one side of his face, thinking hard.

"Wait. Do I have the night shift with Eddie, or do you?"

"I do," Allison assured him. "I thought you were meeting with the grief group tonight."

"Oh." Jimbo stared down at his beer can glumly. "Oh, yeah. That's right."

He returned the beer to the case, then came and joined the women at the table. He didn't bother with a fork, but started plucking leftover bits of salmon, pork, chicken and tofu from various half-eaten plates. He popped each piece in his mouth as if it were a pitching game.

Meg shoved the saucer of salsa in his direction, and inconspicuously nudged a fork close enough for him to reach. "You go to a grief group? I didn't know that."

He nodded. "It's a group of vets," he explained around the salmon. "Some of the men I served with. Some of their friends. Most of them have lost a family member, a wife, a mother, a kid." He took Allison's water without asking and swigged the remaining inch or so. "It's funny. They deal with danger and the reality of death all the time when they're in uniform. Then they get out, where it's supposed to be safe, and someone they love dies. A lot of them can't handle it."

Meg's face was somber, and Allison realized that the other woman had misunderstood.

"Jimbo leads the group," she said. "He's been meeting with these same men for years now. They're really more like a family."

Meg's expression cleared. "I see. I thought you—I mean, I didn't know who in your circle might have died, and—"

"No." Jimbo shrugged. "I've lost people, of course, like everybody. But it didn't hit me that way somehow. But then, I've got both my legs, and my arms, and most of them don't. That undoubtedly screws with your ability to absorb new losses."

They ate in silence a few minutes. Then Jimbo cleared his throat. "Hey, Allie. Did I mention to you about Carl Kelly?"

He didn't meet her gaze, instead pretending a penetrating interest in lining up the tines of his fork. Considering the cutlery was brand-new, Allison considered it unlikely that anything was seriously out of whack. A personal problem, then? Probably. And one he hated to broach.

Deep inside her, something pinched, then altered its

beat. "No, you haven't mentioned Carl in weeks," she said. "What about him?"

"He got chicken pox."

Meg and Allison both smiled instinctively, just because chicken pox was a child's illness. But then Allison remembered that the disease supposedly was much harder on an adult, and she sobered.

"That's awful. How is he?"

"Contagious," Jimbo said concisely. "Which means he can't take the guys to L.A. this weekend." He frowned at the empty plates, and then, laying his hand flat and broad on the table, he took a deep breath. "They want me to go in his place. They need someone who is already cleared, who is already certified for all the activities and stuff. I told them it's the worst possible time, in terms of Summer Moon. I told them there's no way we can be ready if I take almost a whole week off. I told them—"

Allison laughed, and she was careful to make it sound absolutely genuine, in spite of the twisting feeling in her stomach. Jimbo gone a whole week? That would take them right up to the soft opening.

How could she do without him right now, when so much still remained undone? How would she manage?

But she could do it. She could do it. She could get more help. For one panicked second she even considered calling Red, to see if he could put her in contact with those extra crew members he'd let go.

But she wasn't that desperate. Not yet. Thank heaven.

"Don't be silly," she said, smiling while her mind did rapid man-hour and budget calculations. "You must go. We're so close here. Everything will be fine."

"You need me, damn it." He cast a glowering glance around the kitchen. "Look at this place. We still don't have the lights up over the tables, and the dishwasher they sent is the wrong size. And that doesn't even take into account the flooring and the wallpaper in the bathrooms. Plus, there's about a metric ton of—"

"Jimbo, relax." She put her hand over his, obscuring the tattoos on his knuckles. "I've got it covered. If I absolutely have to, I can call in reinforcements."

He made a low, irritable sound. "Who? The Old Coots Club? It would take all four of those octogenarians just to lift that new toilet. Besides, I heard they've phoned Mickey O'Connor's niece, asking her to come check things out. Apparently Mickey didn't recognize Sarge the other day. It may be nursing-home time for him."

Allison's heart fell. She'd known this day would come, but she'd been dreading it. Mickey loved open spaces, excitement and drama. He'd be stifled to death in a nursing home. But maybe there was still hope. She hadn't ever met his niece. Maybe the woman had inherited the O'Connor spirit, and she'd take Mickey home with her.

After a few pensive moments, in which both Allison and Jimbo shared a pang for Mickey, Meg finally spoke up. She'd been watching the argument quietly, with that sensible air she had, letting the two of them work it out.

"I could help," she said. "I'll have to be at the farmers' market this weekend, but after that I've got plenty of free time. I bet that, between us, we can pull things together fine."

"See?" Allison smiled her thanks toward Meg, then

gave Jimbo her best *end of discussion* look. "Maybe, just maybe, you're not quite as indispensible as you think."

NANA LINA'S HOUSE at Belvedere Cove was rarely quiet. Though she was almost eighty, Red's grandmother still loved bustle and merry-making, so she hosted parties as often as she could think of an excuse.

Red and his brothers each had their own legal domiciles, sensible townhomes closer to the city, nearer to Diamante's corporate offices above the company's one sit-down restaurant. But the sprawling waterfront Marin County estate, where their grandparents had brought them after the deaths of their parents, would always be the place they called home.

Carrying on the tradition, they staged revelries there, too, whenever they needed room to spread out. Matt and Belle had said their vows on the back lawn, where nine months later they'd also toasted the arrival of his little girl, drinking pink champagne under trees blooming with pink and white balloons.

Red had always assumed he'd be married here, too, one day, if he ever found a woman he thought he could stand for more than a year or two.

If he did marry here, he'd want something smaller. More intimate. When the estate was in party mode, decked out in Japanese lanterns, urns overflowing with flowers, and crystal and sterling flickering by candlelight, it was magnificent. But Red liked the house best when the guests were gone, and he was alone with family and the moonlight streaming on the water.

Like tonight.

He opened the back doors and moved onto the patio,

pleasantly weary after a long dinner. By Malone standards, the party had been small, fourteen or so. Just Cherry, Marianne and Dylan Wigham, Matt and Belle, David and Kitty Gerard, Colby and his date—Red was pretty sure it was Mandi, who did in-house PR for a department store. And of course a couple of Nana Lina's friends.

It had gone well, but best of all it had ended early, giving Red some time to unwind and catch his breath. He would go upstairs to kiss Nana Lina good-night in a little while, but right now he felt like standing in the cold, glassy black air and listening to the ring-necked drakes fuss and rustle as they settled down for the night.

He was outside at least a full minute before he realized the patio was already occupied. In one of the wrought-iron chairs, as still as if he were merely one more shadow in the garden, sat his oldest brother, Colby.

Something about the sight bothered him. Colby must have heard Red open the patio doors. He hadn't exactly been in sneak mode. Why hadn't Colby said anything?

And what was he doing out here, anyhow?

"Hey there," Red said. "What's going on? Where's Mandi?"

Colby turned around, smiling. His eyes caught a little bit of moonlight, but the rest of him was a dense, slightly darker outline on the dark.

"She went home. She had her own car, thank heaven."

Red laughed. He didn't need to ask Colby why he was thanking heaven. Mandi was great to look at, and nothing to sneeze at intellectually, either. But she had a hungry eye, and she'd spent the whole meal furtively scanning the dining room, her brain clicking away like a calculator, appraising the paintings, the china, the glassware. As they walked out after the meal, Red had seen her rub the edge of the drapes between her thumb and index finger.

Red was all male, and he had no idea what the hell you could learn by fingering the drapes. But he did know that he wouldn't want any part of a girlfriend who did it.

"There's something wrong with all of them," he said, suddenly, with a heartfelt sense of exhaustion with the whole process. "Women, I mean. At first, when you meet a new, interesting one, you think, okay. Yeah, maybe. But there's always some fatal flaw. Have you noticed that?"

Colby kept his face forward, as if he were mesmerized by the shadows of the windy trees stroking slowly against the olive surface of the lawn. But he smiled. Red could see the moonlit edge of his teeth as his lips pulled back.

"Yeah," Colby said. "I've noticed that."

A bird hooted mournfully, and Red leaned against a nearby chair, taking a deep breath of the clean air. For some reason, he sensed that Colby didn't really want him to sit down and settle in for the long haul, but he wasn't ready to go in yet, either.

"So why is that, do you think? Did Matt and David really get the last two decent women on earth? Or…is it us? Are we too picky?"

Colby lifted one shoulder. "I have no idea. Nana Lina says we do it on purpose, to sabotage ourselves. Depending on what mood she's in, she might say it's either because we're terrified of commitment, or because we're arrogant jackasses who think we're too good for everyone. Or sometimes her explanation is that we've got low self-esteem and don't think we deserve good women."

"Yeah. Sure." Red chuckled. "*That* makes a whole lot of sense." He shifted, moving the cold wrought-iron of the chair with a scrape along the bricks, so that he could rest one foot on the seat. "I'll tell you what I do think, though. I think maybe that feeling of perfection comes later, *after* you fall in love."

Colby shrugged one shoulder again, restlessly. "Whatever that means. Sounds like something out of a magazine."

Red laughed. "Yeah, it does, doesn't it? But I'm serious. Think about Matt. David, too, for that matter. They didn't know they'd found the perfect woman right at first, did they? I remember when Matt first met Belle he didn't think she was even up to the job of doing PR, much less being his wife. And remember how it was at first for David and Kitty? Everyone thought she was a freak, including David."

Colby was clearly not in the mood for this discussion. His sardonic voice had cooled. "And your point is?"

Well, shoot, Red wasn't completely sure *what* his point was. It had just occurred to him and was still hazy in his mind. Analyzing emotions wasn't the kind of thing they ever spent much time talking about. Navel-gazing, Colby always called it when they heard their friends going on and on about some woman, and how she made them feel.

Or, as their surfer friend Stony Jones so colorfully

put it, dwelling on these things was like "sitting on your emotional thumbs until your ass hurts."

"My point—" Red soldiered on "—is that Matt and David had to be patient. They had to tough it out. Let the rough spots smooth over, and give love a little time to show itself. They didn't give up because it wasn't perfect right at first. You know what I mean?"

No answer.

"Colby?"

Still no answer. The silence annoyed Red. It was fine to be all stereotypically macho and stoic most of the time. It wasn't an act. They enjoyed their lives and would rather live them than analyze the spirit out of them.

But sometimes, when things weren't working, you had to lift the hood and check the wires. Sometimes, if you felt like crap, and you couldn't make it go away, you had to engage in a little self-reflection.

"Damn it, Colby. I'm trying to say something here. I'm trying to say that it's possible you and I may have met the right woman, somewhere along the way, and we didn't realize it. We let something, some flaw or problem, turn us off too easily. Do you know what I mean or not?"

Colby still didn't turn around. His shoulders were no longer shifting restlessly. He could have been made of stone.

"Of course I know what you mean," Colby said, as Red was about to give up and go in. His voice was cold, dripping icy stilettos that made him sound like a stranger. "I'm not a fool. But how does knowing it help?"

"Because maybe it means that a woman who looks

wrong now might look very different later. It means that maybe, if we're patient—"

Finally, Colby turned around. And the expression on his hard face was so bleak, so hopeless and dreary, that Red wished he had never said a word.

Hayley. Shit. All this time, Red had been secretly thinking about Allison, who was only forty-five minutes away, in Windsor Beach. But Colby had been thinking of Hayley.

Hayley, who was gone, untraceable, maybe married, maybe even dead, for all they knew. Hayley, who was nowhere.

"But what if being patient won't help, Red?" Colby's fingers gripped the arm of his chair so hard his nails were bloodless. "What if you blew it, really blew it? What if it's too damn late?"

CHAPTER TWELVE

WHEN THE APPLIANCE OUTLET delivered the wrong-size dishwasher for the second time in a row, Allison almost lost it. She barely managed to stop herself from yelling at the dispatcher, who kept mindlessly insisting it must be the right one, because the invoice said so.

The fact that Allison would have to hack off about six inches of stainless steel countertop to shove the darn thing in didn't seem to matter to the dispatcher. By the time she got off the phone with the moron's supervisor, she felt her blood pounding in her temples.

The afternoon didn't get better. She was already tired. Eddie had been given his four-month shots yesterday and was a little cranky. She'd been up with him all night. So when the decorator called to say that the framing for the paintings was running behind schedule, Allison decided she'd had enough for the day.

She needed some fresh air. She needed to clear her head. Ignoring the stacks of boxes, and the paperwork piled a foot high, she bundled Eddie into his stroller and headed to the beach. The nearest public access was half a mile down the road, but Flip's Peacock Café was only a couple of blocks away, and he wouldn't mind if she cut through his parking lot. Luckily, her restaurant would serve a completely different kind of fare, so he didn't feel threatened by her plans.

The day was perfect, not too hot, not too windy. It was one of those rare bright afternoons in which one or two pillowy clouds drifted across a big blue bowl of sky. The minute she reached the edge of the dunes, she felt better. She toed off her sneakers, unhooked Eddie from the stroller, propped him against her shoulder and moved out across the warm sand.

Windsor Beach was almost as powdery as her much more famous sister beach, Carmel. Allison wiggled her toes, luxuriating in the feel. She could almost hear her father's voice, as he told her about the tiny, white grains of quartz and the pastel pinks and greens of feldspar that mixed to create the sparkling softness.

A seabird wheeled overhead, crying shrilly. She looked up, thinking that she should remember what kind of gull it was…her father had taught her all that, too. He'd been fascinated by nature, by the fish and the shells, the tides and the clouds and the birds. After her mother left them, her dad had often brought Allison out here, where the vastness of the Pacific and the mysteries of the natural world had taken her mind off her misery.

He would have loved to share all that knowledge with Eddie. His grandson. If only he had lived long enough.

"Eddie, look," she said, speaking the words her dad no longer could. She pointed to the bird as it looped one more time, then sailed away, like a kite that slipped its string. "See the pretty birdie?"

Eddie chortled as a gust of wind blew his delicate strands of hair around, tickling his ears and cheeks. She leaned in and kissed him, suddenly blinking back a stinging in her eyes. Hard to believe that soon she'd probably need to clip the ends of these silky wisps. Four months now…then, before she knew it, four years…

She walked along the denser, saturated ground at the water's edge, every footfall causing a shimmering halo-burst in the sand. Beside her, the sun sparkled across the water, creating sequins out of the tips of every wave. Eddie watched, fascinated. He had recently learned to hold his head at various angles, so he kept it lifted as much as he could, swiveling and craning, clearly enjoying his newfound power.

But eventually the rhythm of walking lulled him to sleep, and his head drooped against her shoulder. He hadn't rested much last night, either, so his slumber was so sound that when her phone buzzed in her pocket, he didn't stir.

She fished the cell out quickly and answered it without checking the caller ID. Even if it was the appliance dispatcher, she wouldn't lose her temper. As always, the immensity of the ocean had reduced her problems to a manageable size.

"Hello?"

"Allison. It's Red."

Her feet stopped moving. "Hi."

"I'm in Windsor Beach," he said, without preamble. "I thought I'd call and see how things are going."

"They're going fine." Better a lie than the truth, which would sound as if she were fishing for a hand-out, either of his time or his expertise. Jimbo had been gone two days, and they were making progress, but not enough. "Everything's great."

He laughed, an easy sound that held no offence. "Now see, I know you're fibbing. Not one time in the entire history of restaurant openings has everything been great. There are always a million unexpected glitches."

She hesitated, unsure what to say in the face of his vaster experience. He was right, of course. Opening any business was difficult, but the restaurant business was notoriously fraught with hazards.

"So why not tell me the truth?" He sounded as if he really wanted to know. "How are things...*really?*"

She ought to say *fine* again. She ought to gloss over everything, give him the simplest answer, even if it was a lie. He didn't have any particular right to be told all the boring details of her life.

"Well, okay, maybe *fine* was an exaggeration," she heard herself saying. "The situation isn't a disaster, but it's still kind of touch and go. Jimbo had to leave town for a week or so, which didn't really help."

"I bet." He paused a minute. "As it happens, I'm staying in Windsor Beach a few days. I'm finalizing the Diamante opening and scouting a couple of other locations nearby. It's enough to keep me in town, but not enough to leave me slammed. How about if I come by tomorrow and see what I might be able to do to help?"

"No. No, really. I couldn't impose. It's nice of you, but it's not necessary. I'll be fine—"

"I'd like to," he said, and she heard a smile in his voice. "I wouldn't have offered just to be nice."

Then why *did* he offer? It didn't really make sense. Unless maybe he wanted to see Eddie a little more. Or maybe he had some remaining curiosity about the woman Victor had been so desperate to hide from his family.

Or a small, leftover spot of guilt?

Or—her cynical side took over—maybe he thought

that, since she'd slept with Victor, she was easy. Maybe he thought that while he was stuck in Windsor Beach he could entertain himself in her bed.

But that was absurd. He wasn't the type of man who had to hunt down lonely, foolish women and bed them in furtive quickies. She'd seen the newspaper clippings. She'd seen the parade of blondes, brunettes and redheads who clung to him, beaming as if they'd won the dating lotto.

She squinted against the bright sunlight and tried to think more logically. For some reason, her instinct said she should protest, stonewall, bar the doors of her life to this man. But when she tried to think how, exactly, he could possibly pose a danger to her, she couldn't come up with anything rational.

So what if he had been Victor's friend? So had she, once upon a time.

Red had apologized for his early missteps—and he seemed to believe her when she told him she hadn't intentionally committed adultery with someone's husband. He was obviously a well-bred, educated, able-bodied man, and he knew a lot about how to launch a successful restaurant.

Only a paranoid, fuzzy-minded fool would reject an offer like this.

"Okay, then, thanks," she said, trying to ignore the wriggle of discomfort that simply wouldn't be argued away. "I guess I'll see you tomorrow."

TWO DAYS LATER, Red looked around Summer Moon, and for the first time he believed they might make it. Allison had three days to go till the soft opening, and about three weeks of work. But he'd called in some reinforce-

ments, and he had found some efficiencies in the setup
that would save her both time and money.

Of course, he'd also found the stain on the ceiling
that proved she had a leak, and the flaw in the software
choices that meant she had to convert to a whole new
system. But that was how the process went. Two steps
forward, one step back.

At about 6:00 p.m. on the second day, Red was near
the front door, trying to help the carpenter figure out
why the hostess podium wouldn't sit flush against the
wall, when a stranger walked in, leading with his chin.
Red glanced at his face. Forty, maybe forty-five? Pencil
pusher with little time to play, especially outdoors,
judging from the pallor. Small eyes that seemed even
smaller because the muscles around them were so tight.
Thin lips that almost disappeared from being clamped
so tightly. And a spot of blotchy red on each cheekbone.

Twenty years of working at Diamante had taught
Red what that face meant. It meant trouble. It meant
this guy felt robbed or gypped in some way, and he intended to complain at the top of his lungs until someone kissed his ass enough to appease him.

Usually, though, that face didn't walk through the
doors of a restaurant that wasn't even serving food yet.

Red set down the level, indicated that the carpenter should carry on, and moved quickly to head off the
angry newcomer.

"Hi," he said. "How can I help you?"

The man's flush deepened. "You can't. I'm looking
for Allison York."

Red kept his smile easy and calm. Diamante didn't
put up with jerks like this. They didn't have to. But this

wasn't his restaurant, so he couldn't toss the guy out without Allison's say so.

"Well, then, maybe I can help," he said. "If you tell me what you need, I might be able to find her for you."

The man frowned hard. "I'll find her myself."

Red planted his feet firmly, anticipating that the guy would try to shove his way past him, but before it could come to that Allison appeared around the corner, carrying a big carton toward the bathroom area. She didn't seem to notice Red and the newcomer.

"Hey. You over there!" The man raised his voice more than he needed to, and the sound echoed through the emptiness of the large seating area. "Are you Allison York?"

She turned, smiling. "Yes." Her eyes scanned the man, and clearly came up without any identification. "May I help you?"

The man's belligerence went down a notch. Obviously he was disarmed by Allison's appearance. Red could imagine why. She looked like a 1950s teenager today. No makeup, glossy brown hair yanked back in a short ponytail, jeans rolled up nearly to her knees, navy blue Keds and a turquoise madras shirt.

"I certainly hope you can," the man said, regrouping and blinking away his surprise. His voice was still loud, still hard and hostile. "I'm Hank Vanak."

She tilted her head, clearly still stumped.

He tried again. "I'm Nell O'Connor's husband."

She shifted the big, heavy box she held and glanced toward the bathroom, where she obviously had been planning to set this burden down. "I'm sorry, but I—"

The man's shoulders twitched impatiently. "Nell is Dickey O'Connor's niece."

Understanding dawned on Allison's face. She put the box down on the floor, right in the middle of the seating area, and came toward the man, her hand outstretched and her eyes softening. "Oh, yes, of course. I'm sorry, Hank. I've met Nell a couple of times, but I'm not thinking clearly about anything. As you can see, things are crazy right now. How is Dickey? We're all so worried about him."

To Red's surprise, the man took a step backward, as if to retreat from Allison's handshake. His arms remained stiffly at his sides, and, after a bewildered second, Allison let her hand drop.

"Is there bad news?" she asked, frowning.

"It depends," the man said curtly.

Allison waited a couple of beats, and then she shook her head. "Depends on what?"

The man folded his arms over his chest. "On whether you can explain yourself adequately."

Red heard Allison take in a tight breath, and he saw her jaw square off. She was a patient woman, but she'd obviously reached the end of her rope with this guy already. Poor Hank Vanak. Over the past two days, Red had seen her interact with dozens of workers—installers, electricians, plumbers, suppliers—and he knew how she handled the ones who were screwing up or slacking off. It always started with that sharp inhale, and it often ended with the worker's tail between his legs.

"Mr. Vanak, I'm very busy," she said, her voice clipped. "Too busy to play a guessing game about this. If you have something to say, you'd better say it, or I'm going to return to my work."

Vanak's mouth opened, closed, then opened again.

His whole face was now suffused with a dull red flush of anger. "I hope you don't do that, Miss York. I came here as a favor to my wife, who didn't want the police involved if we could prevent it. But from the beginning I thought we should call them, and I'd be more than happy to bring them in now."

"The police?" Red got closer, so that he came as close to standing between this guy and Allison as he could without blocking her view.

But, even as he jumped to intercede, he noticed that Allison didn't blurt out the same shocked words. *The police? Why the police?* Instead, she stared at the man, looking furious but not surprised.

"What is your problem, Mr. Vanak?" Red kept his voice flat, avoiding the insolent nastiness the other man had adopted. "Why would you want to call the police?"

Vanak turned a steely glance Red's way. "And you are…?"

Red smiled. "Still waiting for an answer."

Vanak's eyes narrowed even farther, though Red wouldn't have imagined it was possible. "She knows why," the man said stiffly. "Ask her."

"I'm asking you."

"It's okay, Red." Allison lifted her chin. She didn't take her gaze from Vanak. "It's about Dickey's jewelry. Is that right, Mr. Vanak?"

"Yes." The man twisted his mouth. "It's about his *missing* jewelry."

Allison turned to Red, her expression hard, her gaze like two tiger's eye marbles. "Mr. Vanak apparently thinks I've been stealing Dickey's jewelry. I assume he thinks I've been exploiting Dickey's Alzheimer's—and the fondness he feels for me."

Of course. The diamond the old guy had stealthily passed to Allison that first day Red came into the Peacock Café. Red glanced at her, remembering and wondering what the real story was. That day, he'd thought pretty much the same as Vanak. But now that Red knew her better, he wasn't so sure.

"It's necklaces, and a few rings," Vanak said. "At least a dozen precious and semiprecious gemstones."

Vanak touched his wedding-ring finger, as if to demonstrate to them what a ring was. Red made a low noise. *Condescending bastard.*

"And what business is it of yours what Dickey O'Connor does with his own jewelry?" Red felt irrationally heated. His tone was harsher than he had expected it to be.

"Dickey's will leaves the jewelry to Nell," Vanak explained slowly, as if Red were a mentally deficient child. "That's because she's the only surviving female relative. But somewhere along the way, he took the gems out. The settings are there, but they're empty. Dickey says he gave the stones to Allison York."

Without realizing he was going to do it, Red cast a glance toward Allison. She saw it, and her expression was disdainful, as if the question in his eyes was an insult.

"Of course," Vanak continued, "Dickey also says that he's going to marry Allison York." He paused, letting his gaze scan her up and down. "I'm guessing that part isn't true."

"You idiot." Red's annoyance reached critical mass with that slow, insulting appraisal. "Didn't it occur to you that *none of it* is true? If the guy has Alzheimer's, there's no telling what he did with his treasures."

"Stop." Allison spoke up suddenly. "Thank you, Red, but it's not necessary to defend me. Everything Mr. Vanak says is true."

CHAPTER THIRTEEN

RED RAN THE CIRCULAR SAW with a vengeance, taking out his annoyance on the planks of wood he was cutting to rebalance the hostess podium. Through his safety goggles, he kept an eye on Hank Vanak, who was irritably pacing the sidewalk outside Summer Moon, disappearing from one window, then reappearing at the next, then starting the act all over again from the other direction.

Now and then Vanak glanced at his watch with exaggerated care. Allison had promised him she'd explain about the jewelry, but she wanted Bill Longmire there when she did so. She'd asked Vanak to wait outside, so that she could get some work done while they waited for Bill. Vanak had agreed reluctantly, but warned that he wouldn't wait longer than half an hour.

As soon as the man was safely outside, Allison had picked up the heavy box of fixtures and headed straight to the bathroom area without saying a word to Red. He had considered following her, but something in the ramrod-straight way she held her spine discouraged him. He could wait till Bill got here, as long as he kept busy.

He'd cut all the planks before he saw the Rolls Royce creep down the street. Bill parked directly opposite Summer Moon, his right front tire lifting briefly as the car climbed the curb before settling back on all fours. He got out of the Rolls slowly, as always, ignoring the obvious importuning of Hank Vanak, who had approached the car talking, arms waving. Apparently Vanak had built quite a head of steam while he waited. Red smiled, looking at the pile of sawdust he'd created in the same thirty minutes. Allison should have put Vanak to work. They needed the help, and Vanak needed to calm the hell down.

Bill, bless his soul, simply raised one elegant, long-fingered hand and waved Vanak away. He walked serenely toward the restaurant, with his usual old-world dignity undisturbed by the fuming cloud of noise that followed him. When Bill got close enough, Red could see that he carried a rectangular, flat black box.

Vanak trailed behind, still talking, though it was clear Bill intended to ignore every word. When they entered, Red could hear the tail end of Vanak's last sentence. "—a big mistake. If you hadn't shown up exactly when you did, I would have called the police."

"Then you would have looked very silly, young man." Finally, now that he was comfortably indoors, Bill acknowledged the other man. He placidly gazed at the red face, the pugilistic jaw. "As, I'm afraid, you already do."

Allison must have been alerted to Bill's arrival, because almost immediately she emerged from the bathroom area, a wrench in her hand, and her ponytail disheveled from installing the cabinets.

"Hi, Bill," she said, wiping perspiration from her forehead with the back of her hand. The wrench glinted in the sunlight, almost as if she held a weapon. "I'm sorry to ask you to come out." She glanced around the area and frowned. "Where's Steve?"

"He has the afternoon off," Bill said, but he put up his hand and waved her protests away as he'd waved off Vanak's complaints. "I was very careful. I drove at a snail's pace, even though it was profoundly vexing. But I wasn't going to let Steve's absence keep me from coming."

As if suddenly exhausted by the conflicting worries that plagued her from all directions, Allison sat on one of the recently upholstered chairs. "Darn it, Bill," she said wearily. "Do you want someone calling *your* niece, too?"

The old man chuckled. "I don't have a niece," he said, sounding quite pleased by the fact. "Apparently it would be better if Dickey didn't, either. Phoning her was a grave mistake."

Vanak had started to flush red again. "Look, I don't appreciate your tone. My wife loves her uncle. She wants to protect him. And she doesn't want anyone to exploit his condition."

Bill made a skeptical *tsk*ing sound. "What she wants, I'd venture to guess, is to be sure no one else gets the goodies. Dickey isn't dead, Mr. Vanak, and neither has he been declared incompetent to manage his own affairs. If he wanted to give Ms. York everything he owned, including the shirt off his back, there's really nothing you two vultures could do to stop it."

Vanak's eyes flickered with doubt, but he didn't back down. "I guess the police would decide that," he said rigidly.

Bill made another snort of disbelief. Then he turned to Allison. "I'll explain it, then, shall I?"

She nodded.

Bill set his black box on the podium Red had been

adjusting. He fiddled with the clasp, but when he saw
Vanak crowding up close, he paused. "Stand back," he
instructed with a sniff of disdain. "At least try to pretend you're able to control your greed."

Vanak stepped back, both sheepish and deeply offended.

Bill opened the box with a flourish. "These are Dickey's jewels. Eight diamonds, two emeralds and one sap-
phire. I've been holding on to them. When Dickey gave
Allie the first diamond, she brought it to me, worried.
We weren't sure what to do. He loved being able to give
her things—and though she had no intention of accepting them, she hated to hurt his feelings. So I had replicas made. Nice ones. Not cheap, but not real diamonds.
We put the fakes in Dickey's stash, substituting them
for the real ones. That way, whenever he felt the urge
to play the king dispensing largesse, he could do it."

Red couldn't blame Vanak for looking skeptical. If
Red hadn't been here awhile, observing the wacky ways
the Old Coots Club had of making life interesting, he
might not have believed it, either.

Scowling, Vanak approached the podium. He picked
up one of the diamonds and held it to the light.

"Put that back," Bill ordered the other man irritably.
"You'd need a jeweler's loupe to tell if it's real or fake.
We had to buy convincing replicas. Dickey isn't a peasant. A gumball-machine diamond wouldn't have fooled
him for a minute."

Zing. Red loved these old guys, whose old-fashioned
language had a way of insulting you so subtly you
didn't get it until later. Vanak the peasant dropped the
stone into the box. "Then we'll get someone who—"

Bill ignored him again. He turned to Allison. "I

brought these here, Allie, for one reason only. To ask you if you'd like to keep them. Dickey wanted you to have them, as you well know. You have every right to them."

Allison blushed—and, looking from her to Vanak, Red wondered how two sets of suffused cheeks could be more different. One sweet like cherry stains, the other congested and unhealthy, like some kind of poison.

"Don't be silly, Bill," she said crisply. "I don't want them. You know we went to all this trouble to save them for Dickey's family."

"And to let him have the joy of bestowing them on you," Bill added. He looked at Vanak. "Dickey has the soul of a musketeer, a knight of the round table. He needs magic in his life. He needs to live big, to slay dragons and save the princesses. He needs to solve mysteries, to join conspiracies."

He stopped, grimacing. "You don't understand a word I'm saying, do you, young man?"

Vanak, who was at least fifty, bristled at the label. "Of course I do. You're asking us to indulge an old man's pathetic delusions of grandeur."

"No, I didn't think you did." Bill sighed heavily. "Words cannot express how sorry I am that we ever called your wife. I don't believe I'll give you the jewels today. With paranoid people, whose only imaginative skills consist of dreaming up the ways in which others might swindle them, I think I'll do better to remand them to the custody of a jeweler for appraisal. When they're documented and valued, then I'll let you know where to claim them."

Red felt like laughing. Vanak had come in here,

thinking he'd show his manly fangs and intimidate a puny female. Instead, Allison and one eighty-year-old, arthritic senior citizen had made him cry uncle.

Red thought back to his own reaction, the day he saw Dickey press the diamond into Allison's hand. Accepting jewels from doting old men did look damning, especially if you didn't know her. Red wondered what kind of verbal whipping Bill would have given him, had he been able to read Red's thoughts that day.

It was crystal clear that Vanak didn't like the plan one bit. But his mind obviously clung to the last part of Bill's speech—the part that promised the jewels would come to him eventually.

"Fine," Vanak barked. Then, as if he realized how weak that rejoinder was, he turned and stalked out the door.

They all watched him wordlessly until he got in his car, revved the engine and drove off. Then Bill sighed expressively and shut the black box. He turned to Allison. "I'm going to head back home. You are obviously busy, and I'm in the way."

She smiled warmly. "You're never in the way," she said. "But I'm about done for the day. How about if I drive you home?"

The old man shook his head. "I'll be fine—"

She put her hand on his arm, stopping him as effectively as if she'd applied a muzzle. "Bill. You promised. No driving."

Bill grumbled under his breath, but then he nodded reluctantly. "Oh, all right. But we'll have to take the Rolls. I'm not leaving it on the street overnight. How will you get back?"

She searched her mind for a minute, then glanced

at Red. "Would you be willing to follow me, then give me a ride home? I have to be there by seven, because that's when Sue's dropping Eddie off. I can leave my car here and get it later."

"No problem," Red said, casually unplugging the circular saw and setting it in its case.

But his cool tone was a pretense. The instant she'd posed the question, he'd felt a ludicrous rush of pleasure. *Good grief.* How juvenile was that? Here he was, blood pumping faster, simply because she'd needed a helper, and she'd chosen him out of all the men working here today.

He hadn't been this easily flattered since he was about six. It reminded him of when, in the first grade, he'd been thrilled when his pretty young teacher picked him to deliver a note to the office.

He shook his head internally, laughing at himself, but at the same time mildly uneasy. How did she do this to him? Allison might look like the innocent girl next door, but what she did to the male brain felt more like magic.

ALLISON DEEPLY REGRETTED the impulse that had led her to invite Red into the apartment for dinner. When he dropped her off, it had seemed only civil. He'd been so thoughtful and helpful the past couple of days. She'd felt the urge to say thank-you in some small way.

But at least part of her had assumed he'd probably say no.

He hadn't. Without hesitation, he'd accepted, and then she was stuck.

It had been the longest meal of her life.

At the restaurant, while they were working hard as

part of a larger team, conversation was easy, focused on measurements and timelines, on fixtures and printing costs and supplies. Even when he picked Eddie up at the restaurant, distracting the baby when he started to cry, the gesture seemed impersonal, no more intimate than if he'd mopped up a spill.

But now that he was in her home, she was suddenly self-conscious and tongue-tied, acutely aware of how small the apartment was, and how unglamorous it must seem to a man like him.

Not that he'd been condescending, even for a minute. They'd decided to make a salad, and, when he learned she'd never tasted a Diamante pizza, he called the new store and told them to bring one over. They drank their iced tea out of plastic glasses she'd bought at the drug store, and he fetched his own refills from the fridge.

As darkness fell outside, and rain started to patter on the roof, they'd eaten at the kitchen table—the only table she had. She'd given Eddie his bottle with one hand, while balancing a slice of the delicious pizza in the other.

The whole experience had been disturbingly domestic. And far too cozy. Their elbows touched whenever they weren't careful, and she was acutely aware of how close his thigh was to hers.

Before long, her nerves were jangling strangely. She couldn't wait to get up and start clearing away the paper plates.

Red, on the other hand, didn't seem to feel any of that discomfort. She remembered the first time he'd come here, when he lounged so easily on the sofa, making himself at home. It clearly was his special talent—being able to fit in anywhere.

He ate with relish, moved around freely, seemingly unaware that it would be a problem if he bumped into her. He kept up a dialogue of babbling nonsense with Eddie whenever the adult conversation stalled. He was one of Eddie's new favorite people, and sometimes, at Summer Moon, he could soothe the baby when even Allison's efforts failed.

Finally, to her intense relief, Eddie's bottle was empty, and the pizza was gone.

"I'm afraid I don't have any dessert in the house," she said. Partly she hoped that would encourage Red to depart, but it was also simple fact. Though she loved to cook, lately she hadn't had time to think of anything but the dishes for Summer Moon.

Eddie began to whimper. He undoubtedly needed burping. It was nearly time for his bath, too. She got up and filed the pizza box carefully under the sink next to the small trash can. "I feel bad, but I don't think I even have any coffee."

Red was tugging lightly on Eddie's toes, keeping the baby from accelerating into full-throttle fussing. "No problem. I bet I can concoct something out of whatever you've got. I'm a bachelor. I'm used to tossing odds and ends together and calling it food."

She hesitated. "I don't know. I probably should give Eddie a bath."

"Perfect. You take care of him, and I'll see what I can create." He smiled. "Mind if I root around the shelves a bit?"

What could she say? She unlatched Eddie and hoisted him up. He was really getting big, and she could feel the muscles in her upper arms responding. She started to pat his back, hoping the air bubbles would come out easily…and not bring anything with them. Everything a baby did was charming to his mommy, but Red might not find the whole thing particularly appetizing.

Why didn't he take this opportunity to make his escape? Surely he didn't want to be a part of this mundane nighttime ritual, and all the gritty details of tending a baby.

"Do you need the sink for the tub?" He smiled, as if that would be perfectly normal. Which, of course, it was. But surely in homes like the ones the Malones would own, babies had their own suites, complete with running water.

"Just the faucet. He has his own tub." Again, the tableau of domesticity unsettled her more than it should. The only spot in the apartment that would easily accommodate Eddie's plastic tub was on the coffee table in the living room, not many feet away from the kitchen. That meant she'd be splashing Eddie's rubber duckie and singing his favorite silly song while Red rooted around in the cupboards.

As if they were mommy and daddy and baby…

She set things up, filling the plastic tub at the sink quickly so that she wouldn't be in Red's way. Just a quick bath tonight. She had waited too long to put Eddie to bed. He was getting tired, rubbing his fists against his eyes and whimpering. To distract him, she began to sing their bathtime song, "Little Duckie Duddle."

To her surprise, Red sang along, too, from his post at the sink, where he was apparently washing the last of her strawberries. When they got to the end of a verse, she couldn't help laughing.

"What?" He cast a playful smile over his shoulder.

"My brother Matt has a three-year-old. Uncle Red is a virtual encyclopedia of children's songs. My double-time rendition of "John Jacob Jingleheimer Schmidt" is impressive, if I do say so myself."

And he proceeded to prove it.

Eddie, who was still learning to hold himself in a sitting position by grabbing his own feet, froze in place, mesmerized by the rapid-fire singing. Red had a nice baritone, warm and full, kind of a honey sound, and clearly Eddie liked it.

When the song drew to its nearly unintelligible finale, Allison began to laugh. Eddie joined in, slapping his hands merrily in the water, then blinking, shocked by the water that splattered into his face. Once he realized that he'd actually made that happen with his own movements, there was no stopping him. He slapped repeatedly at the water, trying to make it spray as far as he could.

Allison caught his hands and kissed them. "Hey," she said to both Red and Eddie. "It's not silly time. It's sleepy time. Don't you know a lullaby?"

Red feigned indignation. "I bet I know more than you do," he said. And then, with a smooth change of pace, he began to croon "Train Whistle Blowing."

Eddie smacked the water once or twice more, but he could feel that the mood had changed and didn't continue. As Red's voice filled the little kitchen, Allison quickly ran the washcloth between the baby's fingers and toes, and every darling roll of baby fat. By the time she got to his ears, the warm water and the gentle stroking had begun to make him sleepy, and his eyes were drifting shut.

Red kept singing, but his voice grew softer and

softer, until the words could hardly be heard. As she gathered Eddie into a fluffy towel and held his relaxed body against her chest, the last notes died away.

She looked at Red, who was watching Eddie with an affectionate smile. She wondered, suddenly, if the playboy life satisfied him. Were isolated pockets of unclehood enough, or did he harbor dreams of being a daddy himself one day?

He would make a good father. She felt the fact so strongly that she almost opened her mouth and told him so.

Luckily, he chose that moment to set out the dessert he'd created. It was simple—fresh, plump strawberries in one large bowl, with a small bowl on either side. He didn't speak, clearly aware that Eddie had fallen asleep. But when he was sure he had her attention, he demonstrated the technique.

He picked the biggest, juiciest strawberry, and held it up for her inspection. Then he dipped it into the bowl on the left, which was a pillowy mound of sour cream. Then he pulled the snow-capped strawberry out and dipped it in the other bowl, which was piled high with brown sugar.

He brought the final product over and, smiling, held it up, inviting her to bite.

Something low in her midsection began to thrum softly. She felt her breath come shallowly. It was just a strawberry, she told herself. It wasn't the forbidden apple from the garden of Eden. There was no harm in taking one bite.

But there was something in his eyes. Something in the way his strong fingers looked, pink with strawberry juice that gleamed under the kitchen light and tipped with sugar. Something that made the thrum inside her intensify, as if someone were running an electrical charge through her body.

When she opened her lips and let them close around the strawberry, pleasure coursed through her, piercing and sweet. The flesh of the berry released its tart nectar as her teeth sank in, and she felt the wetness dribble slowly down to her chin.

Red caught it with his forefinger. Her heart thudded in her breast, and she realized how painfully she wanted to lick that finger, to suck away the sugar and the juice. She had to breathe through her mouth to keep air moving through her suddenly tight lungs.

"Red," she began, and was horrified to hear the longing in her voice.

His dark blue eyes were suddenly ablaze, and she felt the electricity jump from her own body to his. He still held the rest of the strawberry, the match to the piece she had swallowed.

But she didn't want more fruit. She wanted his beautiful lips on hers. She realized suddenly that she loved his lips, his wide, elegant, bow-shaped mouth, so full and soft in its center, but rimmed in a hard, sculpted edge.

She stared at his mouth now, knowing instinctively that, unless she stopped him, he was going to kiss her. She knew it, and she couldn't force herself to prevent it. The truth sizzled through her. She *wanted* him to kiss her. She wanted it so badly it frightened her.

He lowered his head slowly. She could smell the strawberry, and the sugar, and the cream as he came closer. She could feel the warmth of his sugared breath on her skin. She shivered, as if the heat were a cold fire.

And then, after a lingering moment that seemed to last forever, he finally let his lips come down on hers. Gentle at first, his kiss deepened as the seconds stretched like taffy, and her whole body leaned toward his.

They didn't touch anywhere else. He didn't lift his hand to caress her head, or inch closer to bring them hip to hip. But somehow the possession still felt complete. His mouth moved over hers with power and mastery, stroking and coaxing her trembling lips until something starry burst behind her breast.

She groaned softly, and her arms and legs felt suddenly weak, as if the bones that held them up had melted. She had to grip Eddie harder to be sure she wouldn't drop him.

Maybe that was why he woke, or maybe he sensed something new in the frantic thumping of her heart.

Whatever the reason, he raised his downy head, bumping into Red's cheek, which startled him, as he'd never encountered an obstruction in that space before. With an angry jerk, the baby began to cry.

Red pulled away slowly, as if reluctant to let her go even now, as their ears rang with Eddie's distress and anger. She blinked, trying to return to reality. Red's lips were as swollen as hers felt, and his eyes slightly glazed, as if he, too, were having trouble leaving the dream behind.

"I'd better put him to bed," she said over the wailing. She patted the baby's back, and kissed his head, hoping he would calm quickly. "I think...I think you'd better go."

Red nodded. "I'm sorry," he said. "I know I said I wouldn't do that. I haven't forgotten what you said. I—"

"It's all right," she responded quickly. Reassured by her kisses, Eddie was settling down a little, and the noise was less deafening. Within seconds he was sucking his thumb quietly, but he still blinked over at Red, as if to warn the man not to invade his space again.

"Allison, I—"

"Really," she rushed in to say. "It's okay. I think we both let the moment get away from us. It's been a long day, and we're both tired, and—"

"No," he said, his voice still warm, still thick coming through the lips that had been on hers. "That's not why I kissed you."

Of course it wasn't. She knew that. But it made as good an excuse as any.

He smiled. "Don't you want to know why I did it?"

"Red, I don't think—"

"I kissed you," he went on as if she had said yes, as if she'd asked him to explain, "because there's something magical about you, Allison. Something so sweet, so innocent, it's almost impossible to resist."

She didn't know what to say. She stood there, her hand on Eddie's head, staring at Red. With another smile, he tugged the towel over Eddie's bare shoulder, and stroked his seashell ear with his fingertip.

Then he walked to the door and put his hand on the knob. The living room was so small, getting there took him only a couple of steps.

"I know you don't want this," he said. "I know you want nothing but friendship from me, so I'll try not to do it again. But I want you to understand. I kissed you, I'm pretty sure, for the same reason Victor betrayed his family, and Dickey O'Connor gives you diamonds."

CHAPTER FOURTEEN

FOR ONCE, EDDIE SLEPT THROUGH the entire night, but Allison tossed and turned till dawn. Whenever she closed her eyes, she felt Red's lips on hers again, and imagined she tasted strawberries. For hours she drove herself crazy, alternating between fearing she might not see Red again and telling herself it would be the best possible outcome if he went back to San Francisco.

But when she got to Summer Moon the next morning, he was already there. The hostess station had been leveled, and he'd pitched in to help hang the huge bathroom mirrors.

She'd hoped she wouldn't have to bring Eddie today, but Sue had been called in for an extra shift at the café. So Allison arrived with the baby's basket dangling from one hand, and his huge tote of toys, bottles and diapers in the other.

Luckily, he didn't seem to mind hanging out at the restaurant. In fact, the noise and commotion seemed to entertain him. But having him around definitely made Allison less useful. She had to keep moving him to wherever she was working, and she worried all the time. What if someone came too close with a power tool, or let a mirror crash, sending out shards of glass? What if his lungs were bothered by the sawdust, not to mention the showers of drywall powder created by the drilling and hammering?

She tried to slip past the bathroom door without being seen, but as soon as she got within five feet, Red called out.

"Hey, there," he said.

She paused, looking in. He stood on the counter, making a mark on the wall with a pencil, the battery-driven drill sticking out of his belt like the grip of a handgun.

Dale, one of the workers who had been with Allison from the beginning, waited on the other side of the counter, his hands clutching the rim of the five-foot mirror.

"Hi," she responded, struggling for a placid tone. "Hi, Dale. It's starting to look great in here."

Red smiled. "Did you forget we had an appointment at Diamante this morning?"

Oh, God. She *had* forgotten. Red had a friend who was selling a brand-new ice machine at a used price, and she was scheduled to go look at it. It was the last piece of major equipment she still needed, and the savings would go a long way toward paying the extra workers.

The truth was, all practical matters had been blown straight out of her mind by the emotional hurricane of that kiss. But of course she couldn't say that, not when Red looked so blithe and indifferent, as if last night had happened with some other man entirely.

"I'm sorry," she said. "My sitter cancelled this morning, and in the confusion I lost track of everything. Is it too late to go now?"

"No, it's fine. Travis said he'd wait." He made one

last mark on the wall, then, putting the pencil behind his ear, leaped down from the counter. He landed lightly on his feet. "Dale, I'll send Sandy in to help you get that monster up there."

He slid the drill out of his pocket and handed it over, then turned to Allison. "Ready?"

She nodded. As ready as she'd ever be.

Though Diamante had already opened, she hadn't ever visited the location. But she knew, after one bite of the delicious pizza last night, that Diamante would quickly become Windsor Beach's new favorite take-out place. She was glad her restaurant didn't offer pizza, because there would be no contest.

"Oh," she said as they drove up to the strip mall, which she recognized, of course. "This is where the old Bath Goddess used to be."

He nodded. "Yeah. An amazing piece of luck for us. Spots around here don't come open often."

At times like these, she was reminded what a stranger he really was to these parts.

"It wasn't all that lucky for Lucy Milburn, who used to run the shop," she said. "Lucy had a heart attack. She was only forty-five."

He finished angling the car into the narrow space, then turned to gaze at her. "I'm sorry," he said. "I didn't know. I guess I didn't think to ask."

Of course he hadn't asked. Why would he question his good luck? He was used to swooping in when something he wanted became available. Just like the fast-food chain that had snagged her father's restaurant property, when she had finally been forced to close its doors.

She sat still a minute, thinking of her father—and of

Victor, who had sat there at one of her tables, chatting her up, pretending to be her friend. Yet all the while, he'd been watching the restaurant go up in flames, waiting for the moment when he could swoop in, too, and claim the bits of wreckage he wanted.

And then she thought of plump, motherly Lucy Millburn, who always thought only of others. During Allison's pregnancy, Lucy had brought over baskets of skin cream, perfumed shampoos, even lotions to ward off stretch marks.

"Allison," Red said quietly when the silence stretched on. "I didn't cause her heart attack, you know."

"I know."

She smiled, trying to offset her sudden tension. He was right. It really wasn't his fault he didn't know the people of Windsor Beach. This was one of dozens of little California beach towns in which the Malone family had opened Diamante stores. Simply one more stop on their corporate march up and down the coast. Windsor Beach today, Pescadero or Half Moon Bay tomorrow.

So why did that make her feel so strangely hot and prickly, as if she were filled with a nebulous sense of anger? Why did this part of him remind her of Victor? Why did she feel like another piece of real estate that had suddenly become available, ripe for the swooping?

It was ridiculous, and unfair, especially when she was benefiting from his generosity right now, every bit as much as she'd benefited from Lucy's all those months ago.

To avoid further awkward conversation, she opened her door, slid out, and went around to unbuckle Eddie from his car seat. Red got out, too, and together they entered the doors marked with the well-known Diamante diamond graphic.

Travis, the man with the ice machine, had apparently been waiting patiently, as instructed. He seemed to have passed the time chatting with the Diamante manager, a pretty woman named Elsie with whom Allison used to work at the Peacock Café. They all exchanged greetings, Red apologized for being late, and then they went out back to look at the ice maker, which Travis had on his truck.

Five minutes later, Allison knew the piece of equipment was an absolute steal. It was everything she wanted, an under-counter machine with a huge capacity, both for production and for storage, and even all the frills, like an independent drain connection. As Travis extolled its virtues, she had a fleeting suspicion that he might be giving her a phony price, and getting the rest reimbursed from Red.

"Is there still a warranty?" She propped Eddie over her shoulder, then ran her free hand over the black top, trying not to get her hopes up.

"Sure. Three years parts and labor. Five years on the compressor and the evaporator." Travis gave the top an affectionate pat, as if it were a living thing. "It's a hell of a machine for the money."

It was more than that. It was perfect. Though she wasn't going to let Red set up any sweetheart deals for her, and would, if she found the price had been rigged, insist on paying Travis full price, she had to have the machine.

Eddie had begun to whimper, so they didn't dawdle. They worked out the details, she handed over a check, and Red walked with Travis as he climbed behind the wheel, so that he could give the man directions to Summer Moon.

"I swear, Red Malone," a perky female voice said suddenly, coming from somewhere behind them. "You're one difficult man to track down."

All three of them switched their gazes to the Diamante doorway. Even Eddie turned his head to track the sound. A young woman stood there, smiling archly. Allison had never seen her before. She was stunning, dressed in a green suit that fit so well it couldn't have been bought off the rack. She had black curly hair and flashing green eyes. And a figure that probably guaranteed she didn't have a single female friend in this world.

Red, on the other hand, seemed to know exactly who she was. "Sorry about that," he said with a smile. "I had no idea you were looking for me. What are you doing in Windsor Beach?"

For a split second, Allison felt a dissonance she couldn't put her finger on. She imagined she heard two things in Red's voice—a shock that sounded absolutely genuine, and a delight that sounded…artificial. Forced.

Her curiosity prickled. Who was this? The woman looked vaguely familiar, but she couldn't put her finger on anything specific.

"I'm here for the afternoon, checking the cottage," the woman answered, her voice full of a chirpy confidence that already got on Allison's nerves. "No one's been there in months, so it seemed smart to take a look, you know, make sure all four walls are still standing. Colby told me you were spending a few days over here working on the new store, so I thought I'd track you down and make you take me to lunch."

Before he answered her, Red tapped the hood of Travis's truck, which was the man's signal to start the motor and pull away. The pickup rumbled down the access alley and finally disappeared around the corner. Then Red walked up to the elegant newcomer, put his arm around her waist and kissed her on the cheek.

"It's good to see you," he said, with another hint of that dissonance. He turned to Allison, his movements oddly stiff, as if he were the tin man and badly in need of a lube. "Cherry, this is Allison York. And her son, Eddie. Allison, this is my friend Cherry Wigham."

For a minute the cobblestone alley seemed to tilt under Allison's feet. She heard a noise in her head that sounded like the roar of her blood coursing through her veins. Cherry Wigham? No wonder she had seemed familiar. This was Victor's daughter from his first marriage. The one who was beautiful and good with math. The one who supposedly couldn't handle learning that her father was a lying, adulterous pig.

More importantly…this was Eddie's unacknowledged half sister.

She realized her mouth wasn't completely shut, so she gripped herself hard. She dimly registered Cherry's broad smile, and her outstretched hand, and she forced herself to reach out, too, and shake hands as if it were no big deal.

But she could hardly look into the woman's green eyes, which she now realized looked exactly like Victor's.

"Hi, there," Cherry said warmly. "What a darling baby."

Cherry looked from Allison to Red with a fleeting expression of speculation, and then hid it expertly behind another beaming smile. "Have I come at a bad time? I can make myself scarce if you two are working."

"No, it's fine," Allison started to say.

But Red was already talking. "It might be better if we get together a little later," he said. "Maybe dinner, if things ease up? Allison and I have a lot to accomplish. You know how hard it is getting a new restaurant up and going."

Allison noticed that, while he hadn't exactly lied, he had managed to give Cherry the impression that Allison worked for Diamante. She sensed that he was looking at her, probably trying to signal her to play along, but she kept her own gaze on Cherry.

The other woman nodded sympathetically. "Well, I don't know firsthand, but I've certainly seen you guys go through it often enough. This one looks great, though. How long has it been open?"

Before Red could answer, Elsie, the manager, stuck her head out of the doorway. "Mr. Malone," she called. "I think there's a problem with the temperature on the refrigerator. Would you mind taking a look? I'd hate to throw everything away if I'm just reading it wrong."

Red hesitated, and Allison knew exactly what he was thinking. He didn't want to leave Cherry and Allison alone, even for a couple of minutes. Allison wondered if he thought she might spill all Victor's secrets here in this stupid, dirty access alley.

Probably he thought Allison would be eaten up by envy of this classy, confident, *legitimate* Wigham heiress, and would find herself blurting everything out, forgetting the contract she'd signed and the check she'd deposited a few weeks ago.

No one ever seemed to remember that they were her secrets, too. That she was ashamed of having slept with a married man, and threatened another woman's marriage. No one seemed to understand that she might not care to broadcast that little secret everywhere.

"Let's get in out of the sun, too," she said, smiling at Cherry. "The air's smoggy back here. It's a lot more comfortable inside."

If Red appreciated her gesture, he gave no sign. He had already followed Elsie into the kitchen. It was a small area, so Allison and Cherry waited on the other side of the take-out counter, where a few straight chairs lined the walls for customers who arrived too early. The walls were covered in glowing panels that showed menus, prices and mouth-watering pictures of Diamante specialty pizzas.

Cherry must have seen plenty of Diamante stores, because she didn't seem even remotely curious. She headed immediately to one of the chairs and sat.

"So," she asked, crossing her legs. "Do you work for the Malones and Diamante?"

Allison decided to stick with the truth as far as she could. She bounced Eddie a couple of times to keep him from fussing. "No. I'm opening a new family restaurant here in Windsor, and Red's been nice enough to help me with a few things."

Cherry's gaze was friendly, her manners impeccable. Allison didn't actually catch the other woman scanning her from head to toe, checking out the jeans, sneakers and shapeless gray T-shirt. But somehow she knew she was being evaluated, from the sleepy baby in her arms, all the way down to the absence of a wedding ring and the last three pounds of baby weight that would probably keep her from wearing her bikini all summer.

Cherry flicked a glance toward the kitchen, where Red and Elsie were still in conference, their heads bent over the thermometer they kept in the refrigerator as backup, in case the electronic thermostat ever went bad.

Then she swiveled her head back to Allison. "So," she said, still smiling, "I hate to be forward, but I hate beating around the bush even more, so I'll ask. Are you two dating?"

Allison almost laughed. That was definitely blunt. But she didn't mind. She preferred candor herself. "No," she said. "No. We're friends."

Cherry nodded, obviously pleased with the answer. "Good," she said, still frank, still smiling. "Because I'm thinking I might…" Her gaze sharpened. "We used to be a couple, way back when, but he was…too young. And too spoiled. Women just love those Malone boys. It's something… Well, who knows what it is? Some kind of chemistry they've got. You know?"

Allison kept her face impassive. But yes, she knew.

Cherry folded her hands in her lap, the pink-tipped fingers graceful and composed. She tilted her head, checking out the view of the kitchen with a Cheshire cat grin so complacent it made Allison look, too.

Red had squatted to check items on the lower shelves, unwittingly offering Cherry and Allison a rather breathtaking view of his sculpted back and neat, trim hips. Allison looked away quickly, determined not to reveal any reaction.

But she needn't have worried. Cherry was staring exclusively, and uninhibitedly, at Red. Her manicured thumbs had begun to flick restlessly against each other, and her expression settled into a serious speculation.

"If he's not dating anyone, I might give him another try. I'm thinking…" She watched a few more seconds, then licked her lips delicately. "I'm thinking that the lovely man might have grown up a little bit while I was gone."

CHAPTER FIFTEEN

"I'M SORRY ABOUT THAT," Red said as he pulled up in front of Summer Moon half an hour later. For the entire trip, Allison had sat quietly in the passenger seat, staring out the window, apparently as fascinated by the scenery as if she'd never set eyes on Windsor Beach before.

"I know it must have been awkward," he said, trying again to get her to talk. He could only imagine how she'd felt, running into Cherry out of the blue like that. But it couldn't be healthy to sit on all those feelings. "I had no idea she was coming over to the beach house, and I certainly never imagined she'd try to track me down."

Finally, Allison turned to look at him. Her face was pale, her eyes shadowed. He wondered whether she had been sleeping much lately.

"How long," she asked, "have they had a beach house here?"

He thought back. "Maybe five years? But they mostly rent it out, and they rarely get over here. They also have a place in Monterey, and Marianne likes that one better."

She looked thoughtful, her brow knitted. "So they had the house back then, when he was with me."

"Yes."

Her face was blank. "He never mentioned that. Never."

He felt the same sense of disorientation and discomfort that came over him whenever he thought about the whole messy triangle of Victor, Marianne and Allison. He had no idea what to say, or how to defend his friend. He was beginning to think he hadn't known Victor anywhere near as well as he'd thought he did.

And somehow it seemed obscene to talk to Allison of the—not one, but two—mansions on the ocean. Even Cherry's beauty, her unbounded confidence and passionate zeal for life, seemed like a slap in Allison's tired face.

"Allison, let me take you home," he said. "You've got half a dozen people in there working. Let them handle it. You need rest."

She nodded absently, but he knew she hadn't really heard him. She'd never agree to go home that easily. She glanced once into the backseat, where Eddie lay in his car seat, sound asleep. And then she turned to Red again.

"Cherry looks like her father," she said. "She looks so much like Victor. Even before you introduced her, I thought I must have met her somewhere."

"Yes." Victor had been so proud of his beautiful daughter, and the strong family resemblance they bore. "She does."

Allison braided her hands in her lap. "And his son? Does Dylan look like him, too?"

Red shook his head. "Dylan looks more like Marianne. He's fair, and his eyes are more blue than green. He has his mother's personality, too. Cherry is more like her father in every way."

"How are they taking their father's death?"

He wondered how much to say. "Cherry adored Victor, of course. But she's resilient, and she'll be fine. It's Marianne and Dylan I'm worried about. They aren't as strong."

She nodded again. It seemed almost an unconscious movement, like the outer expression of her inner attempt to make sense of it all.

For several minutes after that, she was completely silent. And then, abruptly, she spoke, cracking the heavy silence as if it had been a solid thing. "Didn't it make you uncomfortable to lie to her like that? How did it feel to stand there between Victor's daughter, and his secret infant son, and pretend that nothing was happening? How did it feel to pretend that we were all strangers who happened to meet in an alley?"

A bitter taste seemed to fill his mouth, a hint of blood, or iron. How had it felt? He remembered the look on Allison's face as she stood there, confronting Victor's daughter, clutching her own son to her breast fiercely. For a minute, he hadn't been able to breathe. He'd glimpsed Victor in the baby's features so many times that he thought surely Cherry would see it, too.

They were blood related, those two children of Victor Wigham, in spite of every lie ever spoken about their bond. It seemed impossible that the kinship wouldn't leap out and announce itself.

And yet, in the blink of an eye, the breathless moment had passed. Cherry had obviously felt nothing, suspected nothing. He knew her expressions, and the only thing he saw in her face was curiosity about Allison, and whether she and Red were an item.

At first he'd been relieved. But, though no disaster

had occurred, the near miss had made one thing very clear.

That kiss last night had been a terrible mistake, a self-indulgent blunder that he must never make again. If he tried to integrate Allison into his life in any way, it would be ugly and painful, and a minefield of danger. In Red's world, she would be exposed to the Wighams over and over, relentlessly reminded of the legacy her son could never claim. Red would have to ask her to essentially adopt a false identity, hiding her true connection to all of them.

Impossible. So the bottom line was...he simply couldn't see any way he and Allison could have a lasting relationship of any kind. And she'd already made it clear that, as a single mother, she understandably wasn't interested in a fling.

He had to stop letting the attraction he felt get away from him. Even asking her to be his friend on those terms would be as insulting as what Victor had done.

So...to get back to her question, how had it felt, running into Cherry today?

"It felt rotten," he said. "It felt wrong."

The glance she cast over him was frigid. "Not wrong enough to tell her the truth, though."

He thought of Victor's pleading eyes, his urgent words that had been forced out on ravaged breaths. He thought of Marianne, crying, and Dylan, hard-eyed and cold.

He even thought of Lewis Porterfield, petty and vindictive, and how eagerly the little bastard would sue Allison for breach of contract, smearing her name everywhere he could.

"No," he admitted. "Not wrong enough for that."

EVERY MINUTE, day or night, Allison could hear the countdown clock ticking in her mind. Summer Moon's soft opening had been pushed back a couple of days, to four days away. She hadn't wanted to change the date, because the whole point was to get a chance to identify the kinks before inviting the general public in. The way they had it set up now, only two days separated the soft opening and the real opening. Forty-eight hours wasn't much time to correct anything serious that might go wrong.

The upside was that Jimbo was due back in three days—which would give him time to get the first food out at the soft opening.

And Red would return to San Francisco in...

She had no idea.

He'd never pinned down how long he planned to stay in Windsor Beach, at least not to her. At first, he'd spent only a few hours at a time at Summer Moon. She assumed he must be working on Diamante business the rest of the time. Occasionally she'd heard him on his cell phone, talking to someone in San Francisco. He always kept his timeline vague. "I've got a few more properties to check out," he'd say. "I'll let you know how it goes."

But as the days went on, he stayed longer and longer at Summer Moon, until everyone took him for granted and relied on his expertise so much that, if they ran into a hitch, they would shrug and say, "Let's wait till Red gets here."

Such dependence made Allison nervous. She might not know exactly when Red would leave Windsor Beach, but she hadn't the slightest doubt that he *would* leave. And he'd do it whenever it suited Diamante's needs, not hers.

Today, her anxiety was worse than usual. Allison had been lucky enough to inherit her father's optimism, and ordinarily nothing got her down. Not hard work, or lack of sleep, or little glitches in the plan. But today she felt strangely enervated.

Look at her now, for instance. She'd received the menus from the printer, and the minute she opened the first one, a typo on the second page screamed out at her. Instead of calling Mary Jo, the printer, and explaining that the menus would have to be done over, she'd put her fingers to her stinging eyes and prayed she wouldn't start to cry.

That wasn't like her. That wasn't Allison York. Her father would be ashamed of her.

She wondered suddenly whether seeing Cherry this morning had acted on her like some debilitating toxin—had seeped into her blood and robbed her of her usual strength.

If so, Allison had to push doubly hard to recover. She wasn't going to give the Wighams that kind of power over her.

She laid the menu carefully in the box. Resting the heels of her hands on the cool stainless steel of the prep table, she bowed her head and counted to a hundred. *I can do this. I can do this. I can do this.*

A hand touched her back. "Everything okay?"

It was Red, his fingertips gentle, sending a tingle down her spine. She straightened, sorry that he'd caught her looking so weak.

"I'm okay," she said, smiling over her shoulder at

him to prove it. "I didn't sleep much last night, and I guess it hit me for a minute there."

The instant she said it, she could have bitten her tongue off. He would know, of course, why she hadn't been able to get much sleep.

Or maybe it wouldn't occur to him. Maybe the kiss hadn't meant enough to him.

If he did understand, he was considerate enough not to let his awareness show. Instead, he got to the point, the reason he'd sought her out.

"I think you left your cell phone in the other room," he said. He held it out. "I heard it ringing several times. Sounds as if someone's pretty eager to talk to you."

"Thanks." She took the phone without much concern. As long as she had Eddie at her side, there weren't very many calls that could be considered urgent. But it might have been Jimbo, she supposed. She hoped he wasn't calling to say his return had been delayed.

She ran through the missed calls list. Six of them. She looked at the numbers, and frowned.

"What?" Red obviously saw her confusion.

"They're all from Dickey O'Connor," she said, suddenly worried. She scrolled to the voice messages. He'd left only one. Glancing at Red, she pressed Play and held the phone to her ear.

As she listened, her blood ran cold. Halfway through the message, she put her hand on Red's arm.

"Call 911," she said. "Send them to Dickey's house. They'll know where it is. Tell them…tell them he's probably on the roof."

Red already had his own cell phone out. He pressed numbers and gave her a quick, sober look as the phone began to ring. "On the roof?"

"Yes." She turned back to the phone and listened to the last few words.

I just wanted to stay goodbye, Allie.

She closed her phone. "Oh, Dickey," she whispered roughly.

Red was talking to the dispatcher. "Yes, the roof," he said. "The roof of his house. Apparently he—"

He glanced at Allison for the rest of the sentence.

She swallowed. "He says he's going to jump."

A CROWD HAD ALREADY begun to gather by the time they got to Dickey's mansion on the oceanfront bluff, its three stories a dark, snaggle-tooth shadow against the violet and yellow streaks of sunset. Two Windsor Beach cop cars blocked the driveway, their blue and white lights circling, bringing the bushes into visibility, then out again, like a relentless strobe.

"You go," Red said. "I'll take care of Eddie."

She didn't give her son's safety a second's anxiety, the same way she hadn't hesitated when Red had offered to drive her to Dickey's house. For some reason, in spite of the relatively short time she'd known him, she trusted him. That said something—something disturbing—but she didn't have time to think about it now.

"Thank you," she said, slipping out of the car. She made her way up the driveway, and was relieved to see that one of the policemen was Larry, who wouldn't question her right to intercede.

"Allie, thank God you're here." Larry was pale-faced, but stoic. "How serious is he about this? What exactly did his message say?"

She pulled the voice mail up and let him listen.

It was the quickest way to convince him how upset Dickey really was. When he got to the part that was the hardest to hear, she watched his young face register the same fear that had flooded her.

That harpy isn't really my niece, Dickey's trembling voice insisted. *She's an imposter, someone who has stolen Nell's skin. But no one will believe me. They're going to let her throw me in her dungeon to rot.*

Larry blinked. "Oh, my God. He's lost his mind."

"Yes," Allison said, steeling her voice to keep out the horror she knew they both were feeling. It couldn't be more cruel. Dickey's fear of Nell, his terror of going to a nursing home, had finally broken the last barrier between his true self and the dementia that had been threatening to claim it. "But we can't think about that now. Has anyone been able to talk to him?"

"He won't answer his cell. We don't know if he still has a phone with him. We know he's up there, because before it started getting dark we could see him. We've got a man on the third floor, at a window, talking to him, but we don't know if he's hearing us or…"

Larry didn't seem to remember how he'd intended to finish his sentence, so he let it fade out.

Allison wasn't surprised about the phone. She hadn't been able to reach Dickey, either, and she felt sure he would have answered if he'd seen her number on the ID. She wondered whether the phone had slipped away from him. "Maybe get someone to look on the ground below him. It might have fallen."

Larry nodded. "Yeah." He kept nodding, like a bobble-head policeman doll. "Yeah. Good idea."

Allison touched his hand, which held the walkie-talkie. "Larry? Tell someone to look."

He pressed the button, got a response and walked a few feet away to issue the instructions. His voice sounded steadier, so she assumed his training had taken over.

How much time had passed since Dickey's call to her? It was getting cool, and dangerously windy. The colors were dying out of the sky, like a scene fading out in a movie.

Allison kept moving toward the house, until she spotted a second uniformed officer standing near the door.

"Elinor," she said, with another rush of relief. This was her lucky day. She didn't know everyone on the police force, but these two were friends. "I'd like to go up and see if I can get to one of the gable windows. Maybe he would talk to me."

Elinor pushed her cap back, tipping it to expose her forehead, which she then wiped with her hand. "We've got an officer up there already. He can see Dickey, or could, but he can't get him to answer. There's an intelligence officer on the second floor, though, talking to Dickey's niece. Maybe you could give him something to work with, but they don't usually let friends or family do the talking."

"Allison." Red had made his way up the drive, and he was suddenly at her side, Eddie in his arms. The baby looked bewildered by all the lights and people, but not alarmed. "Allison, don't do anything foolish."

Allison frowned. "Why is it foolish to try to save my friend's life?"

"You heard her." He glanced at Elinor. "You don't know what Dickey's got planned. It's dangerous. Hell, he might decide to take you with him, Allie. They need to send a professional."

"What professional?" She wheeled on him, all her terror suddenly finding a focus. "You think Windsor Beach has psychiatrists standing at the ready for things like this? He could jump a hundred times before they found someone. Dickey isn't going to hurt me. He's afraid. He's alone. All he needs is a friend."

Red's only response was silence, but his face said he didn't like it.

She didn't care. She turned to Elinor. "Your guy is up there. He can make sure I don't do or say anything stupid. I know it's not quite by the book, but we've got to get Dickey down before he does something crazy. Or slips." Her heart skipped a beat, thinking of that compact, elderly body at the mercy of the wind and the cold and the fatal, random presence of mold, or damp, or a single loose shingle.

"Bill," she said suddenly. Bill would help her figure out what to say. "Has Bill been told yet?"

"He's inside talking with Nell and her husband." Elinor almost smiled, her eyes shining in the blinking lights. "Talking quite frankly, in fact. I don't think they're enjoying it much."

"I bet." God love the Old Coots Club. "Bill can go up with me, too. Dickey and he are close. Please, Elinor. You've got to let me try."

CHAPTER SIXTEEN

HALF AN HOUR LATER, Red thought he might lose his mind. At Allison's request, the police had let him into the house, but he hadn't been allowed higher than the second floor. "We can't have a zoo up there," the intelligence officer had said, eyeing Eddie nervously, as if the baby might explode unexpectedly at any minute.

The man was right, of course. Only the people who could really do some good should be gathered up there. And Red was no one in this drama. However he might be starting to feel about Allison and Eddie, he was a stranger to Windsor Beach. He didn't know Dickey, and he barely knew Bill.

All he could do was wait. The police guided him to Dickey's upstairs game room, which had all the latest TVs and technology, as well as a couple of arcade games and a miniature putting green. For the first few minutes, he had sat opposite Nell O'Connor Vanak and her husband, neither of whom spoke a word.

Vanak must have told his wife who Red was—and his part in the diamond fiasco. She stared at him, unblinking, as if she hoped her glare could spear him through the heart and impale him on the wall.

He checked out her angry mouth, and her spiderlike hands. Maybe Dickey wasn't succumbing to dementia after all. Maybe this nasty female really had been possessed by a harpy. She certainly didn't look normal. In Red's lap, Eddie grabbed hold of his own feet and watched her for a while, but pretty soon he began to fidget and whimper. Apparently he didn't like the look of her, either.

Red stood and carried Eddie over to the pinball machine along the far wall. Dickey had obviously been a boy at heart, which endeared the old guy to Red. They had a room a lot like this at Nana Lina's house in Belvedere Cove, and everyone from state senators to university professors vied for invitations to hang out there. Everyone needed a safe place to be a kid now and then.

Ignoring the irritated whispers from the Vanaks, Red grabbed hold of the ball shooter and got things going. He played one-handed a few minutes, holding on to Eddie with the other. The lights and colors and zingy noises obviously delighted the baby—and infuriated Nell.

Red smiled grimly. Win-win.

But, no matter how many points he racked up on the display, the back of his mind was always upstairs, with Allison.

Finally, when he thought he couldn't stand the suspense anymore, he heard commotion on the staircase. He instantly released the flipper, letting the little silver ball slide unimpeded down the chute. He draped Eddie over his shoulder and moved out into the hall. Behind him, he sensed that Nell and her husband had risen, too.

First, descending the stairs, expressionless, he saw a gray-haired policeman. And then, moving slowly, Bill Longmire. After that, things got chaotic, with people crowding tightly together. But Red was sure he glimpsed Allison. She was smiling, and she had her arm around a stocky little fireplug of a man Red thought he recognized—the guy who had given Allison the diamond at the Peacock Café. This must be Dickey O'Connor.

He hadn't meant to be holding his breath, but suddenly it gushed out of him in one long, relieved exhale.

She'd done it. Whether they'd let her talk, or they'd simply taken her advice, he knew she'd made the difference.

He took a deep breath, filling his empty lungs awkwardly, as if he'd forgotten how to breathe by instinct. As he'd waited up here for news, he'd tried to imagine what failure would do to her, the guilt she'd carry around forever. It hadn't been a pretty picture.

But she'd done it. He dropped a kiss on Eddie's head. *Thank God.*

He turned, ready to share the good news with Nell. Her uncle was all right. But the Vanaks had obviously already seen. They faced each other now, and Red caught a glimpse of the naked disappointment they believed they were sharing in private.

"The ridiculous old bastard," Vanak said. And his wife hissed something in response. Red couldn't hear the words, but her expression was so vicious he felt a shimmer of disgust run down his spine.

"You know, Mr. and Mrs. Vanak," Red said conversationally, as he moved to pick up Eddie's tote, "I feel the need to point something out before I go."

Vanak glanced at him, his eyes hard. "And what is that?"

"Your uncle may have dementia. I don't know. But if I were ever so unlucky as to find myself at the mercy of you two hyenas, I'd climb up on the roof and jump off, too."

THE PARAMEDICS WERE going to take Dickey to the hospital, of course. Even when their discussion had been at its most desperate, up there as she listened to the negotiator talk to him, she'd never let them promise him they wouldn't.

She hadn't let them lie to him, even once. She made them tell him she'd be there for him. When he admitted that his biggest fear was that Nell might have rats in her dungeon, she'd fought her tears and told them to promise him she would visit every day.

If there were rats, she vowed to herself, literal or metaphorical, she'd break Dickey out of whatever hospital they had him in. She'd do it with her bare hands.

Because he loved her, he believed her. He was cold, shivering and very weak by the time he agreed to let the officer come out and help him inch his way over to the gable window. The minute they got him down the stairs and out of the house, they put him on a waiting gurney.

Once flat on his back, Dickey held out his hand, and Allison took it, walking alongside the stretcher as the EMTs rolled it toward the waiting ambulance. Her chest was aching, and her head burned from all the tears she couldn't shed, but she forced herself to smile at him.

"It'll be okay, Dickey," she said, bracing her voice to keep the shivers out. "Just get plenty of rest tonight, and I'll come see you in the morning."

"Okay." The old man grinned. "We'll fool them, won't we, Allie? They have me now, but I'll escape someday. Take that diamond I gave you, the big one. We can use it to pay off the right people, if we need to."

She wondered if he could hear her heart breaking.

"You get better, Dickey. We'll work it out, one step at a time. Getting well is the first step."

Dickey nodded. "First step, get well. Second step, diamonds."

She squeezed his hand, unable to speak around the jagged lump in her throat. As the medics hoisted the stretcher into the bay of the ambulance, she had to let go. She moved to the edge of the vehicle, so that she could be as close as possible till the very last second. The Vanaks had already made it clear she wouldn't be allowed to come with them to the hospital tonight. She held Dickey's gaze, trying to send him all the strength and courage she had.

He smiled and blew her a kiss. Then, as he always did when he was enjoying some melodrama he'd cooked up, he lay his stubby forefinger alongside his nose and winked.

The tears won. Hoping he couldn't see them, she raised her own trembling hand and rested her index finger at the side of her nose. "Bye, Dickie," she said.

And then they shut the doors.

She stumbled toward the house, not sure exactly where she was going or what she intended to do. Without the police-car lights circling, or the floodlights pouring onto the roof, the night seemed suddenly so black she was almost blind.

"Allie," Red said, his voice coming out of nowhere. She blinked, and he was suddenly a few feet away, with Eddie in one arm and the other outstretched to her.

She made a low sound that should have been his name, but wasn't. He seemed to understand, though. He closed the gap between them and wrapped her in a solid, firm embrace.

Oh, it felt like heaven here—it was such a relief not to be alone. She put her arms around his waist and clung, as if he were a life raft and she were adrift in a deep, deep sea.

In response, he said her name again and tightened his grip. Burying her face in his chest, she finally let the burning tears have their way.

For a long, soothing time, he stroked her hair gently. She thought perhaps he kissed the top of her head. She couldn't really think, couldn't even ask herself why this was the haven she had turned to. All she knew was that she needed to be here.

After a few minutes, he spoke softly. "What can I do, Allie? What do you want me to do?"

She couldn't make herself let go. She couldn't imagine breathing air that didn't smell like Red. She couldn't imagine standing up without his body there to brace her.

"I want you to stay with me," she said, her words muffled by the cotton that covered his strong, safe, beautiful chest. "I don't want to be alone tonight."

HE TOOK HER HOME in silence. Exhausted by all the alien stimulation, Eddie conked out the minute they put him in his car seat, and for a while Red thought maybe Allison slept, too. But when they pulled up in front of her little apartment, his car brushing the folded blooms of the hibiscus bush, she stirred.

"I'll get Eddie," he whispered.

She nodded, and together they climbed the set of wooden stairs that led to the second floor. The wind had kicked up, carrying the salty smell of the ocean inland. It molded her T-shirt to her breasts, and lifted her hair around her like a gauzy veil.

It was probably only about ten o'clock, but emotional exhaustion made it seem much later. She turned the key carefully in the lock and eased the door open on its hinges, as though she didn't want to disturb the slumbering world around them.

Still in silence, they worked together to put Eddie to bed. By unspoken agreement, they ignored the bath he should have had hours ago, settling for a diaper change and sleepers with little blue feet. When Allison dug through the tote bag, she held up the empty bottle, a question in her gaze.

Red nodded, confirming that he'd fed Eddie at Dickey's house. The baby was full, and so limp with sleep that it would be futile to offer him more.

While she tucked Eddie into his crib, Red went into the kitchen and rinsed the last dregs of formula from the bottle. He used the bottle brush that lay beside the sink. For once, he was glad he'd spent so many nights on uncle duty.

When he turned off the spigot, he realized that Allison was standing in the tiny kitchen, no more than two or three feet from him. He could have reached out and touched her. But did she want him to? That earlier moment of easy intimacy might have passed. It might have been merely the product of adrenaline and stress, and the feeling might have ebbed with the chemicals that produced it.

He forced himself to wait, to let her make the first move. Outside, the treetops swayed in the wind, and their shadows undulated across the floor.

"Thank you," she said softly. Her voice was thick, as

if emotion still clogged her throat. "I don't know what I would have done without you tonight."

"You would have done fine," he said. "But I'm glad I was there."

The room was dim. Only a small blue digital read-out on the stove and the suffused glow of a nearby streetlamp illuminated the apartment. Though he couldn't read the nuances of her expression, he watched her and waited.

"Red, I—" She put her fingers to her temple as if she couldn't calm the thoughts inside her head enough to create sentences out of them. "Tonight, when I asked you to stay with me—"

"It's all right," he said, though a shimmer of disappointment fell through him like the last fading colors of a firecracker. "I understand if you've changed your mind."

"No, that's not what I'm trying to say. I want you to stay. I—I need you to stay, if you are willing to."

"I'm willing," he said, softly. What an understatement. He was so much more than willing.

"Thank you. But—" She tilted her head uncertainly. Her hair caught the light and it slid across her cheek like wet satin. He remembered how those soft strands had felt under his fingertips.

"But?"

"But I want to be clear that…I'm not asking—" She inhaled deeply. "I want you to understand that I can't make love to you tonight."

"I know," he answered. "That's all right. It doesn't matter."

And it didn't, even though he knew in his heart that she was asking the nearly impossible. She wanted him

to stay with her all night, hold her, watch her sleep…
but somehow control the ravaging desire he felt every
single damn time he looked at her.

That was white knight stuff. And, as too many
women would attest, Red Malone was no white knight.
Somehow, though, he knew that, for this one night, he
could be whatever she needed him to be.

"It's not that I don't want to," she said, and he
thought he glimpsed a stain rising on each of her
cheeks. "It's just that…I can't. I can't take the chance
that I might get pregnant again. You see, Victor and I—
we took every precaution, and it wasn't enough. I can't
be irresponsible enough to run that risk again."

He almost smiled. She always walked right up to the
truth, didn't she? However scary or embarrassing that
truth might be, she looked it in the eye and called it by
its name. She might be the most honest woman he'd
ever met.

"I understand," he said. "It's all right. Besides, you're
hurting tonight. You're in pain. I generally prefer to
have sex with women who aren't using it purely as an
anesthetic."

She scanned his face, as if trying to read between
the lines. She must have seen the tiny hint of humor
there, because suddenly she sighed. Her body relaxed,
and he realized she'd been holding her shoulders tight,
like a soldier facing an enemy.

"Allie," he said, using the nickname consciously for
the first time, though he realized it had slipped out
before. "I'm here. I want to be here. I want to stay with
you tonight, whether or not we make love."

She nodded. He extended his hand, and when she
took it, and when their fingers twined, he led her to

the sofa. He sat, and she sat sideways beside him, her bare feet under her, her face turned toward him, glowing pale.

He cupped her cheek in his palm. It felt cool, almost bloodless. "Do you want to talk about Dickey?"

She shook her head. "Not yet," she said. "Later, maybe, but not tonight."

"Okay." He settled against the padded sofa. "Then why don't you lie down? It might do you good to get some rest."

She looked at him, her brown eyes wide and shining, and then she nodded. She shifted and reclined slowly, letting her head rest against his lap.

"Get comfortable," he said, and held himself in strictest check as she wriggled gently, finding the perfect spot, which nestled her ear somewhere between his hip and his thigh. When she grew still, he dropped one hand and began to stroke her hair.

She made a low, purring sound and sank deeper, her neck softening, her body stretching out till her feet touched the arm at the other side of the sofa. Then she reached up and felt for his other hand. When she found it, she pulled it around and tucked their mated palms to her breast.

And then, while the rising wind clattered through the trees and rumbled the windows in their old wooden frames, she slept.

CHAPTER SEVENTEEN

THEY WERE ALL SITTING in Summer Moon, taking their lunch break the next day, when Jimbo finally came home, two whole days early.

"Oh, my God!" Letting her fork fall into her salad, indifferent to the splash of apricot dressing, Allison jumped up. She catapulted herself into his arms, whooping with delight. "You're back!"

Jimbo laughed. "You always were one for stating the obvious," he said wryly, but he twirled her in circles, then danced her all the way to the kitchen door.

He stopped dead the minute he glanced in. "Wow. You guys have been getting it *done*."

She smiled, pleased by the approval she heard in his tone. "Of course we have. Did you think we'd twiddle our thumbs until the Great Jimbo's return? Our soft opening is in three days."

"Right. Still, this is some pretty amazing progress." He moved through the door, obviously mesmerized by all the shining stainless steel and pristine new appliances. He hadn't even said hi to anyone out in the other room yet, but they would all understand. Everyone knew the only thing that really mattered to Jimbo was the kitchen.

He prowled through the room, touching everything, opening every door, inspecting every brand name and model number, every pot and pan and spatula. He stopped when he got to the ice maker, glanced at Allison and whistled.

"What did you do, take out another loan? This baby is the dream machine. I know darn well she wasn't in our budget."

Allison suddenly felt a frisson of discomfort. She'd anticipated this moment many times over the past few days, but she hadn't yet decided exactly how much she was going to tell Jimbo about Red.

She knew Jimbo didn't like him, and wouldn't appreciate the fact that Red was the one who had spearheaded the work in his absence. He definitely wouldn't be happy to hear that Red had spent last night in their apartment, even if the sleepover hadn't involved anything but a chaste, fully clothed sharing of the sofa.

"We've had a lot of help," she started carefully. "So much has been going on. It'll take hours for me to tell you everything. Bottom line—I was able to buy the ice machine at an amazingly good price."

"Oh, yeah?" Jimbo's voice sounded suspicious. He opened the bin and peered in. "What, did you buy it used? I thought we decided that wasn't really a savings in the end."

"No, it's new," she said. No use trying to postpone this. Because Jimbo had known her since she was a little girl, he always knew when she was hiding something. He said her left eye twitched, but she didn't believe that. He had brains, and he had decades of experience with her. He just knew.

"You see, Red Malone has been helping us the past few days," she blurted quickly. "His family owns Diamante Pizza—you probably already know that. So of course he's got a ton of expertise with restaurants, and he's got a lot of friends. One of them is this appliance guy named Travis, and—"

"Wait a minute. Slow down with this verbal landslide of misdirection. I know what exactly kind of expertise that guy has, and it's got nothing to do with the restaurant business. Are you telling me that the minute I shipped out, Malone moved in?"

She flushed and felt her spine stiffening defensively. "That's a ridiculous way to put it. But yes, essentially that's what happened. I needed help, and Red has been generous enough to offer his."

"God, Allie." Jimbo ran his hands through his spikey blond hair. "Have you forgotten who this guy is? He's that bastard Victor Wigham's errand boy."

"Keep your voice down," she said. "He's in the dining room right now. And I don't want you being rude to him. He's been very helpful. He's been…he's been good to me, Jimbo."

Jimbo rolled his eyes. "I bet he has."

She felt her temper flash. "You know, Jimbo, when you say things like that, you aren't only insulting him. You're also insulting me."

He leaned forward assertively, planting his hands flat on the range top, at least three feet apart. "Don't try to shame me into shutting up, Allie. You know that's not what I meant. The guy is a sleazeball, and he's not good enough to wash the dishes in this place. But it sounds as if you've been letting him run it."

"No, I've just been accepting the help I need. Help that has been pretty graciously offered, if you ask me, since there's not a darn thing in it for him. And I'll thank you to—"

At that moment, Meg Bretton appeared in the kitchen doorway. Allison had no way of knowing whether their voices had been vehement enough to carry the sound of the argument out into the seating area. But, even if it had, Meg had clearly decided to play it cool.

"Everything looks fantastic, doesn't it?" She smiled at Jimbo as if she hadn't noticed that the air was thick enough to cut with one of his brand-new meat cleavers. "You wouldn't believe how hard Allie has worked."

Jimbo scowled. "And not only Allie, I hear."

"Well, I can't accept *all* the credit," Meg said, bowing extravagantly with her hand over her heart. "We've had a virtual army here most days. But thanks. I've done my part, and I'll accept the compliment."

She caught Allison's eye, and her expression made it clear she'd chosen to deliberately misunderstand Jimbo. Allison's answering look was loaded with gratitude. Time, that's what they all needed. With a little time, Jimbo would get used to the changes. Once he saw that Red wasn't planning a permanent coup, and would be returning to San Francisco any day now, he'd relax.

She wished it would be that easy for her. But the bottom line was—she was going to miss Red. In a short time he'd become a part of the rhythm of her life. He'd become a rock, an ally...a friend.

And maybe something more.

When she awoke this morning, she'd been in her own bed, still wearing her jeans and T-shirt from last night. Red must have carried her there so adroitly he hadn't jostled her awake. But when she went out into the living room, the sofa was empty and Red was gone.

Foolish as it was, she'd felt a piercing stab of disappointment.

All he'd left was a note on the kitchen table with the phone number of Dickey's hospital, the floor and room they'd put him in. At the bottom, he'd added this quick message:

They say he slept well. Hope you did, too.
—R

She had stared at the note longer than she should have, wondering if he'd even for a minute considered signing it with *Love*. She found herself remembering the feel of his hands on her hair, and his muscular thigh beneath her cheek. Like a dopey teenager, she used the tip of her forefinger to slowly trace the bold, slanted *R* several times. It was only the sound of Eddie babbling in his crib that had pulled her out of the trance.

When she got to Summer Moon and saw that Red was already there, little explosions of pleasure went off behind her heart. They were followed, almost instantly, by little detonations of fear. How could she have let herself get so attached? One day soon, she'd show up and the restaurant would be empty.

But maybe that was a good thing. Maybe the sooner Red went home, the better. Otherwise, as Jimbo immediately had guessed, she might be in danger of making a very, very stupid mistake.

"So everyone is asking for seconds." Meg's tone was pointed, as if she sensed that Allison had drifted away. "Any chance you could bring out some more salad?"

"Oh, yes, sorry. Of course I can." She already had some made up, waiting in the refrigerator. She opened the door and pulled out the bowl. "I even have enough for the prodigal brother."

"Great. Now you come on out, too, Jimbo," Meg said, starting to sound like a den mother rounding up her unruly Cub Scouts. "Don't hide out in here. Everyone wants to say hi."

He glanced one last time at Allison, then nodded. He must already have stopped by the apartment, because he had arrived dressed for hard work in one of his most disreputable sweat suits. Good thing she'd slipped Red's note in her pocket, and the apartment held no traces of its overnight visitor.

Together, the three of them returned to the main seating area, which also looked terrific, especially compared to how Jimbo had last seen it. Dale was here, and Sue, and Bill and Sarge. Red sat at the closest table, with a telltale empty spot beside him where Allison had been eating.

Red, who appeared to be in the middle of burping Eddie, smiled politely as Jimbo came over and stood beside him. He stood, still patting Eddie's back.

"Hi," he said. "Welcome back."

"Thanks." Jimbo managed to bite the word out, though his tone was noticeably grudging. He held out his hands. "Mind if I say hi to the little man?"

"Sure." Red swiveled Eddie around to face Jimbo. "You might want to get a towel, though. He packed away a whole bottle, and sometimes it doesn't all stay down."

"I know how it works," Jimbo said curtly. Then he gave Eddie a smile. "Hey, buddy. Did you miss Uncle J.?"

Eddie stared up at Jimbo with wide eyes, as shocked as if he'd never met the man in his life. He twisted his mouth, and his face went red. He kicked his feet furiously and arched his spine, trying to get back to Red's shoulder.

Allison watched, horrified. She reached out and
touched the baby's damp forehead. He'd already worked
himself into a sweat. "Eddie, sweetheart. It's Uncle
J...."

But no amount of soothing reassurances could stop
the disaster. Eddie was not going to be handed over to
the new man without putting up a loud and heartfelt
fight. The minute Jimbo's hands touched him, he began
to wail as if he were being dipped in boiling oil.

Red, at least, knew better than to put Eddie on his
own shoulder. When he saw that Eddie was going to
reject Jimbo, he handed the baby immediately to Allison.

Eddie hid his hot face in her neck, refusing to turn
around. She stroked the sweaty crown of his head and
wondered what on earth had caused him to act this way.
From the day he was born, he'd adored Jimbo.

"You know how babies are," she said, trying to make
light of the moment. It hurt to see Jimbo's stricken
face. "Yesterday, he'd fallen in love with Meg, and he
wouldn't give me the time of day."

"That's true," Meg said helpfully. She smiled at both
men. "But he's not a bit interested in me today. Fickle
little devil."

"He's not fickle, he's confused," Jimbo said, looking hard at Allison, then transferring his gaze to Red
briefly and pointedly. "Babies need stability."

Oh, Jimbo. Allison wished she could make him understand that this wasn't personal. She bounced Eddie
softly, relieved that the wailing had subsided to soft
hiccups.

Red's expression was placid. "Of course. But they

also need socialization, don't they? Or at least a healthy balance between the two?"

"No," Jimbo answered without any effort to soften the syllable.

"No?" Red tilted his head, as if quite interested in this new theory.

"No," Jimbo repeated harshly. "Especially when they're very young, babies need to know exactly who they can rely on. They need to know which people are in their lives to stay." He narrowed his eyes. "And which people are blowing through."

ANOTHER TIME, another place, and Red might have found Jimbo's pugilistic protective streak funny. When they were younger, he and his brothers had encountered a fair number of gatekeeper fathers, brothers, cousins and ex-boyfriends who issued dire warnings about what would happen if their favorite innocent female got hurt.

It had become a running joke. Colby, especially, had created hilarious caricatures of the dads as mobster-voiced thugs. "Sleep with my little girl, son, and you sleep with the fishes," he'd mumble out of one side of his mouth. The brothers, gathered in the boathouse to play darts after they took home their dates, would chuckle. "Do the math, boy. Five minutes late equals six feet under."

But as Red drove to the nursing home the next morning, where he had plans to pick up Allison after her visit with Dickey, he wasn't laughing. He was cranky, and tired from wrestling with his conscience all night. Because, this time, the guardian was right.

Red was blowing through. Already, his work was piling up in San Francisco, and he was staying here on stolen time. One more day, maybe two, and he'd have to leave.

Now that Jimbo was home, maybe it would be easier to go. In many ways, even after all this time, Allison was still a mystery. On one hand, she was tough and principled and determined as a pit bull. On the other, she was inexplicably innocent, naive and vulnerable, and he hated to leave her in that apartment all alone.

But playing temporary boyfriend, or even substitute best friend, wasn't fair to Allison, or to Eddie. Not when he was leaving so soon, and probably wasn't ever coming back.

He hadn't needed Jimbo to clarify the situation for him. He knew how impossible it was. When they'd run into Cherry, he'd told himself he simply had to stop—

Oh, hell. *Cherry.*

He'd forgotten to phone her last night. She'd offered lunch, and he'd put her off, suggesting they might do dinner instead. He'd meant it, at the time. But then Allison got the call about Dickey, and afterward he'd driven her home, and…

And, generally, the whole night's madness had burned all other considerations out of his mind. He scooped his phone off the passenger seat and found Cherry's speed-dial entry. Not calling wasn't exactly an unforgivable sin. He wasn't her boyfriend, and he'd made no promises. The only claim she had on him was common courtesy, but she at least deserved that.

He got her voice mail, which she updated daily, and which now said she'd returned to San Francisco after a couple of days at the beach, and she'd get back to him as soon as she could. He left an apology, friendly but generic.

Again, no promises. He had no intention of leading her on.

All the way to the nursing home, he half expected to get a call from either Jimbo or Allison, letting him know he was no longer needed for this errand. A couple of days ago, he and Allison had arranged to talk to the dairy distributor Diamante used for fresh milk, yogurts and cheeses. The rep would be close to Windsor Beach this morning, and Red was picking her up at eleven so they could meet the man together.

Unless Jimbo—who probably didn't want her alone for an hour with Red, even if they discussed nothing but goat's milk—bullied her out of it and insisted on taking her there himself.

But the phone didn't ring, and as he turned into the facility's parking lot, he saw her standing out front, Eddie in her arms and the baby's tote bag slung over her shoulder.

Red couldn't help it—he smiled at the sight of her wearing a dress for a change. It was simple, street-length and flowered, and probably lightweight, judging from how it ruffled around her knees. Her hair was down, shimmering in the sun, and she even wore a little peach lipstick.

She looked feminine and sexy enough to start a slow burn he tried to ignore. But then, God help him, he found himself turned on no matter what she wore. The ponytail she scraped her hair into at work shouldn't have been even remotely erotic. Her hair was technically too short for that style, and stuck out in the back like a feathery little whiskbroom. Still, about twenty times a day, he fought the urge to run his fingers through it.

He pulled up and leaned over to open the door. She settled Eddie in the back—he'd long ago bought a car seat, though he'd rationalized it by saying he needed one for Matt's new baby, anyhow. Then she popped in with a grin and a rush of gardenia-scented soap.

He knew it was gardenia because he'd seen the creamy white bar in her bathroom, right next to the clear honey-colored baby shampoo.

"Morning," she said, full of energy and cheer. "You should see how great Dickey looks. The nurses already adore him. He's completely forgotten the dungeon thing. Today he thinks he's a P.I., and the nurses are his agents, like *Charlie's Angels*."

"Awesome." He smiled, as delighted to see her as if he hadn't been thinking that he must put her out of his mind, and his life, as soon as possible. But he found her spunk and optimism contagious, especially considering how many worries he knew she was carrying. "Dickey must be quite a guy."

"He is," she said as she buckled her seat belt. She let her head fall back and shut her eyes. "It's such a relief to see him so happy."

He pulled away from the curb, ridiculously glad she hadn't cancelled, and a little ashamed that he felt as if he'd won a contest of some kind. He wasn't in competition with Jimbo for this woman.

Still. He smiled again. He should have known she wouldn't let Jimbo bully her into anything. If her big, blond guard dog got too bossy, she'd probably lock him in the supply closet.

"We have plenty of time," he said. "Anywhere you want to stop first?"

She turned her head toward him. She'd opened her

eyes, but her head still tilted back against the leather of the ventilated headrest. "How much time do we have?"

He glanced at the dashboard. "Twenty minutes or so. But we can steal a few more minutes, if you need some. Jack is occasionally a little late—it's hard for him to predict exactly how long all his deliveries will take." He glanced at her. "What do you need?"

"I don't *need* anything," she said carefully. "It's just…something that's been on my mind. I don't know whether it's something you'll be comfortable with."

He was certainly curious now. "As long as it doesn't involve disposing of dead bodies, I think I can handle it. I could do the dead bodies, too, except I've already got the trunk loaded up with Summer Moon supplies."

She didn't laugh, though ordinarily she at least cracked a smile at his lame jokes. Her eyes looked thoughtful. "Nothing that dramatic," she said. "I wondered if you'd show me Victor's house."

For a second he didn't speak. He wasn't sure why, but for some reason Victor's name landed in the car like a bad smell.

"That's okay," she interjected quickly, obviously reading his hesitation as a no. "I'm sure I can find the address somewhere, and I can find it by myself another time. I thought it might be easier if I wasn't alone. But that's silly. Never mind."

"I don't mind a bit." He smiled at her. "I was surprised, that's all."

"Surprised that I want to see it? Or that I haven't seen it already?"

He shrugged. "I don't know, really. Maybe both."

She'd asked for the address when he'd first told her about the house, and he'd given it to her. He trusted her completely. She might drive by out of curiosity—he assumed, in fact, that she would—but he no longer worried that she might stalk up to the front door and try to cause trouble in the Wigham family.

But if she wanted to see it now, he wasn't going to deny her. He had already pointed the car in the correct direction. He reached the beach road, then turned south. Victor's large, modern house was at the extreme edge of Windsor Beach. It might not even be in the city limits. But it wouldn't take more than seven or eight minutes to get there. Windsor Beach didn't cover many miles, from tip to toe.

They were there in no time. But the house had been built as close to the beach as zoning would allow, so there wasn't much to see from the street. Just the slate-colored roof, made to look like an extension of the bluffs—very Frank Lloyd Wright—and a glint or two of sun on half-hidden picture windows.

When he idled the car in front of the peekaboo driveway that wound into the thick green shrubbery, he saw the disappointment on her face.

"I guess Cherry is still there," she said finally. It was a question. She wanted him to explain why he didn't turn in and drive up to the house itself.

But Cherry wasn't there, and he knew that. Her outgoing message had said she was already in San Francisco. And Marianne never came here. She found its rugged architecture cold and unappealing.

So why was he so reluctant to take Allison up the drive, to get a look at the house itself? The strange hint of disquiet he felt made no sense. She hadn't been Victor's lover in that house. She hadn't even realized it existed, until Red told her. And Victor wasn't here to feel ashamed.

Though he should have. Red felt a sudden surge of unaccustomed anger against his friend. *Damn it, Victor. She's a very special woman. You should have been ashamed.*

Impulsively, he pulled into the driveway, which twisted steeply toward the house. Getting up close felt a little like rubbing her nose in Victor's wealth. But if she wanted to know, she had a right to the facts.

The minute he reached the house, he knew something was wrong. A starburst of broken glass lay just outside the three-car garage. A long stripe of crushed foliage bisected the grassy border, as if a tire had run over it. And at the edge of the walkway to the house, an elegant garden statue of a heron in flight had been knocked off its pedestal, and lay in pieces on the river-rock path.

"Oh, my God," Allison said softly. "Vandals? We had trouble with some teenagers last year, breaking into some of the unoccupied houses."

But this damage hadn't happened last year. In fact, since Cherry had been here only yesterday, it must have happened today. Red was about to throw the car into Reverse, removing Allison from harm in case whoever did this was still around, when two things happened simultaneously.

First, he saw someone move around the side of the house, heading for the beach side. Could it be…? He'd had only a second to make an identification, but he was almost sure he knew that head of fair, tousled hair. Could Dylan possibly be here?

And, oh, lord, what a mess if that meant Marianne

had unexpectedly come, too. Bringing Allison here had been stupid. Worse than stupid. It was as if, on some unconscious level, he had wanted to force this confrontation so that the secret would finally be out in the open.

Before he could fully sort the tangled knots of his thoughts, much less articulate anything out loud, his cell phone rang. He looked at the ID. It was Marianne.

He answered instantly, hoping she wasn't calling from inside the house, because she'd spotted his car in the drive. But when he heard her tearful, frantic voice, his subconscious instantly began to fill in the blanks. Her words confirmed his suspicions.

"Red," she said when she heard his voice. "Are you still in Windsor Beach?"

"I am," he said, though he was already pulling the car through the circular drive and heading to the main road. "What's wrong?"

"It's Dylan. We had a fight this morning, a bad one. He took Victor's car, and it looks as if he's taken the key to the beach house, too. Not the Carmel house. The one in Windsor, where you are."

"Hell," Red said under his breath. "The little fool doesn't even have his restricted license yet, does he?"

"No. Victor wouldn't let him, because of the trouble he'd been in lately. But I'm pretty sure he knows how to drive. He's stolen the car before, though he only went to his friend Brock's house that time."

God, what a disaster—Dylan trying to maneuver the forty minutes down the beach highway. Thankfully, the traffic on weekdays wasn't as bad as it could be on the weekends.

"Have you called the police?"

"No, I don't want to get them involved. I'm already on the road, trying to find him. But I'm at least half an hour away. Is there any chance you can go to the house, to see if he's there? I have no idea how good a driver he is, or whether he might get lost, or…" Her words dissolved briefly as the tears took over. "I need to know he's all right."

"I'm sure Dylan's fine," Red said, his mind racing. "What was he threatening? What was his plan?"

"I don't know, I don't know." Marianne's words sounded like soft moans. "But you've seen how reckless he's been lately. I'm so afraid he'll do something stupid. What if he has drugs on him?"

Oh, crap. He'd looked fine when Red had last seen him at the house, much more alert and, though Dylan had been angry, he hadn't seemed truly out of control. Red kicked himself for staying away so long. He should have stayed in San Francisco, where he could see Dylan every day.

"God, Marianne, has he been using again? Why didn't you tell me? I'm only an hour away. Why didn't you call me?"

"No, he's not. Or… Red, I just don't know. We hardly communicate anymore. Please. I know you're busy, but can you go by the house and wait for him till I get there?"

He glanced at Allison, whose face looked somber. She knew who was on the other end of this call, of course.

Eddie started to fidget. It wouldn't be long before he broke into full-blown crying. Allison cast a worried look into the backseat, obviously aware that a wailing baby would be difficult to explain.

Red rubbed his eyes. God, this was the most ridiculous farce he'd ever been a party to. Why the hell hadn't he told Victor to man up and acknowledge all his children?

And why, knowing that his own first obligation was to protect Dylan and Marianne, had Red allowed himself to become entangled with Allison, too?

How much better was he, in the end, than Victor?

"Red? Will you go to the house?"

"Yes, of course," he said dully. "I'll go."

CHAPTER EIGHTEEN

"DON'T WORRY," Allison said as Red hung up the phone and sat for a second as if frozen, staring at the thing. "I got the basic idea, and it's all right, really. Go ahead and see if Dylan is okay. I'll call Sue, or Jimbo. I'll wait in the car until one of them shows up to get me."

He looked up at her, his face unreadable. "I'm sorry," he said. "It's unbelievable, really. Could there be worse luck? To get here when—"

"Don't say that. Maybe it's not bad luck at all. If Dylan is in some kind of danger, maybe he needs you." She tried to eliminate all selfish thoughts from her heart, and to think only of the troubled teenager. "Maybe it was meant to be."

He shook his head and pinched the bridge of his nose. He squeezed his eyes shut, as if to banish some thought or emotion he found it impossible to live with. Then he drew in a long breath.

"Damn it, Allie. Don't be like that."

She was surprised by the vehemence in his voice. "Like what?"

"Don't be a saint." He shook his head again. "It makes me feel worse. This is an impossible situation for you. Marianne's on her way now. I should never have brought you here."

"Don't you remember? I'm the one who suggested

it. I'm the one who wanted to see where Victor lived. How Victor lived." She smiled ruefully. "Well, as they always say, I should have been careful what I wished for."

Red drummed his fingers on the console, clearly unwilling to accept the inevitable. But Allison knew they had to hurry. Dylan was up there, doing only God knew what. And down here, every time a car passed them on the road, her stomach tightened, and she wondered if it was Marianne Wigham.

Besides, Eddie was still fuming, and a tantrum was inevitable if they didn't distract him soon. She cast a glance into the backseat. He'd begun kicking his feet and pressing his fists against his eyes. He was clearly tired, and probably hungry.

"I'll drive you two home and then I'll come back here," Red said, reaching around to distract the baby by tugging on his toes, which Eddie loved. "Fifteen, twenty minutes can't possibly make that much difference."

"Of course it makes a difference. Even the time we're taking now, arguing about it, makes a difference. Just go. Sue can be here in less than ten minutes."

In truth, she had no idea whether Sue was free this morning. She might be preparing for the lunch shift at the Peacock, unable to get away. But if Sue couldn't come, Allison would try Meg. Then Jimbo. If he couldn't come, either, she'd call a cab.

One way or another, she'd be out of this car and gone before Marianne arrived.

Finally, his expression cleared a little. "I know. You take the car. Eddie's already situated, and you'll get home faster that way."

He opened the door and got out, not waiting for her answer. While she was still processing the idea, he came around and opened her door, too. The curb was awkwardly close, so he extended his hand to help her out.

"Come on, Allie. You know it's the best plan, really. Leave the car at Summer Moon. If I'm late, and you're gone, you can put the keys under the mat and lock it. I have another set."

Reluctantly, knowing he was right, she put her hand in his, swung her feet around, and climbed out of the car.

The tiny space before the curb off-balanced her. She tightened her grip on his hand to steady herself and awkwardly leaned into the stable column of his chest to avoid stumbling.

Without warning, she felt his warmth. The scent of him filled her lungs. Their eyes met, and suddenly their hands clung as if one or both of them were drowning. He brought her hand to his chest and pressed it there so hard she could feel his heart beating against her fingers.

"Alli," he said, his voice hoarse and oddly helpless.

She tried, in that moment, to memorize his beautiful face, but she knew that she would never be able, in later years, to recreate the magic of those angles and shadows, the exact play of sunlight on his hair and eyes.

She reached up and touched his cheek gently. "You need to hurry. You'd never forgive yourself if anything happened while you—while we—"

He nodded, but he still held her hand as they walked to the driver's side. They released each other briefly as she got behind the wheel, adjusted the mirrors and the seat, but then he took her hand again.

She smiled at him, determined to hold her emotions in check. "Anything I need to know so that I don't crash your beloved Mercedes? After what Bill did, that would really be adding insult to injury."

With quiet efficiency, he explained the car's few idiosyncrasies. She hoped the subconscious part of her brain was following the instructions, because all she was consciously aware of was how low and mellow his voice was, and how it went straight through her.

It was strange, she thought. Most of the world would probably think that the witty, charming playboy, with his laughing blue eyes, his wind-tossed waves of hair and his dimpled grin, was the irresistible side of Red Malone. But she liked him best when he was subdued and pensive, as he was now. In those moments, he seemed more real to her, more accessible—as if she were on the verge of learning something important about him.

It was an illusion, of course. Charismatic or quiet, he lived in another world, one she could never enter. And that would never change. This week—God, had it been only a week?—had been a fluke. Nothing more.

They still held hands through the open window, like teenagers. But he was finished explaining the car, and they both knew he had to go. Luckily, she was starting to feel a little numb, and some of the emotions she would endure later had no power over her now.

"How will you get back?" She glanced at the hidden driveway. "Will Marianne give you a ride?"

"It depends on whether she feels comfortable leaving Dylan," he said. "I'll probably get a cab to Summer Moon."

She nodded slowly. "Red... I think when you get there..."

He waited. But suddenly her voice had disappeared. She had to clear her throat and begin again. "When you get there I don't think you should come in."

The sudden darkness in his eyes told her he understood. She didn't mean that he shouldn't come in today. She meant that he shouldn't come in ever again.

The silence was so heavy it seemed to press onto her lungs, as if it were trying to force her to say something else. Trying to force her to take the words back.

But she couldn't. As she'd sat there, listening to him talk to Marianne Wigham about Dylan, she'd felt an irrational envy that coursed through her like poison. And at that moment, she'd finally understood how reckless and unwise she had been this past week.

She had let herself make another painful, ridiculous mistake with a man. But this one was the worst of all. With Chuck, she'd let her nest egg slip away. With Victor, she'd given up her self-respect.

But with Red Malone, she'd lost her heart.

She'd fallen in love with a man from another planet, a man whose allegiance lay with other people, other places. A man who liked her, wanted her, maybe even felt sorry for her, but who had undoubtedly never once considered the possibility of *loving* her.

And, to prove what a fool she was, when she realized it was over, the first thing she thought was, *I wish we had made love. I wish I had that to remember.*

"Allison, when I'm finished here, maybe we should talk—"

"No. You know where that will lead." She smiled, though her lips felt stiff and hard to move. "Please, Red. Let's be realistic. You've been wonderful. And I'm grateful, more than you'll know. Let's leave it like this, before we do anything we'll regret. Another day, another week—that would only make it harder for me, in the end."

He shook his head, but she could see in his eyes that he knew she was right. "The last thing I want to do is hurt you."

"I know. But you don't want to hurt them, either. Look at us. Is this what you really want? Do you want to sneak around with me behind their backs? Like Victor did?"

The blow hit home. She could almost see the internal flinch as he processed the truth of her words. He glanced up the winding drive, then returned his dark, hooded gaze to her and nodded.

With a bleak smile, he lifted her hand to his warm lips, brushing them almost imperceptibly across her knuckles.

And then he was gone.

RED HAD A KEY to the beach house, so he didn't bother knocking. After watching Allison drive off, probably for the last time, he wasn't in the mood to pussyfoot around Dylan's dysfunctionality. If the kid had pills in there, why give him time to flush them down the toilet?

The air seemed quiet. Too quiet for a house that supposedly had a tumultuous teenager in it. Every cushion on the beautiful wicker beach furniture was perfectly lined up, and everything smelled clean and untouched.

That probably meant Dylan was outside. Red's mind

sifted through the possibilities. He'd like to think the boy had run away to the beach so that he could work out his aggression with a surfboard. That was how Red had handled his own teenage squalls. But he knew that was unlikely. Lately Dylan seemed to have totally forgotten the therapeutic joys of exercise.

So what, then? Liquor by the pool? Pot, maybe? Had Dylan gone outside to smoke to avoid leaving the telltale scent in the house? He was a smart kid, and he had to realize his mom would be barreling down the highway, hard on his heels.

Other, more dire possibilities tried to form in Red's mind, but he pushed them away. He wouldn't consider anything like that unless he had to.

He shoved open the French doors and walked onto the deck. It was high noon, and the Pacific lay like a long band of gun metal that had been beaten flat by the sun. No one could surf on that.

As Red made a path across the deck, a huddled, beach-towel-wrapped form in one of the lounge chairs suddenly sprang up like an angry jack-in-the-box.

"Damn it," Dylan said, tossing his towel aside, letting it fall to the deck in a heap. "Knock much? What the hell ever happened to privacy?"

Red turned and stared at the boy. He looked intact, thank God. And he looked sober. Red would have liked to grab him and kiss him—or yell at him until his brains kicked into gear. But he did neither one, of course.

Instead, he adopted a mildly disapproving but basically dispassionate air. As if the boy annoyed and bored him at the same time.

"Sorry, buddy. You lost the right to privacy when

you started doing crap like cleaning out your mother's medicine cabinet and stealing your father's car."

Dylan glared daggers at him, but as a comeback it lacked punch. Red ignored it. He walked to the banister for a minute, and quickly texted Marianne a brief message.

He's here. He's okay.

Maybe she'd drive more carefully if she knew she wasn't racing against disaster.

Then he pocketed his phone, came to where Dylan sat and drew up a chair. Now that he was closer, and the sun spotlighted Dylan's face, he could see that the boy had been crying.

A lot. Dylan's eyes were red-rimmed, like one of the zombies in the comic books he used to read. His face was a patchwork of tear tracks and the few spots of acne that his mother's expensive dermatologists hadn't been able to eradicate.

Intact, maybe, but miserable.

Unfortunately, Red wasn't in the mood for a pity party. His heart said *go easy,* but his gut told him everyone had been so busy feeling sorry for Dylan they'd forgotten to hold him accountable.

"What's the matter with you, Dylan?" He scraped his gaze over the boy's skinny arms and toothpick chest. In a couple of years, he would be a man, but he definitely wasn't there yet. "Are you desperate for attention, or what?"

"Are you kidding?" Dylan flicked his towel irritably. "I came down here because I can't ever get a minute's peace. She always wants to talk to me about Dad, and I can't stand that. I came down here to be alone."

"Yeah?" Red got comfortable in his chair. "Then it's

too bad you didn't take the bus. There's nothing guaranteed to bring parents and cops swarming down on you like a little grand-theft auto."

Dylan's face tightened. "She's coming?"

Interesting that he obviously didn't take the cop comment seriously. "Of course she's coming. What did you think?"

Dylan moved his shoulders. He wasn't looking at Red anymore. He was picking pointlessly at a half-healed scab on his knee. "I don't know. I thought maybe... I mean, she knows you're here. I thought she might call you. I figured she'd be cool if she knew I was with you."

With him?

Oh, man. Was that what this was all about? Was Red's week-long absence from San Francisco the reason Dylan had shown up here in Windsor Beach, boiling with a mixture of anger and vulnerability?

Red had thought Dylan was getting better—he'd believed the boy had recovered enough that a bi-weekly visit was no longer necessary. He'd called Marianne almost every night, and she'd always assured him Dylan was doing well.

Apparently they'd both been wrong.

It looked as if Dylan feared that Red had abandoned him. And apparently he had hoped that, if he created a new drama, and staged it here in Windsor Beach, Red might step in and take over.

So what was the right response? Red's heart went out to a boy who, having lost his father, couldn't bear the thought of losing his father figure, too. But if Dylan's ploy worked, wouldn't that train him to act out whenever he wanted attention?

"Well, you were wrong," Red said, feeling his way. "There's no circumstance in which she'd be *cool with* your stealing a car. If you wanted to hang out here with me, you sure picked a crummy way to go about it. I'd say you more or less guaranteed it won't happen."

"That's crap. I didn't steal anything. It's our car."

Red shook his head. "Wrong again. It's *her* car."

The boy mumbled something, but it probably was more emoting than speaking, so Red let it go. He shut his eyes for a few minutes, pretending he was soaking up some sun. He hoped a little time might bring the temperature down on Dylan's temper.

When he heard the boy settle in his chair, he sneaked a peek. Dylan's arms and legs were stretched out, looking almost relaxed. Red decided to take a risk.

"So," he said, keeping his eyes shut to avoid any hint of interrogation. "Why can't you stand it when your mom wants to talk about your dad?"

A few seconds of silence were, at first, his only response. He forced himself to be patient.

"I don't know. She wants to, like, pretend everything was perfect. That's just stupid."

Red put his feet up on the lounger next to him. Eyes still shut, he murmured, a vague sound that he hoped was nonthreatening. "Yeah?"

"Yeah."

More silence. God, what a lot of work kids were. Too bad you couldn't treat them like a malfunctioning soda machine, and jostle them until they coughed up the information you wanted.

"Yeah," Dylan said again, his voice a little fuzzier now, as if he were partially talking to himself. "They were always fighting. Not as bad as before, but he was always mad at one of us, her or me. It was like he hated even being there. They were going to get a divorce, if he hadn't died."

Red opened his eyes. "You think? Or you know?"

Dylan flushed and picked at his scab. "Whatever. Nobody said the word *divorce,* but it was pretty obvious he hated us. I guess dying was the next best thing, if you think about it. At least it got him away from us."

Something hot pinched at Red's chest. So much pain lay below the bravado of those words. Losing your dad when you were still locked in the rebellious phase was so unfair. At that age, you were so busy blowing up bridges, trying to prove you could make it on your own. If your dad died then, you were cheated of the time every kid needed, time to grow out of it. Time to rebuild those exploded connections and make amends.

Not that Dylan understood that, of course. But Red did. The last words he'd spoken to his own much-loved father had been *I hate you.* It had taken years to forgive himself for that.

Shoot. Kids were so helpless, completely at the mercy of the fates. It was amazing, really, that anyone ever made it across the burning coals of youth, all the way to manhood.

Red didn't know what to say, but silence in the face of all this misery wasn't an option. "You know your dad was sick for a long time before he told anybody, right?"

Dylan frowned. "I guess. So what?"

"So I imagine it makes you pretty angry to know you're going to die. You'd be sad, and maybe in a lot of pain, too. You might take it out on the people around you, don't you think? Even the people you love. Where else is all that anger going to go?"

The towel rustled as Dylan lifted it and draped it over his head, ostensibly to keep the sun out of his eyes, but probably so that he could hide his confusion behind it. He looked like a scrawny little boxer, weary from his first round in the ring.

"How should I know?" But his voice carried less bluster. "Maybe."

Red wondered if he might be getting through. He hoped so. But either way, they were running out of time.

"Look, Dylan, your mom is going to be here any minute. You're in big trouble. Stealing a car is no joke, and frankly I think you know that, no matter what you say. It's time for you to grow up here and start thinking about what you're doing to other people. Especially your mom."

Dylan stared, stony-faced, at the horizon. "What does that mean? Does it mean you're going to make me go home with her?"

"I can't make you do anything," he said. "I'm not your dad."

"Yeah." Dylan's eyes flickered. "Sometimes I wish you were."

Red felt like a man on top of a tightrope. He had no idea what the best strategy was here, so he tried to remember what it had been like to be fifteen and afraid. He remembered the words his grandpa Colm had used when the three orphaned teenagers had arrived at the house in Belvedere Cove. Maybe it would be worth a try to repeat them. Grandpa Colm had been the wisest man Red ever knew.

"I love you, Dylan," he said, adapting the script a little, hoping to make it fit what he knew would matter to this boy, at this time and place. "I always will, just as if you were my son. But I won't respect you, man to man, unless you deserve it. And respect is the real prize. Respect is what will allow us to be friends now, and equals later."

Dylan cut a quick glance toward him. The glance was full of longing. "So…what would I have to do?"

"Shape up. Help out. Stop doing stupid things. Take care of your mom for a change, instead of making her always take care of you."

Dylan looked doubtful. "For how long?"

Red laughed. "For the rest of your life, dummy. But maybe we could start with…a week? A week handling things on your own, using your common sense to make decisions. And then, after a week, maybe I'll come by and you can tell me how things are going."

In the distance, a car door slammed. Dylan sat up straight, as if the noise announced the day of doom. He swallowed, then squared his gaunt shoulders.

"Okay. A week." Dylan held out his hand. "And then you'll come see me. Deal?"

Red nodded, and accepted the boy's hand. His fingers almost swallowed up the bony ones on Dylan's hand. With a piercing suddenness, the sight reminded him of the way Eddie's fist had closed around his index finger, gripping a stranger with all the blind trust in the world.

Two fatherless sons, vulnerable and exposed. Still so unready for the pummeling the world had waiting for them.

And Red torn between them, unable to be there for both.

He shook the three-quarter-size hand firmly. "Deal."

CHAPTER NINETEEN

RED HAD BEEN in San Francisco two days. Two incredibly hectic days.

He'd gone to three parties, and let four women slip him phone numbers he promptly threw in the trash. He and David Gerard had taken the sailboat out, he'd surfed with Colby, and later, with Matt at the helm of a borrowed motorboat, he'd damn near broken his leg waterskiing. After that, he'd limped Matt and Belle's daughter, Sarah, around Golden Gate Park because apparently she couldn't live unless she got to see the white alligator.

And, when all else failed, he'd even put in a few hours of legitimate work.

The only thing he hadn't done was sit still and think. In fact, he'd been at Diamante forty-five whole minutes this afternoon, and he was already restless. He wondered if he could drum up a handball game at the Y.

"Hi, little brother."

Red looked up from his paperwork—demographic stats on the new Diamante location he was considering in Carmel. The most boring crap he'd ever read. For once, he was actually pleased to see Colby leaning against the doorframe, smiling sardonically at him.

"I was just thinking about you," Red said. "You in

the mood for an ass-whooping at handball this afternoon?"

"Dream on," Colby responded succinctly. He started to leave, but a couple of feet away he paused. He turned around and planted himself once again in the doorway.

"Red," he said. "Tell me the truth, buddy. Have you been given six weeks to live or something?"

Red smiled. "Dream on."

"No, seriously." And, to Red's surprise, Colby did look serious, a rare occurrence. "I never saw anyone pack more action into forty-eight hours than you just did. What's the deal?"

Red fiddled with his pen. "No deal. I've been gone a week. I guess I'm making up for lost time."

"Okay." But Colby didn't look convinced, unfortunately. That meant he'd keep at it until he got the truth. Big brother syndrome. "So is that how you feel about the time you spent there? That it was lost?"

Red shrugged. "It was okay."

Sighing, Colby took off his jacket and hung it on the coatrack in the corner of Red's office. Then he pulled out a chair and got comfortable. The sibling equivalent of taking out the thumbscrews. Red rubbed at a headache that popped up on his left temple.

"See, here's where I'm confused." Colby crossed one foot over the other knee and brushed the fabric of his pants as if he saw a piece of lint, which he obviously didn't. "I got the impression you were staying in Windsor Beach of your own free will. It sure wasn't Diamante that kept you. Those phantom *other locations* you said you were researching... Well, no reports showed up in my inbox."

Red held out an open palm toward the computer, as if to say *Damn email.*

Colby tapped his fingers on the arms of the chair, and studied his brother in silence for a minute.

"Look, Red," he said finally, "I get that you don't want to talk about this. But I know you. And I'm worried. What the hell happened down there?"

"What do you mean?"

"It's that girl, isn't it? What was her name again? Victor's hot little baby mama?"

"Crap, Colby." Red leaned forward, his eyes narrowing. "When did you start to talk about women like that? Nana Lina would sew your lips shut, and I'd help her. If you—"

Ah, hell.

Red dropped back against his chair. It had been a trap, of course. Colby was already smiling.

"Okay," Colby said smugly. "Now we're getting somewhere. So cut the crap and tell me what really happened."

Red put his pen down, giving up any pretense of working. And suddenly he had a weird feeling that it might actually be a relief to tell someone about Allison.

"Nothing happened," he said flatly. "I mean nothing. She needed help, so I rebuilt her whole damn restaurant. I changed her infant's diapers and let him vomit putrid liquids on me. I even helped her babysit the lunatic old geezers who form her fan club."

"No." Colby's eyes widened. "Bumper-car Bill Longmire?"

"Bill's just the start. She's got hundreds of them. They give her diamonds, and jump off roofs, and wave meat cleavers at anyone who threatens to hurt her."

Colby laughed. "Fan*tas*tic. And you mean to say something actually went *wrong* in a dream scenario like that?"

Red laughed, too. It did sound like madness. So why, when he thought about it, did it feel like the only true happiness he'd ever known?

"You know that's not what I meant, though." Colby's gaze was on him, sharp and intuitive. "When I asked what happened, I meant between you and Allison York."

"Nothing."

Colby's eyebrow went up.

"I mean it," Red insisted. "Nothing happened. Okay. I kissed her, but only one time. I held her hand. One night, I went through hell on her miserably uncomfortable sofa, while she slept with her head on my lap."

"All night?"

"All night."

"No sex?"

Red growled. What was this, the Inquisition? "No sex, damn it. I told you nothing happened."

Colby's mouth went slack. "Oh, my God," he said softly. "You poor, masochistic fool. You fell in love with her, didn't you?"

No, of course I didn't...

That was what Red wanted to say, but somehow, with Colby's keen gaze on him, he simply couldn't. Because, for the first time, he knew it was true.

He really had done something that dumb. *Masochistic* didn't even begin to cover it.

He'd had thirty-two years...a lifetime of beautiful, willing, available, sophisticated women. Women with no illegitimate children, no vows of silence. Women he could bring home to Nana Lina, and take to dinner at the Wigham house. Appropriate women everywhere.

Instead he had gone to the beach one day and fallen in love with Victor Wigham's dirty little secret. The angry, proud woman he'd legally bound to eternal invisibility and silence.

"God help you, Red. It's true, isn't it?" Colby was still shaking his head, incredulous. "All night. *All night.* And no sex."

In spite of everything, Red had to laugh. "God, Colby, what's become of us when it takes the absence of sex to prove we've fallen in love?"

They chuckled together for a minute or so, enjoying the irony. But all too quickly reality washed back into the office, and Red was left with this impossible new truth.

When they'd stared at the walls as long as two men possibly could endure, Colby shifted in his chair. Then he cleared his throat.

"I'm probably going to regret this," he said wryly. "But I'm going to tell you something, and you'd better never repeat it to anyone else on this earth."

Red tried to think of one of his usual rejoinders. Sarcasm was practically required among the brothers. But for once he didn't feel like joking. Colby's face looked…strange. Hard. And, weirdly, he also looked simultaneously five years older and twenty years more vulnerable. That look disturbed Red right down to his toes.

He tried to sound blasé. "Okay. What?"

Colby chewed on the inside of his cheek for a second, as if he still wasn't reconciled to sharing his secret. "Do you know where I'm going after work today?"

"No idea."

"I'm meeting Hayley Watson's father." Now it was Red's turn to let his jaw go slack.

As far as Red knew, Colby hadn't spoken Hayley Watson's name in seventeen years. Red had always suspected Colby hadn't forgotten her, but it was like looking at the ocean on a sunny day, aware that ten feet below the surface a rip current was roaring and kicking up sand. The current was there, but only a few people knew it. And even those few couldn't actually see or hear it. They had to rely on their instincts to tell them where the danger lurked.

For seventeen years, the Malone instincts had told them that the subject of Hayley Watson was off-limits.

Now here Colby sat, saying her name as if it were as common as Jane Doe. And, in a tortured bit of psychology, suddenly the danger seemed to be in suggesting that Colby hadn't always treated it as casually as this.

Colby frowned. "You remember Ben Watson, right?"

"Of course." Who could forget that brutal, drunken bastard? "Why?"

"Because Ben says he knows where Hayley is. He says he'll tell me. But only if I give him five thousand dollars."

Good Lord. Red couldn't find his tongue. What on earth was the right response?

"Okay," Red said, slowly and cautiously. "And you said…"

Colby stood. "I said, do you want cash, or will you take a check?"

Red's vocal cords no longer belonged to him. He couldn't do anything but stare.

"I hope you hear what I'm telling you, little brother."

Colby reached for his jacket. "I don't know why you're up here, desperately filling every hour with mindless distraction. I'm not sure why you're terrified to be alone with your own thoughts. But I can guess."

"Colby." There had to be something he could say, some single word of sympathy.

"I don't want to talk about it." Colby put one arm into the jacket, then the other. He twitched his shoulders expertly to finish the job. "Consider me the ghost of Christmas future. What I'm saying is this. If you don't want to end up like me, you'd better find a way to fix this thing in Windsor Beach."

RED HAD PERSUADED Marianne to enroll Dylan in a hardcore summer soccer camp. It would be good for the boy to sweat out his frustrations, and besides, he had talent. If he made the most of it, his welcome at the Baker Country Day School was pretty much guaranteed, pharm parties or no pharm parties. The expulsion hearing had been postponed, and Dylan had been put on temporary probation.

But Red knew that school administrators always made exceptions for great athletes. And good camps made talented slackers into great athletes.

Five days a week, nine to four. So, as Red parked his car in front of the Russian Hill townhouse that Thursday afternoon, he fully expected to find Marianne at home alone.

"Hi." She looked surprised to see him, which was fair. He rarely showed up without calling. She had no way of knowing that today was going to be different in a lot of ways.

"Sorry I didn't phone first. But I wanted to catch you

when Dylan isn't here. I hope you've got time. I need to talk to you about something important."

"Goodness, I hope that's not as ominous as it sounds." She raised her cheek for a kiss, then took his hand and led him into the marbled foyer, her smile warm under the multicrystaled chandelier. "Come on in. We just finished lunch, but if you're hungry, I can make a sandwich or something."

Red hesitated. Marianne never dressed down, so he couldn't tell if her silky blue summer dress, with its glimmery silver belt and silver sandals, meant she had real company or not. It might only be Dylan.

But if that kid was skipping soccer camp already...

Red smiled, trying not to look disappointed. "We?"

He sensed motion in the front parlor. Glancing over, he saw Lewis Porterfield standing from the green-brocade sofa, a gold-rimmed coffee cup in his pallid hands.

"Hello, Malone." Lewis didn't offer a welcoming smile. He clearly wasn't pleased to see Red, and he wasn't the type to feign an emotion he didn't feel. "Marianne and I have been going over some of Victor's accounts."

Marianne, who hadn't ever seemed to find Lewis as distasteful as most people did, pulled Red into the living room, apparently unaware of any undercurrents.

"We've been talking about the Baker situation. Lewis has agreed to represent Dylan's interests at the hearing."

"If they ever actually hold the thing," Lewis observed drily. "I suspect the Baker trustees know they're on shaky legal ground and will use the hearing more as a threat than anything else. At any event, we'll be ready for whatever they think they've got."

Marianne beamed at him, as if he'd invented rainbows. But Red shook his head internally. She'd better hope that Lewis was right, and that no hearing materialized. Lewis, with his sour-milk face and his conversational two left feet, wouldn't exactly be an asset on Dylan's team.

"And maybe," Marianne went on easily, "if you've got something serious to talk about, it's good that Lewis is here, anyhow. I've told him everything, so don't worry. He knows that Dylan stole the car and ran away to the house in Windsor Beach."

Red glanced at the lawyer. Lewis was already staring at Red carefully, as if curious to see how he'd react.

"I understand that you happened to be in Windsor Beach yourself when the boy showed up," Lewis said. "What a happy coincidence."

That paper-dry sarcasm was Lewis's idea of subtle humor. Irritated that the lawyer would dare to make a joke of it, Red steeled himself to remain deadpan.

"Yes, it was." He turned to Marianne. "What I need to say isn't related to Dylan, Mari. It's personal. Any chance we could talk about it alone?"

Marianne's eyes widened. She wasn't accustomed to frontal attacks—at least not since she joined Victor's social set. If Red had been playing by their rulebook, he should have sat around politely, making small talk while Lewis finished his coffee, and outwaited him if he wanted to see Marianne alone.

But Red didn't have that kind of time. And besides, he knew that, once Lewis got a whiff of Red's agenda, it would take dynamite to blast him out of this house.

"You want me to leave?" Lewis's eyes hardened, but he kept his voice composed. "Marianne and I have had this meeting planned for a week. Whereas you... you were busy elsewhere. Windsor Beach, wasn't it? Though how you entertained yourself in that sleepy burg for a full week, I can't imagine."

Red laughed. "Oh, I think you can. In fact, I'd be willing to bet you've spent hours imagining it in living color."

Marianne inhaled, shocked. "Red!"

"Don't worry, Marianne. He's trying to be funny." Lewis smiled thinly. "The point is, I'm afraid you're the gatecrasher today, Malone. Not me."

"Red." Marianne's gaze had darkened. She was clearly uncomfortable, and real worry was setting in. "You know that I don't have secrets from Lewis. Whatever you have to tell me, you can say when he's here. Is...is something wrong? Something new, I mean?"

Briefly, Red considered bagging it for today, and coming back another time. But then he thought of Dylan's tearstained face, and his bewildered words. *Not as bad as before, but he was always mad at one of us.*

"Fine. I thought it might be better to do it privately, but on second thought maybe including Lewis is a good idea." He glanced toward the sofa. "Can we sit down?"

"No," Lewis said sharply.

But Marianne shot a repressive glance at the lawyer and spoke over him. "Of course." She led the way to the formal seating area and arranged herself on the sofa. She looked like a painting—the blue dress, the green brocade, the gold-satin hair. And all the pretty material possessions around her, which should have protected the sad little family, but hadn't.

Red sat beside her.

Lewis remained standing, his shoulders hunched over and his chin thrust forward. "What exactly do you think you're doing, Malone?"

"What I should have done two months ago."

"You can't. You know you can't."

Red gazed at the lawyer impassively, thinking that, in the pale sunlight that came in between the green drapes, he looked a little like a fish. A dead, pale green fish. "Why not? I didn't sign anything, Lewis. You didn't buy *my* silence."

"What about the promises you made? Don't they mean anything anymore?"

Red shook his head slowly. "No. No, they don't."

He'd spent the past two days letting his subconscious come to terms with this. He had faced a lot of things, including the painful, basic fact that he'd made a terrible mistake. And he'd let Victor make a terrible mistake, too. Because Red had lost his father so young, Victor had become the substitute. Because Red had failed his real father, and had no way to make things right, he had been desperate not to fail his new one.

But in the end, Victor had simply been wrong. Maybe it was because he was sick, in pain and frightened of dying. Maybe, if he'd been thinking clearly, he would never have suggested buying Allison's silence.

Or maybe he would have done the same, no matter what. Victor hadn't been perfect, even when he was robust and well. It was far past time for Red to admit that. He could see the man's flaws, and still love him.

He could even defy Victor's dying wishes, and still love him.

Because his dying wishes were wrong.

Lies and silence never healed anyone. Only love and the truth did that.

Dylan knew his father and mother had problems. It wasn't the problems that cut the deepest. It was the charade required to cover them up.

She wants to, like, pretend everything was perfect. That's just stupid....

"Is that the kind of man you are?" Lewis's voice was sharp and vicious, like the flick of a whip. "One who can break a promise made to a dead friend?"

"Yes," Red said. "I guess it is." He turned to Marianne, and took her hands in his. Her fingers were as cold as a china doll's. "Mari, remember how you said you and Victor had some problems?"

She looked at him blankly. She swallowed roughly, obviously knowing this wasn't going to be good. But her eyes were dry. For once, she didn't appear to be on the verge of tears.

"I want to talk to you about those problems," he began.

"Goddamn it, Malone—"

"Be quiet, Lewis." Unexpectedly, Marianne cut the lawyer off. She lifted her chin, and she met Red's gaze without faltering, though he could tell it required a superhuman effort.

That's right, Mari. He squeezed her hands, sending courage. *You can do this. You are stronger than you think.*

"Malone, you'd better think twice before you say something you'll regret."

Marianne looked at Lewis. She seemed puzzled, as if she suddenly couldn't remember who the man was. Her thoughts had obviously gone to somewhere completely different.

Somewhere painful.

All of a sudden, Red wondered if she might know more than anyone had ever guessed.

"Mari?" Red spoke as gently as he could. "Mari, can we talk about the problems, please? Were they bigger than you've let on? Can you tell me what you know?"

"I don't know much," she said. She frowned, as if trying to clear her mind and recall the details. "I—I hired a private detective once."

"When?"

"About…about a year ago." She blinked twice, as if to banish tears, but she still didn't appear to be on the verge of weeping.

"And what did the detective find?" Red took her hand. "We need to talk about this, honey. I know it's hard, but—"

"It doesn't matter anymore."

She turned to Lewis, though she didn't let go of Red's hand. "I'm tired, Lewis," she said to the lawyer, apologetically, as if she owed him an explanation. "I'm so tired of pretending."

She turned to Red. Her fingers fluttered once, as if a spasm of nerves passed through them, and then were still. "Is this about that woman in Windsor Beach? Is this about Allison York?"

CHAPTER TWENTY

ON THE NIGHT OF ITS GRAND OPENING, Summer Moon looked exactly like what it was—a dream come true.

After all the sweat and panic, at the very last minute, everything had come together perfectly. There wasn't a detail Allison would have chosen differently. Of course, she'd overspent her budget on the framed prints that decorated the walls. But the beautiful abstract art, with its soothing greens and elegant geometric shapes, was so far from the ordinary offend-no-one, please-no-one generic print that she knew the money had been well spent.

The flooring was mellow, honeyed wood. The light fixtures cast ovals of soft light above the tables, over which the melon-green tablecloths draped perfectly. The china, which had been the very first thing she'd picked out, was patterned with a gentle yellow moon rising over a green field—and had inspired the restaurant's name.

Jimbo came up behind her as she surveyed the room. "Yep," he said contentedly. "You did all right, little girl."

Tears pricked suddenly at her eyes. That was what her father had always said to her, which, of course, Jimbo knew. He was telling her that her father would be proud.

"Thanks," she said. She put her arm through his. He smelled delicious, like honey and chicken, and apples, and all the wonderful things he'd been preparing in the kitchen. "Will they come, do you think?"

He didn't answer for a second. And then he smiled, a small, wry thing. "They? *They* have been coming for days, ever since the soft opening. I think what you really mean is *he*. Will he come?"

Flushing, she shook her head. "No. Honestly, that wasn't what I meant. He's definitely not coming. I told him I didn't want him to."

Jimbo laughed. "Yeah. Right. And he's the kind of guy who takes orders."

But it hadn't been an order. It had been a mutual decision. She had lived that moment over and over. The car idling in the street, Eddie whimpering in the backseat, the other boy, Victor's other son, somewhere above them, in the mansion on the bluff.

The idea of a relationship was hopeless. Both of them had seen it, finally.

But what she hadn't seen was how difficult it would be to forget him. She thought about the first time she'd met him. Such a short time for someone to have become so important to her happiness.

Mere weeks ago, they'd been enemies. And then they'd been friends. And then...

Then he'd spent a week here, helping her pull the pieces of her dream together. One week. But day after day he'd brought laughter and strength, excitement and courage. And the most amazing, calming sense of no longer being alone.

For the rest of her life, she'd never walk into Summer Moon without seeing him here.

"Damn it, Allie," Jimbo said with a sigh. "If you're going to gloom around here like a little weeping cloud, you might as well call him. You're going to put the customers off their food."

She scowled at him. "I do not *gloom around.* I do not weep."

In fact, she was quite proud of the fact that she hadn't moped at all. She'd worked hard, and laughed at mishaps, and stressed over glitches, the same as she always had.

If she dreamed of Red, if she woke in the night aching like one big bruise, that was her problem, and she didn't inflict it on anyone else.

Jimbo rolled his eyes. "Maybe not on the outside, sugar lips." He pointed a finger toward her heart. "But in there? I'm pretty sure everything's in pieces. I'm surprised you don't rattle when you walk."

She made a small scoffing sound. Desperate to change the subject, she glanced at her watch. "Five minutes to seven," she said crisply. "Aren't you supposed to be in the kitchen? I already see cars parking out there, and if we don't have any food it's going to be sort of embarrassing."

"Allie, look." He touched her chin with a rare gentleness. "Don't forget how well I understand you. I've never seen you this way, not with Chuck, and not with Victor. You know I'm not the guy's biggest fan, honey. But even I'm saying it. Call him."

"It's not that easy."

"Okay. So it's hard. So what? You're smart. He's smart. Put your heads together and work it out."

"Jimbo, it's almost time—"

"What is it? The money? You know this place is

going to make it big. We can take care of Eddie without Victor's money. Give it back."

"I'm not sure contracts work like that."

"Well, then get a lawyer and find out how they do work." He retied his apron irritably. "Hell, what's the matter with you, Alli? You're a fighter. I've never known you to run away from anything that really mattered."

She willed herself not to go weak. Not now, not tonight. "That's just it, Jimbo," she said quietly. "It matters to me. But he never said...he never once said it mattered to him."

"Never said..." Jimbo stared at her a minute, as if he couldn't believe his ears. "You think he never said..."

And then, his eyes tilting up at the corners, he simply began to laugh. He laughed hard, from the belly. He kept laughing, the sound dwindling as he turned and slowly walked to the kitchen, shaking his head.

She stared at his retreating back, and then again at her watch. She took a deep breath, smoothed down the new white dress she'd bought for tonight and forced herself to put all that aside.

Time to open the doors.

Four hours passed in the blink of an eye, and before Allison knew it, they were five minutes from closing.

It had been the most amazing grand opening anyone could ever have wished for. About an hour ago, Sue had brought Eddie over so that he could share the excitement. The Old Coots Club had sent buckets of green shellflowers and yellow snapdragons, and at least two hundred people, some from as far away as Half Moon Beach, had been served Jimbo's fabulous food.

Jimbo had been right. Summer Moon was going to be a success.

Only one or two customers, a few of the staff and Jimbo remained. Allison paused briefly in the small hall between the kitchen and the seating area and rested her back against the wall. She held Eddie close to her chest and pressed a kiss on his head, wondering if her heart might overflow.

Only one thing was missing....

"Oh, there you are, Ms. York." Cindy, the pretty young hostess, came around the corner, menus in hand. "A man just came in. I told him we were closing, but he said he's here to see you."

Allison smiled. See how lucky she was? She had the best friends in the world, and every single one of them had stopped by at some time tonight. How could she have been brooding over the one thing she didn't have when fate had given her so much?

"Sorry. Just catching my breath." She smiled reassuringly at Cindy. "You've done a great job. Why don't you clock out, and I'll go see who it is?"

The minute she turned the corner, she saw him.

He stood by the door, tall and athletic and gorgeous. She'd grown used to him in jeans and a T-shirt, so this dressed-up magnificence took her breath away. He looked like something out of a magazine, with an elegant navy suit, a sharp white shirt, and a swirly blue tie that exactly matched his incredible eyes. He held a bouquet of yellow roses.

And suddenly all the pent-up pain of the past few days swept over her like a tidal wave. She tried to walk calmly toward him, but by the time she was halfway across the room she found herself moving very fast,

Eddie bobbing against her shoulder, as if she feared Red was an illusion and might disappear before she got there.

She didn't know why he had come, and she didn't care. For this one, blissful moment, it was enough that he was here. But then, when she reached him, a strange self-consciousness took over. She slowed, and when she opened her mouth, the only thing that came out was "Hi."

He smiled, holding out the flowers. "Congratulations," he said. "Everything looks fantastic."

She took them with a trembling hand. Their scent rose to her nostrils, perfumed and expensive.

"Thank you," she said. "As you know, we couldn't have done it without your help."

Oh, stilted, and so stupid. This wasn't what she wanted to be saying. These were the same words she'd exchanged with a hundred people tonight. His words should be different.

But so many sentences crowded against her throat, so many emotions clamored to be expressed, that she couldn't sort them out and begin.

At her shoulder, Eddie had been watching this newcomer with silent curiosity, his fists clinging to the collar of Allison's dress. But all of a sudden, as if Red's voice finally clicked and the association fell into place, Eddie leaned urgently forward and reached for Red, calling out a joyous recognition.

Laughing, Red took him into his arms, where the baby immediately began to fiddle with the knot on his tie, bending his damp mouth toward it and babbling contentedly.

The sight of the two of them, Eddie in Red's arms one more time…

Allison knew she needed to pull herself together. She mustn't read too much into this. It had been nice of Red to come, but it didn't necessarily mean anything except that he wanted to support the restaurant in which he'd invested so much time and energy.

"Watch out." She smiled. "He'll have that tie too soggy to wear before you know it."

"I don't mind. Whatever he wants, he can have." He kissed Eddie's exploring fingers, then caught Allison's gaze over the baby's head. The look in his eyes made her breath hitch jaggedly.

"Allison," he said softly. "You look beautiful, too. I've missed you. I've missed both of you so much."

"Me, too." She still tried to smile, in case those two lingering customers were watching, but she had the most idiotic impulse to throw herself into his arms and cry as if she were no older than Eddie. "It's been…hard. I thought…I thought I wouldn't ever see you again."

"I know," he said simply. "I'm sorry."

"No, it's not your fault. I told you to go. It seemed right, at the time. I guess I thought that if you left, if you weren't here, I would be able to put you out of my mind and move on."

"And did it work?" He tilted his head. "Were you able to put me out of your mind?"

"No." She couldn't lie. She just couldn't. "Never."

"I'm glad to hear that. Because that's how it was for me, too. I thought about you every minute." He moved in, so close that only Eddie's body was between them. "And do you know what I thought?"

She shook her head.

"I thought about how much I love you. I thought that I love you so much I would go insane if I tried to live without you."

"Red…" She touched the hostess station with a trembling hand. Thank God he'd balanced it, because right now it was the only thing holding her up.

She wasn't the only one. He loved her, too, the way she loved him.…

But would knowing that he felt the same make it easier when they finally had to accept reality and let each other go? Or would it, as she had always feared, simply make it worse?

"I wish I could whisk you out of here right this minute," he said, his tones low and husky. "I have so many things I want to say. And do."

A trill ran down her spine, and she bowed her head, hoping she could hide her flushed cheeks and shallow breath from anyone who might be looking. Though Summer Moon was her dream, right now she would have given anything to be able to wish it all away. She wanted to be completely alone with him. At home. They would put Eddie to bed. And then…

Then, even if this was the only night they would ever have, she would tell him that she loved him, too. She would show him.

"Are you staying in Windsor Beach tonight?" She touched Eddie's back, trying to make it appear that they were having a casual conversation about the baby. Her fingers and his met there, skin grazing against skin. A sizzle streaked up her arm and buried itself in her midsection.

"Yes," he said. "I am."

"Can you come to the apartment?"

He glanced toward the kitchen. "What about Jimbo?"

"Oh." Her heart sank all the way down to her toes. "Oh. I forgot."

He smiled. "That's okay. Tonight may not be the best night, anyhow. I have a feeling you'll be very busy tonight."

Her last two customers rose, folding their credit card receipts into their wallets, and headed out. She turned to them with her biggest smile and thanked them for coming. It took a couple of minutes to exchange pleasantries, and to accept their compliments on Jimbo's food, but finally, finally, they were gone. As if they sensed she wanted privacy, the few remaining waitstaff wandered to the kitchen with Jimbo.

At last, if only for a few minutes, they were alone. She turned to Red, embarrassingly eager but unable to hide it.

"I'm not that busy," she said in a rush. "We're closing right now. If I hurry, I could be free by midnight. A lot of the paperwork can wait until tomorrow...."

"I'm not talking about the restaurant," he said. "I'm talking about... Well, maybe I should just show you."

He coaxed his tie out of Eddie's wet hands, then handed the baby to her. He moved to the door and opened it halfway, letting a cool wind sweep into the restaurant, fluttering the pages of the reservation book.

Allison watched wordlessly as Red held up his hand, clearly signaling to someone outside. She held her breath when he stepped back, holding the door open courteously while he waited.

Oblivious to whatever was happening, Eddie began to pull on her earrings, attracted by the little green, shiny crescent moons that dangled there. She touched his hand automatically, peeling his fingers away before he could get the earring in his mouth.

But her concentration was fixed on the door.

Surely…surely it couldn't be…

Within a few seconds, a tall, thin, quietly glamorous blonde woman entered, followed by an equally blond teenager who was obviously her son. They both looked poised, but nervous.

Allison's breath stopped altogether. How could this have happened? Did they know where they were? Did they know who she was?

Surely, he wouldn't have brought them here unless they knew.

But who had told them? She had sworn herself to silence, and she would have gone to her grave without breaking that contract, whatever the cost. She hadn't meant to hurt them, but she had done so. And she had been willing to pay the price for that terrible mistake.

And yet, here they were, and there was no accusation in their eyes, no readiness for combat in their posture. They had come to her, these two people she had so badly harmed, however unwittingly. And they had come in peace.

The teen was at that awkward age, when his gangly body seemed to be younger than his face. He cut a glance at Allison, but then immediately looked away. He swallowed hard, and reached up to smooth an adorable cowlick he obviously detested.

Then he glanced at Red, practically pleading for guidance.

Red nodded supportively, but he didn't speak. He looked like a parent encouraging his child to step onstage and speak his first lines in the school play. Obviously, whatever was about to happen had been carefully rehearsed.

Allison's heart went out to the teen—and, amazingly, to his mother, too. That they were here at all was clearly an act of great courage, generosity and forgiveness.

Now it was her turn. She moved forward, though her heart was skipping madly in her chest. "Hello," she said, encompassing both the boy and the woman with her tentative smile. "I'm Allison York."

"Hello," the teenager said, formally. He cleared his throat. "I'm Dylan Wigham. I'm sorry to bother you on such a busy night, but…"

He paused, clearly panicked. He seemed to have lost his place. She saw him dig deep, and somewhere during that struggle the expression on his face changed. It was as if the man he would someday be emerged to handle the crisis.

"If it's all right with you, Ms. York," he said with a grace that would have made his father proud, "I would like very much to meet my little brother."

CHAPTER TWENTY-ONE

Three months later

ALLISON MIGHT NOT BE the most objective person in the world, but in her opinion Summer Moon was the ideal place for a wedding reception. The green walls showed off the white roses and white satin bows to perfection. Candles gleamed at every table, and the swagged garlands that looped across each picture window sparkled with fairy lights.

Inside, each table was ready for Jimbo's pork chops with melon salsa, which had rapidly become Summer Moon's most requested dish. Outside, a man with a guitar was playing love songs, waiting for the guests, who would soon be dancing in the street.

Too bad the groom, Jimbo Stipple, refused to let anyone else make the meal, and was stuck in the kitchen even now, while they waited for seven o'clock, when the guests who had attended the wedding, and about fifty more who were coming only to the reception, would flood through the Summer Moon doors.

They'd all been required to cool their heels while the bride and groom prepared the reception feast. They didn't trust anyone else to do the cooking, even on their own wedding night.

Jimbo was wearing a tuxedo and wielding a butcher

knife while he argued with his white-clad bride, Meg Bretton Stipple, about exactly how much cilantro was too much cilantro.

"Time out, people." Red held up his hands. "Stop arguing. Do you want to get divorced before you've even had a wedding night? A pinch, a dash, what's the difference, really?"

Meg, who had tied a knot in her veil so that it wouldn't catch fire, rounded on Red with a frown. "Maybe in a *pizza* it doesn't matter, but in this recipe—"

"Pizza boy," Jimbo said with an evil grin as he waved his knife. "I guess she told you."

Allison laughed, knowing it was all in fun. Jimbo had forgiven Red months ago, and the two had become great friends. They both had that man thing, in which an insult was as good as a hug.

She, on the other hand, was female to the core, and she wanted some time in her fiancée's arms before the night got too chaotic. She tugged on Red's sleeve.

"Come on," she said. "Leave them to it. They deserve each other. I want to dance."

He followed with a grin, looking absolutely dashing in his groomsman's tuxedo. But then, she'd discovered, he looked dashing in everything.

Or nothing.

Her insides began to simmer, as if the very thought of his body lit a fire she couldn't put out. She decided, halfway through the restaurant, that the street was simply too far away. The doors stood open, and the sweet sounds of the guitar filtered in, but Red and Allison were all alone in the restaurant. She stopped, right in the middle of the room, and held out her arms.

"I can't wait," she said. "I started thinking about how

you look under that tuxedo, and if you don't hold me right this minute I'm going to faint."

He never turned down a request like that. He moved in with a rakish grin.

"Hussy," he whispered as he put his arms around her waist and pressed her hips against his. She grinned, too, discovering to her immense satisfaction that she hadn't been the only one having dirty thoughts.

For several blissful minutes, he rocked her gently to the music, and his hands did a slow, stroking, nudging thing along the curve of her bottom, so that every time they moved the tingle deepened. He dragged hot kisses along her neck, and down to her collarbone, and pretty soon she felt something hot and wonderful coiling up inside her.

"What if I…" She buried her head into his shoulder and tried to keep from panting. They were alone for the moment, but—"Maybe you'd better stop, because I'm pretty sure the guitarist could see us, if he looked—"

"He's not looking." His hands tightened hungrily. "But if he did, all he'd see is two lovers dancing."

He kissed the side of her neck, and she murmured her delight, forgetting that she was supposed to be resisting.

"Let's see." He glanced at his watch. "Fifteen minutes…that's more than enough time." And then, with a seductive chuckle, he tilted her into him so expertly that she gasped slightly. He might as well have touched her with a torch.

Obviously aware of how close to the edge she was, he danced her softly into the corner, behind the cash register. And then he kissed her. She made a helpless sound, feeling herself falling. When he opened her lips and drove his tongue inside, that was all it took.

Clutching his shoulders, she shimmered like one of the candles on the tables behind her. She closed her eyes and tried to remain completely still. She tried not to make a sound, even as ripples of lovely, tingling heat ran through every nerve ending in her body.

He held her up, even while he subtly, invisibly moved tiny muscles that made the feeling seem to last forever. When the last shimmer had passed, he smiled and kissed her one more time.

"You're amazing," he said. "Did I ever tell you that?"

"And you're irresistibly evil." She shook her head and tried to settle her breathing. "Did I ever tell you *that?*"

"Why, yes," he said with a smile. "Yes, I believe you did."

But she wasn't really angry. It had been divine…and she would get her revenge later tonight. She arranged herself in his arms, her back to him, their hands braided in front.

From the kitchen, the sounds of the endless argument wafted out. They listened with drowsy amusement, well aware that Jimbo and Meg were madly in love.

She let her head drop against his chest, realizing that she was happier than she'd ever been in her entire life. Their own wedding was planned for Christmas. They'd wanted a little time—their relationship had gotten off to such a rocky start, and there were so many emotions, so many complicated relationships to consider.

Though it had turned out that Marianne had known all along about her husband's affair with a waitress in Windsor Beach, the existence of Eddie had come as a shock. For the first few weeks, Allison had watched the other woman hold herself together desperately, trying to be fair to this illegitimate child who had appeared out of nowhere to rock her world.

It hadn't taken long for Allison to realize she liked Marianne very much. And as the weeks went on, Marianne's emotions had settled down, and an inner strength had emerged that stunned everyone—Marianne, apparently, most of all. She'd seemed to grow and mature before their very eyes.

It would be a slow road to real intimacy, but, with Red's help, they had taken the first steps. For the first time, Allison could believe that maybe, someday, Victor's widow and first son could think of Allison and Eddie as family.

And then, of course, there were the Malones themselves. It had almost been more daunting to meet them than it had been to meet the Wighams. The Malones were the closest family Allison had ever met, but they opened their arms unconditionally to anyone who joined their ranks.

Allison had fallen in love right from the start, especially with his grandmother.

She'd been so flattered, so relieved, when, after their first dinner together, Red told her Nana Lina had announced that she approved of Allison. She said she liked Allison's way of saying what she meant.

And so, come Christmas, the ceremony would be held at Nana Lina's house, though Red and Allison had decided that, because of Summer Moon, they would live in Windsor Beach. Red would commute a lot, and Allison had promised she would drive to Marin County at least every other Friday night, for the family dinner.

In preparation, Red had already bought a new car, a hybrid SUV that got great gas mileage and would carry all the car seats the ever-growing family of Malone brothers, wives and children could ever need.

Surprisingly, telling Cherry the news had been simplest of all. She'd accepted the new relationship without much fuss, as if she, too, might have suspected all along. Her main interest seemed to be in proving she'd never fallen for their charade.

"I knew there was something going on with you two," she'd said to Allison, without even a hint of rancor. "Good thing I didn't actually have my heart set on getting him. I'd have given you a run for your money."

And she was so beautiful, Allison hadn't doubted that for a minute. In fact, sometimes when she watched Red sleeping, his elegant profile as perfect as a sculpture against the softness of her pillow and his powerful body rimmed in moonlight, she wondered what he could possibly see in an ordinary woman like her.

But then, as if he felt her thoughts, he'd wake, and he'd make love to her with so much passion that she couldn't possibly feel ordinary anymore. When he touched her, when he trailed kisses across her skin, she felt cherished, enchanted, adored. She felt more precious and sought-after than gold.

"Hey." Red rubbed his chin against her temple lazily. "Did I tell you Eddie said his first word today?"

She swiveled her head to look up at him. It made her heart skip a beat, just gazing at his sexy, tender profile. "You most certainly did not tell me. How awful that I missed it. What was it?"

"Well, I might be wrong, but I'm pretty sure he

looked right at me and said 'Da-da.' Of course, he did keep repeating it about a hundred times, so it actually sounded more like 'Da-da-da-da-da-da-da.'"

She laughed. As they both knew, Eddie made that noise all the time. It was part of his regular babbling and seemed to apply to everything from strained carrots to his little choo-choo pull toy.

"Silly," she said. "Don't tease me like that. It would be terrible if I missed his first word."

She felt Red's enveloping arms tighten slightly. "Would you think it was terrible if his first word really was *Daddy?*"

She smiled. "Well, of course, I'd rather it was *Mommy,* but I'd try to forgive you."

"But what I mean is…would you be all right with that? With Eddie calling me Daddy?"

She turned herself so that she faced him directly, and could look straight into his eyes. "Of course I would."

He didn't say anything else, but she sensed the worry deep behind his eyes. How could he even think that she would deny him the name, when he had so completely, thoroughly earned it?

She felt a sudden rush of love for this wonderful man who was willing to give so much without demanding anything in return.

"You are his daddy," she said softly. "What else would he call you?"

She lifted her face, asking for a kiss, but at that moment a troop of wedding guests came swarming through the door, whooping and laughing, oohing over the decorations and hollering out friendly hellos.

From there, it was fabulous madness.

Sue had come, and at least half a dozen of the

Summer Moon staff. The Peacock Café was repre-
sented, too, with Moira and Sven and Flip. Even Larry
Longmire had made it, though he'd obviously just
gotten off duty and was still in uniform. Meg's friends
were newer to Allison, but they were here in full force,
too.

And of course The Old Coots Club. Sarge Barker
was already swaying his hips to the music, which
caused Bill to groan. Stuart Phelps was rolling his eyes.
Dickey, who had arrived on the arm of a sweet-faced
young woman he'd probably forgotten was his private
nurse, was calling for the guitarist to switch to "Danny
Boy."

With a quick kiss, Allison and Red pulled apart and
got to work. She brought out the trays of hors d'oeuvres.
He moved to the bar and began dispensing champagne.
With the first loud pop of the cork, a cheer went up.
And even though the bride and groom were still no-
where to be seen, the party had officially begun.

A few minutes later, Allison was thinking about
going to the kitchen to grab another tray of crab and
mint crostinis when Dickey sidled up to her.

"Well done," he said out of the side of his mouth, as
if no one else must hear his cryptic words. He jerked
his head in the direction of the boy-cop, Larry. "It never
hurts to have a uniform in the room. You never know
who might sneak in."

"True," she said gravely. She could tell by the twinkle of his Irish eyes that this was one of his clear times,
when he knew full well he was inventing nonsense.
"What do you think, Dickey? Who looks the most suspicious?"

Dickey pretended to survey the crowd. With his arm

stiff at his side, he surreptitiously pointed to Red, who was gracefully pouring champagne.

"Him," he said. "I'd definitely watch that one. I have a feeling he's got wicked plans for you."

Allison laughed. "I certainly hope so," she said. And then she leaned close and kissed the wonderful old man on his wrinkled, ruddy cheek.

When she straightened, she met Red's gaze across the room. He smiled, and she felt herself begin to shimmer inside all over again.

I love you, she wanted to say. *I love you, I love you, I love you.*

As if he heard her, he nodded solemnly. And then, with a wink, he laid his finger along the side of his nose.

I love you, too, it said.

* * * * *

HEART & HOME

Heartwarming romances where love can
happen right when you least expect it.

COMING NEXT MONTH
AVAILABLE JANUARY 10, 2012

#1752 A HERO IN THE MAKING
North Star, Montana
Kay Stockham

#1753 HIS BROTHER'S KEEPER
Dawn Atkins

#1754 WHERE IT BEGAN
Together Again
Kathleen Pickering

#1755 UNDERCOVER COOK
Too Many Cooks?
Jeannie Watt

#1756 SOMETHING TO PROVE
Cathryn Parry

#1757 A SOLDIER'S SECRET
Suddenly a Parent
Linda Style

You can find more information on upcoming Harlequin® titles,
free excerpts and more at www.HarlequinInsideRomance.com.

HSRCNM1211

*Brittany Grayson survived a horrible ordeal at the hands
of a serial killer known as The Professional…
who's after her now?*

*Harlequin® Romantic Suspense presents a new installment
in Carla Cassidy's reader-favorite miniseries,*
LAWMEN OF BLACK ROCK.

Enjoy a sneak peek of
TOOL BELT DEFENDER.

*Available January 2012
from Harlequin® Romantic Suspense.*

"**B**rittany?" His voice was deep and pleasant and made
her realize she'd been staring at him openmouthed through
the screen door.

"Yes, I'm Brittany and you must be…" Her mind suddenly went blank.

"Alex. Alex Crawford, Chad's friend. You called him
about a deck?"

As she unlocked the screen, she realized she wasn't
quite ready yet to allow a stranger inside, especially a male
stranger.

"Yes, I did. It's nice to meet you, Alex. Let's walk around
back and I'll show you what I have in mind," she said. She
frowned as she realized there was no car in her driveway.
"Did you walk here?" she asked.

His eyes were a warm blue that stood out against his
tanned face and was complemented by his slightly shaggy
dark hair. "I live three doors up." He pointed up the street to
the Walker home that had been on the market for a while.

"How long have you lived there?"

"I moved in about six weeks ago," he replied as they

walked around the side of the house.

That explained why she didn't know the Walkers had moved out and Mr. Hard Body had moved in. Six weeks ago she'd still been living at her brother Benjamin's house trying to heal from the trauma she'd lived through.

As they reached the backyard she motioned toward the broken brick patio just outside the back door. "What I'd like is a wooden deck big enough to hold a barbecue pit and an umbrella table and, of course, lots of people."

He nodded and pulled a tape measure from his tool belt. "An outdoor entertainment area," he said.

"Exactly," she replied and watched as he began to walk the site. The last thing Brittany had wanted to think about over the past eight months of her life was men. But looking at Alex Crawford definitely gave her a slight flutter of pure feminine pleasure.

Will Brittany be able to heal in the arms of Alex, her hotter-than-sin handyman...or will a second psychopath silence her forever? Find out in
TOOL BELT DEFENDER
Available January 2012
from Harlequin® Romantic Suspense
wherever books are sold.